TREAL LOVE

Le'Monica Jackson

Lock Down Publications and Ca$h
Presents
TREAL LOVE
A Novel by *Le'Monica Jackson*

Le'Monica Jackson

Lock Down Publications
Po Box 944
Stockbridge, Ga 30281

Visit our website @
www.lockdownpublications.com

Lock Down Publications
Like our page on Facebook: Lock Down Publications @
www.facebook.com/lockdownpublications.ldp
Book interior design by: **Shawn Walker**
Edited by: **Jill Alicea**

Stay Connected with Us!

Text **LOCKDOWN** to 22828 to stay up-to-date with new releases, sneak peaks, contests and more...
Thank you.

Submission Guideline.

Submit the first three chapters of your completed manuscript to ldpsubmissions@gmail.com, subject line: Your book's title. The manuscript must be in a .doc file and sent as an attachment. Document should be in Times New Roman, double spaced and in size 12 font. Also, provide your synopsis and full contact information. If sending multiple submissions, they must each be in a separate email.

Have a story but no way to send it electronically? You can still submit to LDP/Ca$h Presents. Send in the first three chapters, written or typed, of your completed manuscript to:

LDP: Submissions Dept
Po Box 944
Stockbridge, Ga 30281

DO NOT send original manuscript. Must be a duplicate.

Provide your synopsis and a cover letter containing your full contact information.

Thanks for considering LDP and Ca$h Presents.

DEDICATIONS

Rip my fallin souljas

Tyreshall Ponds aka lady
Tastariqn banjamin aka star
DeAnthony Ryles aka ctc d.a
Deresha Armstrong aka Pooh baby
Diamond Hill aka Ctc d-hill
Terrance Hill aka Montana
Terrance Cook aka freeze
Spencer Thompson aka lil Spence
Takeya aka Remy

This book is dedicated to the ones who mean the most to me my sons, Jamari Maurice Jones & Phillip Antawn Jones. Everything I do is for y'all. Remember always shoot for the stars and aim for the moon #GANGGANG

Thank you to my higher power because without God none of this would've been possible. Thank you to every woman that did time at Gadsden Correctional Facility between 2019-2021 that read pieces of this story and encouraged me to leap out on faith. Thank you mama for always being by my side no matter what. Thank you Shapora King and Tyqueria Rivers for them late nights y'all stayed up and allowed me to bounce ideas off of y'all every time I got writer's block.

To my day 1's my very best friends. The two people God gave me as sisters Natasha Mondesir & Sylvanie Mondesir idk what I'll do without y'all I love y'all forever

Le'Monica Jackson

CHAPTER ONE

Boom! Boom! Boom!

"Open up the motherfucking door! We need to speak with Mercedez Smith!"

Once again, the Orlando Police Department was on Mercedez's ass for the third time within a two year time frame. They knew she was a menace to society, but could never seem to slam real charges on her. The twenty-seven-year-old was living life in the fast lane. By age sixteen, she'd been direct-filed into the Orange County jail, where she was charged as an adult for aggravated battery with a deadly weapon. With the connection Mercedez had, she only spent eight months in jail before being released with a slap on the wrist.

"Shit!" Cedez whispered as she jumped out of her king-sized bed and tip-toed to the front door of her luxury two bedroom apartment. Placing the palm of her hands on the wall for support, she stood on her tippy toes, closed her left eye and peered through the peephole, coming face to face with Officer Whitehead. He had the purest baby blue eyes, a perfect pointy nose, and rose pink lips. His face was beet red as sweat dripped down the bridge of his nose. Cedez noticed how handsome the young white man was. He was eye candy - the model type. He continued beating on the door. Apparently he didn't have a search warrant because after thirty minutes of banging and yelling, he walked hastily back to his all-black F-150 undercover truck.

Officer Whitehead typed on his laptop, made a phone call, and proceeded to slowly pull away from Mercedez's apartment.

"Whew!" Cedez exhaled. She didn't even realize she was barely breathing.

As soon as the coast was clear, she hurried to her bedroom to grab a few of her belongings. She unlocked her safe, pulled out a duffel bag of cash, and threw it over her shoulder. She grabbed the keys to her 2018 BMW truck and burned rubber as she sped out of the apartment complex. All was silent. The only noise was from the rattling of her keys in the ignition caused by the trembling of her right leg. Horns honked as she eased into the busy traffic with strangers yelling insults. The drivers were highly pissed off by the asshole who had cut them off. Ignoring their road rage, she reached over into her Alexander McQueen purse, fumbling around unable to find what she was looking for. Becoming aggravated, she turned the bag upside down, dumping all of its contents onto the passenger seat. Snatching up her rose gold iPhone, Mercedez pressed number one, speed dialing her main man, T-Money.

"Damnit! Answer the phone, T!" she shouted by the second ring.

By the fourth, he answered in a calm tone. "Yo, what's up baby girl?"

She felt a weight lift off her shoulders. She closed her eyes for a brief moment, took a deep breath, and began speaking. "T, I'm headed your way. I gotta get out of Florida. I'm on the 408 right now. Them crackas on my ass again." Breathing uncontrollably heavily, she stumbled over her words, trying to catch her breath. Her throat began to tighten up with tears as her heart beat out of her chest. Instantly,

T knew something serious was going on. He could sense the fear in her tone, knowing she was about to cry. Cedez wasn't one to cry easily. Suddenly astonished at the gravity of the situation, T responded, "Okay, bet! Say less!

Ending the call, Mercedez pulled out a pre-rolled Backwood full of the finest dro in the south. She grabbed her Zippo, sparked up her blunt, and stared at the cherry as it appeared. Tears clouded her eyes and her vision became blurry while she took a long drag from the blunt. Wiping the tears away, she was upset with herself for getting caught up and even more upset that she was folding under pressure. Relieved that no one was around to witness her crying, Cedez laid back in her seat and got comfortable for the long drive.

She drove the speed limit to Georgia, making sure to drive as carefully as possible. The last thing she needed was twelve jumping behind her, which would result in a high-speed chase. Lord knows Cedez wasn't going down without a fight. Them crackas was definitely gon' have to do their job. Mercedez played Lil Baby's new album and let it quake through her speakers. The A/C was blasting as she cracked the back window to allow the smoke to go out. Mercedez thought long and hard about her next move

As fine as Mercedez was, she was a bit your typical girl next door. She looked nothing like what she'd been through. Standing at 5'1" and weighing 135 pounds, Mercedez's lil ass had the heart of a lion and wisdom of an owl. Her appearance is what every man and woman dreaded of waking up to. Everyone wants a foreign bitch. She was Black and Cuban with slanted eyes, high cheekbones with rosy cheeks, and dimples to die for. She didn't even have to smile for the dimples to be noticed. She had a cute button nose with small diamonds on both sides of her nostrils. With powder pink, cotton candy lips and perfect teeth, Cedez was flawless. Her skin looked sun-kissed. You didn't have to touch her to know it was smoother than a baby's bottom. Her small, perky titties and flat stomach blended perfectly with the tiny waist. Her apple bottom and thick thighs kept guys wondering what was between her small gaps. Mercedez was tatted like a biker chick, even in places that couldn't be seen. She was a hardcore bitch, but she genuinely had a heart of gold when it came down to the people she loved. She was getting hella loot and most people looked at her as a blessing. She was what you called "hood rich". With the lifestyle she lived, she was every little girl in the hood's idol.

Mercedez never forgot where she came from, no matter how much money she made. Shit wasn't sweet growing up in Orlando, Florida. It was not the Disney World Orlando folks get all excited about. She was from West Orlando, from a hood called Pinehills, also known as "Crime Hills", a place where you either swim or drown, eat or starve, take or get your shit taken, kill or be killed. Not to mention Cedez had been banging with the Bloods since the age of thirteen. Get down or lay down was her motto.

Being the baby girl of her mom's six children, Mercedez was the one who got blamed for everything. Everyone expected her to fail. While her siblings made the honor roll and barely had a fight, Cedez's lifestyle wasn't a choice. Ms. Karen, her mom, couldn't do anything to slow her daughter down. With all the money Cedez was dishing out to her family, her mom eventually became content with her lifestyle. Ms. Karen was a ride or die mother no matter what. She made sure she always had her daughter's back. Being a single, black mother, Ms. Karen was the definition of a strong woman. If she had to work three jobs in order for her children to live comfortably, that's exactly what she would do.

"Take the next exit," Siri spoke through the speakers on the GPS.

Mercedez was an hour and a half away from reaching her destination. Although she appeared unbothered, she was certainly deep in thought. Her mind was going one hundred miles an hour. When it came down to beating the law at its own game, she always had a plan. She was book smart and sure as hell street smart.

It was one o'clock in the morning when Cedez finally arrived in Atlanta, Georgia. She grabbed her phone and shot T-Money a quick text.

5 minutes away bae!

T responded, *Okay, bet, 100!*

The conversation was always brief between them over technology because of her lifestyle. Way too many people get fucked up from talking over the phone. Simple mistakes.

T-Money and Cedez had a thing going for years, but their friendship always came first and then business. Although they were deeply in love, neither allowed their feelings to cloud their judgment when it came down to business.

They met when they were young, on a website called Backpage where prostitutes would post their ads to meet clients. Cedez had an ad portraying her to be a prostitute, meanwhile, she'd never turned a trick in her life. She utilized the website for one reason and one reason only: to rob mothafuckas.

Cedez was a jack girl. She would lure men into sleeping with her only to meet up with them and rob them for everything they had. Money, phones, jewelry and cars...nothing was untouchable. Apparently, T-Money was on Backpage for a similar reason, but with different motives. T would portray to be a horny client in need of sex, meanwhile, he was really looking for young girls to work for his organization.

Human trafficking was one of Tevin's many hustles. He became a pimp at a young age to take care of himself. From the first time he and Mercedez conversed, he knew she was different from any other girl he'd ever spoken to. When they finally agreed to meet up, he changed her life dramatically. He introduced her to a whole new lifestyle. Cedez began seeing more money than she'd ever imagined. By the age of seventeen, she had her own everything: an apartment, car, and several bank accounts. T had dragged her into the drug game and Cedez was pushing more weight than any nigga she knew. Quickly going from selling to the users to supplying the biggest drug dealers, moving weight was now her lifestyle.

T-Money, was originally from Baton Rouge, Louisiana, but he did business all over, so his reputation was solid just about anywhere. He was a jack of all trades and about his money. Over the years, T had taught Mercedez everything she knew. Eventually, she became the female version of him. There wasn't much he did that she couldn't do - including tricking hoes. Mercedez had done it all.

Le'Monica Jackson

CHAPTER TWO

Mercedez had a set of keys to every spot T-Money owned. Just in case he ever got fucked up, she would have access to everything. Reaching in her purse for the keys, she hopped out of her truck and grabbed a few of the belongings she brought along. She made her way up the long, brick driveway, unlocked the glass double doors, and let herself in, kicking her shoes off and leaving them at the front door. She ran her toes through the furry, plush white rug before proceeding to walk upstairs. The house had two stories, six bedrooms, and three pitbulls walking around freely as if they owned the place. The dogs were trained and recognized familiar faces. Sniffing Cedez up and down, they showed her love by wagging their tails and licking her.

"Hey Draco, Dream, and Bullet!" She greeted the dogs with air kisses as she entered their territory before making her way upstairs to the master bedroom.

T-Money was stretched across his California King-Size bed with a cigar hanging form the corner of his mouth, looking like the boss-ass nigga he was. Mercedez's face lit up at the sight of him.

"Bae!" she screamed excitedly, dropping her bags down in front of her as she plopped right next to him. Mercedez planted soft kisses all over his face. It had been three long months since they last saw each other.

"Wassup, baby girl. Damn, a nigga missed you like a ma'fucka." T-Money smacked her ass, acknowledging how fat it was.

They did lots of catching up and their typical flirting before Cedez started telling him about why the police were after her. She'd gotten into some big shit a year prior. Originally, she planned on never telling T, but now she had no choice but to spill it all.

"Talk to me, Cedez. What happened?" T asked as he ran his fingers through her long, platinum blonde frontal wig. His fingers looked so sexy running through her hair. The blonde complimented his 24K rings and diamonds. T-Money had a caramel complexion, was 6 feet tall, and had the body build of a nigga who just did a prison bid. He was covered in tattoos from his neck down to his ankles. He had a mouth full of VVS diamonds, thick eyebrows, dark eyelashes, and dimples you wouldn't know were there until he smiled. T-Money had a low fade with waves that would drown a bitch. He kept his Rick Ross beard nicely groomed and spoke with a smooth, New Orleans accent. That nigga was so damn fine. Eye candy, mouthwatering, and he kept females dropping their panties on sight.

Cedez rubbed her head, bit the corner of her bottom lip, and looked down at her fingers, fidgeting. She was trying to find the right words to say. T had always told her, "Hesitation causes fear." The last thing she wanted was for him to think she was scared to tell him.

There was an awkward silence in the room. Time began to move in slow motion. She began, "Well, I was making a major play with your homeboy Buddy Ro, and I was moving fast, assuming I could trust him because he was ya boy. I sold him 30 bands worth of blow, then later that day, I realized he'd paid me in counterfeit."

T-Money interrupted her. "So you mean to tell me a nigga bucked up for 30 bands and you didn't tell me shit about it?" His nose was flared and his forehead was creased from him mugging. T was furious.

Holding up her hands in defense mode, Mercedez stopped T from saying anything else." Mercedez pleaded, "You know I would never let no shit like that slide. You've taught me better than that!"

"Okay. So did you get ya money?" T asked.

Cedez sucked her teeth and responded. "Did I get my money? Not only did I get my money, I set that nigga up on a date with one of my girls from Orlando. Long story short, I rolled up on their date and finished his ass."

It was all coming back to T-Money. Everything was making sense now. He stood up and began pacing the room, pulling at the hairs of his beard. "So baby, you mean to tell me this whole time Snoop had me thing he'd gotten Buddy Ro, but in reality you killed the nigga?"

"Yes, T! I had no choice, baby!" Cedez cried, sitting up on her knees on the bed.

T pulled her in, embracing her. "Chill, ma, relax! I'm not made at'cha. I had paid Snoop to kill Buddy Ro because he was plotting to rob me. Shit kind of crazy though 'cause Snoop had me convinced he handled it."

"Wait a minute. How much did you pay him, T?"

The vein in T-Money's neck began to bulge and throb. His facial expression became dark instantly. He said, "I gave that nigga twenty-five bands, bruh!"

There was a brief silence. T's and Cedez's minds had just intertwined at the same time, coming to the same conclusion. No words were needed. Snoop had bucked T for 25 G's and he was definitely going to have to pay for it with his life! It was up there and stuck there for Snoop. There was no coming back from the foul shit he had pulled.

"That nigga was better off trying to mask up and rob me instead of playing me for a green-ass nigga like that!" T-Money said as he pondered on the whole situation.

Now that business was out of the way, the mood changed. T-Money dimmed the lights and poured them glasses of Patron - something to take the edge off. They both knew what time it was. It had been awhile since they'd last seen one another. Things were very intense because their sex was long overdue. Round one was passionate, but the eagerness made things rushed and fast. They needed each other badly and their kisses were laced with hunger.

T-Money grabbed a handful of Mercedez's hair and smashed her face into his. Breathing deep with her eyes closed tight, her heart was racing as she was trying to force her tongue down his throat. Fireworks ignited as their tongues intertwined. T was biting on her bottom lip and pulling at her clothes all at the same time.

Mercedez pulled his tank top over his head, not missing a beat in their make out session. She pushed him back, standing to face him as she took a second to stare at the god lying naked in front of her. She admired every inch of his body, then began to give her man a strip tease.

Slowly winding her hips in a circular motion, she kept her eyes on him, watching his dick jump every now and then as pre-cum oozed from the head of his dick. Mercedez turned around, bending all the way over, grabbing her ankles without bending her knees, and made her ass clap one cheek at a time. In her mind, she was dancing to "Body Party" by Ciara. In his mind, she was dancing to "Dat's My Bae" by Ball Greezy. Cedez got down on all fours and crawled over to him, wrapping her hands around his dick, making sure he saw exactly what she was doing.

T sat up on his elbows as he laid back and watched the show she was putting on for him. She placed soft kisses all over his dick before she dropped down to the base without giving him a hint as to what she was going to do next. He was caught completely off guard and couldn't contain the moan that escaped his mouth, leaving his body shaking.

She began to swirl her tongue around the shaft of his dick while she had him down her throat. She sucked fast and deep, rubbing her clit as she pleased her man. T-Money was weak as hell. He eventually fell back into the bed and allowed his lady to take control. She was dominant in so many ways, especially in the bedroom, to a certain extent.

After T-Money released all of his kids in her mouth. She ended with swallowing every drop. She climbed on top of him and began to grind slowly to get his tool hard again.

Holding her hips, he thrust inside of her, gasping for air as she flexed her pussy muscles.

Their sex life was always epic. After busting their nuts, Mercedez collapsed on his chest as they fell into a deep sleep. She slept well every night knowing that no matter how near or far they were, and regardless of how many bitches T had sexual relations with, she always came first. Besides, hoes came with the type of lifestyle he lived. He was attracted to get-money-bitches like Mercedez. There weren't too many bitches running it up like her anyway. There was no competition on her mind. T's dick belonged to her and she had no desire for any other nigga…period!

CHAPTER THREE

It was 8 a.m. when Mercedez rolled over, squinting her eyes, blinded by the beautiful ATL sunrise. She yawned and stretched, not seeming to care about the drama from the previous day. She knew money could change a lot of shit, and she felt like between her and her man, they had enough to change the world.

Slipping her feet into her Steve Madden bedroom slippers, Mercedez made her way downstairs to prepare breakfast while T-Money lay still sound asleep. Turning on "Always Be My Baby" by Mariah Carey, Cedez hummed along to the music as she stood over the flat-top stove, being sure not to let the bacon grease jump from the skillet and pop her.

She had plans on pulling up on her older sister Tonya, who also lived in Georgia. It was a must she fill her in on a few things that needed to be handled back in Florida. Her family was definitely down to ride, especially her mom and sisters.

"Good morning, beautiful." T-Money crept up behind Mercedez, placing soft kisses on the back of her neck. She could feel his hard morning dick bulging against her ass.

"Good morning, bae!" Cedez turned around to acknowledge him.

He pulled out a bar stool and began rolling his first blunt of the day as Mercedez finished up on the stove. She began a conversation.

"Baby, I'm pulling up on Tonya today to lace her up on everything."

"Shit, I would slide wit' ya, but I got a few things to handle myself. Gotta start putting shit in motion to make sure you don't get cased up, we got to get to Miami, baby, to handle some shit."

She already knew that T knew people that knew people in high places, and he was going to make sure she was good. "Okay, T. No problem."

Mercedez was perfectly fine with riding alone. Besides, she needed a lil one-on-one with her sister. Tonya was truly Cedez's best friend. She was older, wiser, and more settled. Tonya had the body of a goddess. Her having kids didn't do much damage. Hell, if you didn't know, you wouldn't know. She was 5'5", 165 pounds with brown sugar skin. She only had one tattoo: the name of her kid's father. Her ass was so fat you could set a glass on it. She was natural, no make-up and no weaves. Her features turned plenty of heads. Tonya moved to Georgia four years prior after her kids' father was murdered in front of her. She had intentions of starting a better life for her kids, and she did. Cedez and Tonya had always been close, but the tragedy had brought them closer than ever.

T-Money and Cedez chit-chatted at the kitchen bar and sparked a blunt before eating. After eating a hot plate of fluffy pancakes, crunchy bacon, cheese grits, and scrambled eggs, they were ready to start their day.

Cedez took a quick shower and threw on a fitted Tom Ford dress with matching sandals. She sat in front of the mirror and pulled her lace wig up into a top knot, laying her baby edges down the lining of her hairline. Her shit was slayed to the gods. It looked as if it was growing straight out of her scalp. She drew a black line under the bottom lid of her eyes, put on some lip plumper, sprayed on some Jay for Ladies, took one last look in the mirror, and grabbed her Dolce and Gabbana sunglasses and bag to match. She walked to her living room, looking at the keys to all of T-Money's cars, trying to decide which car she wanted to push through the city. Settling on the two-door 2019 Audi Coup, she grabbed the keys and proceeded to the car.

"I'll see you later, baby!" she said while standing on her tippy toes to give him a kiss, wrapping her arms around his neck while he hugged her waist.

Cedez hit the busy streets of Atlanta, weaving in and out of lanes with the sunroof down. Tonya lived only twenty minutes away. It took Cedez no time to get there. As she pulled up to her sister's house, she had the biggest smile on her face, seeing her nieces Asia and Akeela outside playing hopscotch. Cedez sat in the car for a few moments, going down memory lane of her childhood. The kids were oblivious to the fact that their auntie was only feet away. She opened the door, stepped out of the car, and the girls instantly ran up to her before she could fully get out of the car.

"TT Cedez!" They jumped up and down screaming. She was all of her nieces' and nephews' favorite auntie.

"Hey girls!" she responded with a smile reaching her eyes. Seeing them so happy warmed her heart. She reached in her bag and pulled out forty dollars for the girls to split.

"We got money!" they yelled, running off while waving the money in the air.

Mercedez made her way up the drive-way, walking straight into Tonya's house without knocking. Tonya was laid out on the sofa with her feet up, deep in conversation on the phone, when she looked up and realized who was standing in her house. Her face lit up. "Girl, let me call you back!" Tonya yelled on the phone. She jumped up and ran to Cedez, embracing her sister. "I didn't know your ass was in town! Wassup!"

Mercedez laughed, "Yeah, I know you didn't. You know I like to pop up on ya ass every now and then!"

It was as if they were kids again, talking and holding hands, giggling like school girls. Cedez was always on the go, so she rarely had time to spend with her family. Although she and Tonya stayed on FaceTime 25/8, it was nothing like being in each other's presence. They always went down memory lane when they met up, laughing about shit that happened years ago.

Cedez didn't even know where to begin as far as telling Tonya what she needed done. Tonya already knew about the incident with Buddy Ro, but she didn't know that her sister was on the run. Cedez had plenty of bodies on her hands - that was nothing new - but she had never been fucked up on a murder charge before. The only other person that knew was her mom. Cedez's apartment was in Tonya's name. She never kept anything in her own name due to the lifestyle she lived. She never wanted her name linked to anything. Cedez began to give Tonya the rundown.

"Tonya, I need you to go to Orlando, stop by Ma's house, and drop off this bag." She tossed Tonya a bag with 50 G's in it. "Tell mama take it to Mr. Jameson." Mr. Jameson had been Mercedez's lawyer for every case she'd ever had, and he was damn sure a badass lawyer. Mercedez continued, "Okay, once you take that to Mama I need you to go to my place and pack up everything. I got people coming to move everything out. The box that you see in my closet with the money in it...that's for you. I'm not sure how much is in it, but keep it for yourself."

Tonya had a worried look on her face, but she was willing to do whatever to help her sister.

"I'm on the run for the shit I told you about what happened at the hotel," Cedez explained.

Tonya was devastated by that statement. She hated when her little sister was in fucked-up situations. This particular one had to be the worst. "Oh my gosh, Cedez! What the fuck?" Tonya dropped her head into her lap. The whole situation immediately stressed her out beyond measure, but she was ready to do everything she was instructed to do.

Cedez and Tonya sat and talked for a few more hours before Cedez got a phone call from T-Money.

"Get back to the house ASAP!" he yelled.

Mercedez jumped up. "I gotta go, Tonya! I gotta go!" Panicked, she shoved her phone down in her purse and quickly ran out the door.

CHAPTER FOUR

"Who in the hell?" Cedez zoomed into the driveway, noticing an unfamiliar car parked next to her truck. She'd never seen the red Corvette before. Reaching in her purse, she pulled out a baby 9 mm and tucked it in her holster underneath her dress before maneuvering inside. She stuck her key in the lock and let herself in, expecting the worst.

The house was quiet and everything was still intact as before she left, except...

"Snoop!" she said in surprise as she looked the creep-ass nigga in his eyes.

Snoop threw his head up acknowledging Mercedez. He never said much, so that was quite normal. The shit wasn't sitting well with her knowing what she knew about him.

T-Money must have got something up his sleeve, she thought and remained calm. Pulling out a dining room chair, Mercedez took a seat in plain view to see Snoop's every move. Biting on her bottom lip, she was fuming, wanting to pop his ass right there, but instead she just sat back and waited to see how shit was about to play out.

Snoop sat in the living room, his elbows on his knees with his head down, waiting for T-money to come downstairs. If looks could kill, that nigga would've been dead because Mercedez's was mugging him down. She was burning a hole in Snoop with her eyes. Although he was nobody to look at, she refused to take her eyes off of him.

5'9", black as hell, with golds across his bottom teeth only and big Rastafarian-looking dreads, the nigga was ugly as hell and had death written all over his face. Snoop had been T-Money's hit man for about ten years and honestly, he was good at what he did. That was his main source of income. T-Money kept him paid in full. "Bands for bodies!"

T-Money walked down the stairs with a brown briefcase, the same briefcase he kept his special guns and ammunition in. Mercedez didn't say a word as she and T-Money locked eyes. She could sense the negative energy coming from him towards Snoop.

"Here GG, take these with you and hold on to them. I got some work lined up for you," he said as he tossed the briefcase to Snoop. Mercedez was confused as fuck. *I know he didn't just give this nigga...* She shook her head and kept quiet until Snoop exited the house. "Okay, now, what the fuck was that about?" she said with a confrontational attitude.

"Listen, Mercedez, we need Snoop right now, baby! That's why I told you to get here ASAP, so I could explain it to you. Okay, this is the plan. We need to find out who's talking on you, or see what detectives they have working on it, see if they got a witness of something. Shit, the bitch you had do the date may be talking. Snoop gon' get rid of them and once that's done, we gon' handle his ass ourselves. We have to play this right. You follow me, baby?"

T grabbed Cedez's jawline and pulled her in for a gentle kiss on her forehead. Them forehead kisses meant more to her than he'd ever know. "I got you, baby," she replied.

Cedez remained at the bar. She drank five glasses of Rose followed by a shot of Remy Martin. Once she began feeling her liquor, she joined T-Money and talked about her plans to Miami.

"Okay bae, check it out. You need a very common name," T-Money said.

Cedez nodded her head in agreement.

T-Money knew some Arabs that he was going to pay to change Mercedez's identity.

Mercedez got up stumbling. She was definitely intoxicated. She fell directly into T-Money's lap. She was horny as fuck and ready to turn up for her man. She grabbed T's legs and did a little slow grind down to the floor, giggling, looking into his eyes while she unzipped his pants. She toyed with his dick, causing him to get hard within seconds.

Once his man was hard, she shoved it into her mouth, getting wetter the more it grew in her mouth. She began deep throating every inch of him. She made sure his head was hitting the back of her throat. Giving T that sloppy head that he loved, she allowed the slob to drip down to his balls, making loud slurping sounds, gagging every now and then to stroke his ego.

Mercedez wasn't big on giving head, so whenever she did, she always brought her "A" game. T-Money knew that wasn't an everyday special coming from Mercedez, so he made sure to enjoy every second of it. He knew when she got on that liquor, she was a beast. He leaned back in the stool, propped up on his elbows, and admired the brain Cedez was giving him.

"That's right, eat dat dick up," he moaned aggressively, smiling inwardly because he knew just what turned her on when she was on that drink.

She loved that rough shit. Every time she came up for air, he pushed her head back down. She was a hardcore bitch at anything and everything she put her face on.

Everything became very sensitive for T-Money. His body became weak, legs shaking and tightening up. Cedez knew he was almost there, which gave her the motivation she needed just to show off a lil more during her performance.

Cedez cupped his balls, rubbing them together, tightened her mouth up every time she came up. She rolled her tongue around the head of his dick, then dropped down the furthest she could, coming back up slow and tight. After a few seconds, she felt his cum building up in his nuts. She kept sucking and refused to pull out. As he came, she continued to swallow each time more cum shot from T-Money's dick. He moaned and grabbed the back of Cedez's head. Once he finished, he just laid there speechless and exhausted.

Mercedez was definitely out of it, and T-Money was aware of that. No words were spoken. They took two more shots of Remy as they gave each other googly eyes like high school kids.

"You ready to slide, bae?" asked T-Money.

"Yes sirreee," Cedez replied on that drunk-ass shit.

He scooped her up in his arms to carry her upstairs. En route, Cedez kicked her shoes off.

Damn a nigga legs feel like jelly while I'm tryna be all romantic and shit T-Money thought to himself.

Making it to the bedroom, he laid her down in bed, then went to the restroom. By the time he made it out of the restroom, Cedez was knocked out and snoring. T decided to get dressed and handle a few things. He took a shower, threw on a fresh white tee, black gym shorts, and a pair of Gucci slides. He liked to look like an average-ass nigga, careful not to draw any unwanted attention.

No matter how hard he tried to stay plain, his appearance still screamed "rich nigga!" T was what you called wealthy. If you know money when you see it, then you know that he had a big bank. He could be in a crowd of niggas all dressed identical and would still stick out like a sore thumb. On sight, everyone knew he was a walking check.

He bopped down the hall to the camera and alarm system and set them up to come directly to his phone. He made it to the front door and locked up as he made his exit. T jumped in his silver Range Rover and connected his phone to play some Mook Boy as he pulled off heading to East Atlanta.

He had to meet with one of his young niggas that worked for him. T-Money supplied niggas with just about any drug you could think of: weed, heroin, meth, mollies, coke, Percs, blues…you name it, guaranteed he heard it.

T picked up his phone to bang Honcho's line. Honcho was his main man. They were very close. The lil nigga was a real go-getta. Anything T put in Honcho's hands he'd move it with no problem, and that's what T loved about him.

"Yooo, my young one! What's good, blood?" T-Money was like a father to Honcho, the one he never had. Even though he supplied him, there was a friendship. It was deeper than all that other shit. He always called Honcho just to check up on him. He showed him a lot more love than all the other jits he employed.

"What's up, Bossman!?" Honcho replied. He showed T-Money much respect.

"Shid, I'm just in da streets right nah, you wanna slide with me?" T asked. He never allowed anyone to ride shotgun with him so if he did, he considered you a close friend and he trusted you.

"Hell yea, bruh, come scoop me up." You could hear it all in Honcho's voice. He was ready to chill with his O.G. Honcho rushed to throw on all of his jewelry and one of the best fits he had. He always overdid it when he was with T-Money, knowing he wasn't just an ole "anybody-ass nigga." Honcho definitely wanted to fit in and look up to par. "Shid ain't no telling what type of model bitches gonna be around," Honcho said to himself, smiling from ear to ear.

Honcho was dressed to impress. He was a handsome jit, tatted from the neck down. He had neat, full, pretty, shoulder-length dreads with a faded tapeline, a beautiful smile, and a mouth full of golds. Honcho was a pretty boy if you judged him by his looks. Don't get it twisted though He was known for knocking niggas out and spinning a block. However a nigga wanted to get down, he was with it. Bumpin; or gunplay, he didn't mind. He was twenty-one and had been in the streets since he was a young'un. He was one of the youngest corner store boys back in the days. Honcho was what you would call a hot head, ruthless-ass nigga.

T-Money was pulling up to Honcho's grandma's house in the projects where they lived.

"That mothafucka out dat door that be having you in dem damn streets ain't no good for you, Jadarrius. And tell his ass to turn that gotdamn music down when he pull up to my shit, ole disrespectful-ass bastard!" Ms. Gladys, Honcho's grandma, talked shit to everybody and about everyone. She didn't care if it was God himself. She always had something to say.

Jadarrius was Honcho's real name, but only his grandma called him that. She considered him as her actual baby. Ms. Gladys had him since he was a newborn. His mama was on drugs heavy. Honcho probably saw her maybe all of three times growing up. As he got older, he would see her on the block, but he would never acknowledge her. Eventually, she died from an overdose when he was seventeen years old.

His daddy had a life sentence. Honcho was five years old when he found out about his pops' bid. When he was eight months old, his pops caught his elbow for killing a man and his wife along with their three children during a home invasion, which left his mom, Ms. Gladys, to raise his son.

"Here, Ma, go get yaself sumthin' to eat," Honcho said as he handed his ole girl two 50 dollar bills, kissed her on the cheek, and walked out the door.

"Uh huh, mothafucka!" she mumbled, grabbing the money and stuffing it in her bra. She eyed Honcho as he walked out the door. Ms. Gladys was something else, but Honcho loved her more than anything in the world.

He jumped in the Rover, and he and T-Money greeted each other with their Blood gang handshake. T had a few packages to drop off to some young'uns who'd been blowing him up to re-up. T had so many different incomes and he waited on no man. They were on his time. Clearly, he was the boss. T made his few rounds and then decided he and Honcho would stop at a local bar.

They grabbed a few drinks, ordered some hot wings, and watched the football game. Honcho truly enjoyed being around T because he always learned something new. He was a sponge and retained information well. By just listening to T and paying attention to how he moved and how he handled people, Honcho learned a lot.

As T-Money and Honcho were eating and sipping, he tapped into the cameras at his spot to check in on Cedez. T assumed she would still be sleeping, but his bed was empty. He zoomed in on the driveway and all of his cars and her truck were still there. He noticed a red Corvette ride past his house three times. Immediately, he banged Snoop's line. No answer.

"Aye, let's slide, brah," he said, leaving the tab on the table with a nice tip. He and Honcho sped out of the parking lot.

T-Money never said a word to Honcho as to what was going on. However, the air was tight and Honcho's reflex automatically had him clutching on his burner.

T-Money picked up the phone and dialed Cedez number.

"W-wassup ba-baby?" She was gagging and choking in between breaths, trying to get her words out.

"Aye, you good? Wassup?" he questioned. He couldn't make out all of her words. His heart dropped to the pit of his stomach and his forehead crinkled with worry. T-Money put the pedal to the floor as he continued trying to communicate with Mercedez. "Baby, are you okay? I'm looking at the cameras and I don't see you?" he yelled into the phone, becoming agitated.

Cedez began coughing and gagging uncontrollably.

His mind was thinking the worst after seeing Snoop's creep ass riding by his house.

"I'm…I…I'm…" Mercedez stuttered

"You what, baby? Talk to me?" T-Money was tight as a few moments passed, then suddenly he heard the noise of a toilet flushing. His mind was twisted at that point, trying to figure out what the fuck was going on.

Le'Monica Jackson

CHAPTER FIVE

Long silent moments passed while T-Money's mind ran wild. *Damn, bruh, I hope this nigga Snoop ain't trying me*, T thought to himself. "WTF is going on, man, talk to me," T-Money hollered into the phone.

"I'm puking up my guts, baby. I think I had too much to drink. My bad, I had my face in the toilet," Cedez said in a muffled voice.

"Damn, baby, you scared the shit outta me. This peon-ass nigga Snoop been riding by the house and shit. I'm watchin' his ass on the camera," T-Money replied.

"Oh shit, I didn't mean to worry you, baby. I'm Gucci though."

"I'm burning the road up tryna get to ya," said T-Money. "Aye, check it out, I'ma see you in a few. Let me watch these cameras."

"A'ight, baby," Cedez responded.

T-Money hung the phone up and pulled up the camera that showed the bathroom area. He did the dash, making it to his spot within six minutes literally. The door flew open before the car fully stopped. Honcho and T jumped out, guns drawn, checking the perimeter, ready to up on anybody.

Everything was good, but Snoop was definitely up to some creepy-ass shit. T-Money hated to get his hands dirty, but shit was getting serious. He would have to handle Snoop himself. Not too many people would be able to catch Snoop slipping, but T would be the one. T was so used to paying lil niggas to do his dirty work, but it was no pressure for him to do it on his own.

When T-Money finally made it inside the house, he told Honcho, "Make yourself at home, bruh. The theater room is open."

"A'ight, big bruh. You good though?" questioned Honcho.

"Yeah, everything's everything," was T-Money's simple response. He never let anyone in on his personal business. He told people what he wanted them to know. Since he was killing Snoop himself, he definitely wasn't telling nobody that they had any ill blood.

He reached upstairs, taking two steps at a time to hurry up and fill Cedez in on what he witnessed on his cameras. He knew Cedez was a ride or die and always ready for whatever, so he always gave her the full run down on everything. Now she was who he considered his other half.

Once they'd discussed everything and had a plan put together, T went to check in on Honcho. He'd fallen asleep by the time T made it back.

"Fuck, dis nigga think this a damn hotel or something?" He went to the hall closet and grabbed a pillow and blanket. "Here, nigga, and don't slob on my shit, bruh. Tired-ass nigga," T-Money told Honcho after throwing the pillow at his head, waking him up. T-Money laughed on his way out at how Honcho jumped up out of his sleep.

He joined Cedez back upstairs to finalize the plans on how to turn Snoop's light out.

The next morning, Cedez got up bright and early to make sure her sister Tonya was handling business. "Wassup, sis? I hope you taking care of that for me."

"Bitch, WTF are you talking 'bout?" questioned Tonya.

Instantly aggravated, Cedez responded, "What, bitch! The shit I need you to do for me! The lawyer! Duh! Come on, man, tighten up!"

Tonya burst out laughing. "Girl, stop trying me. You know I am on my shit. Of course it's done. Stop tryin' my shit."

"You a dumb, childish-ass hoe! Stop playin' so much," said Cedez.

"Yeah, uh huh. Anyways, bitch, you're welcome."

"Thanks so much, bae. I'ma call you back later though, okay? Love you."

"Love you too," Tonya said before hanging up.

"I should've known that she probably has been in Orlando since last night. My girl always got me," Cedez said to herself. Mercedez informed T that the lawyer, Mr. Jameson, had been paid and that part was all taken care of.

T-Money was paranoid about Snoop. He watched the cameras all night and all morning. The only thing that ran through his mind was that he'd just given Snoop that damn briefcase. "That mothafucka got life all fucked up," T thought out loud.

"Just chill, baby, you know we got hella guns. Ain't no pressure. We gon' get that nigga first." Cedez was real chill about the whole situation. She began thinking to herself, she'd never known Snoop to drive a red Corvette and the fact that he couldn't even look at her the day he came to the house. Everything was just so damn suspicious.

T-Money jumped up, ran downstairs to grab his iPad, and went back upstairs. He lay in bed with Cedez all morning and put a few things together. They booked the trip to Miami and got the rental car and hotel reservations.

They couldn't fly out since Cedez was already hot and they didn't want any attention before the law. Cedez was a little nervous - not about changing her identity, but more so about burning her fingertips. She was clueless about the procedure, but she'd done a little research.

The trip to Miami was only two days away. They'd also planned to meet their plug while down there, kill two birds with one stone. Their plug was an old Cuban dude from New York named Papi. He always dressed in a black three piece suit and kept a cigar between his teeth. He wore a patch over his left eye and the only thing you saw when you looked into his one eye was a very wise man.

T had met Papi years ago when he was in prison. They were bunkies in a two man cell. Over time they became very close and ended up doing business together. Papi was nobody to be fucked with. He had a gang of mothafuckas that moved at his command. Papi pushed everything, but only supplied T with guns and ammo. He had a whole warehouse out in Miami that was stocked like a real store. He had any and everything.

T-Money and Cedez got up to go shopping to grab a few things for their trip. Every time they were out they turned plenty of heads. They were the cutest couple and stayed fly. They always got lots of attention as if they were celebrities.

They jumped in the Rover and headed out. Cedez sat up in the passenger seat as her hair blew in the wind, looking like the queen she was. Cedez kept looking over at her man. He was laid all the way back in the seat, left hand on the steering wheel, right hand caressing his bitch's thighs.

They had the music blasting. The windows quaked as they popped along to YJB TOBY new album.

They dropped Honcho back off at Ms. Gladys' house then made their way to the closest mall. As they bounced from store to store, nobody else existed. They hit Foot Locker, Gucci, Prada, Victoria's Secret, along with all the other big brand stores. Cedez always blew a check whether she was solo or with T. However, blowin' somebody else's money is always better. She made sure to grab everything she needed for the Miami trip.

They had to make a few trips back to the truck to free up their hands of shopping bags. They stopped at Auntie Annie's.

"There's no way I'm leaving the mall without getting some pretzels," Cedez said with a little dance and a huge smile. She skipped off to the stand.

T-Money watched his lady with a little smirk on his face.

"Anything I can help you with, ma'am?" asked the cashier.

"Uh, yes, I would like a whole pretzel with three cream cheese and a lemonade. Large size, please," Cedez answered.

"Aye baby, order me the same thing," T requested once he made it to the stand.

"Hey, can you double that order?" Cedez asked the cashier.

"Would you like anything else with that, sir?" the girl asked while sizing T-Money up with lustful eyes.

Damn, I know Cedez finna cut up if she catch this lil dumb-ass bird, T thought while trying to play it off.

"Naw, lil mama, I'm doing the ordering, not him, and we good, sis!" Cedez said with attitude before T-Money even had a chance to respond. Cedez checked that shit. She rolled her neck and pointed her finger as she spoke.. "Fuck dis Auntie Annie working-ass hoe think dis is? About to get drug across dis counter," Cedez said under her breath, just loud enough so T and the bitch could hear her.

"Okay, okay, I got you. Just gimme a few minutes," the girl said, totally ignoring the threat Cedez just made.

"Funny how when you put a bitch in they place, they straighten up real quick," Cedez said to T with her arms crossed over her chest, refusing to take her eyes off the girl.

"Well, good thing the stand open where we can see the bitch every move while she handling our food," T-Money said, laughing to himself. *Baby girl wild AF. I knew her ass was gon' peep that play. Bitch needs a check on the 1st and the 3rd of the month*, T-Money thought.

They grabbed their food and exited the mall.

Le'Monica Jackson

CHAPTER SIX

Snoop had yet to return T-Money's call, which made him look even more suspicious. When Mercedez and T had finally made it home, everything seemed to be just as they left it. Nothing looked out of place or strange, but that didn't stop T from checking the cameras.

Within an hour of being home, Cedez received a call from her moms. "Hey baby, I got an email from my friend that works on the investigation team. After you make your trip where you need to go, swing through so y'all can meet. He has some really important information for you." Ms. Karen kept her daughter laced up.

Cedez was almost ready to put her trip to Miami on hold for a day or so. *I have to pass through Orlando to get to Miami anyways. I can just stop by or leave a day early*, Cedez was thinking to herself.

"Aye, what Ma talking 'bout?" questioned T.

"Some info her friend have for me about these crackas"

"A'ight, that's good. On the way back up from Miami, we'll stop by your city," replied T. "You're definitely gonna want a new identity before you show your face that way."

"Yeah, you right, bae," Mercedez said.

The couple had so much on their minds. The remainder of the night was soundless.

They jumped on the road, heading to Miami. The ride was smooth and they made it to the hotel. They only had enough time to freshen up before they met with the Arabs. Habeeb, the Arab, had the works when it came to fraud. He had a machine where he printed fresh ID's, Social Security cards, and birth certificates. He had a drawer full of blank I.D's and software downloaded onto his computer where he plugged in the new info. In a corner he had a blue sheet nailed into the wall with a black umbrella over a huge stand-up camera.

"Okay, what would you like your new name to be?" he questioned Cedez.

"Uh, lemme see… Chantal Jackson, and you can change my age to twenty-five. Yeah, that's straight," said Cedez.

T was looking around the room, scoping everything out. He really was looking for the fingerprint changing machine. He remained quiet though and trusted the process.

"Okay, follow me," said Habeeb, leading them through a door into a whole different room.

There, Cedez's fingerprints were burned. Habeeb ran her hands through a machine that laser-changed her prints. The whole process took about three hours.

"Thanks, Habeeb," said Cedez.

T-Money passed him three bundles of cash. "Good looking out, man."

"No problem. T."

The next morning, Cedez went to the hair store and picked up her jet black front lace wig. She had changed her hair from 613 blonde. She was really feeling like a new bitch. She never wore black hair.

"Get ready, bae. We gotta go meet Papi," stated T-Money.

Every time they met up with Papi, they always made sure to dress the part. Cedez wore a red backless dress that dropped to her calves, hugging her body tight enough to show all of her curves, and she pinned her hair up, exposing her full face features. She put on red bottom open toe shoes with a small silver clutch, and small diamond earrings.

T-Money had on a three-piece chocolate brown and tan suit. He, too, also wore red bottoms and chocolate brown hard bottoms. He wore a small blood red handkerchief in his pocket and one small diamond in his ear with a decent size chain and cross. He cleaned up his edge line and they walked out the door arm in arm.

Papi had instructed them to meet him at a five star restaurant that they'd never heard of. However, they never went anywhere, being in the blind. With that being said Cedez made sure to Google the establishment and menu.

They ate, laughed, and drank wine. From there, they went to the warehouse. T purchased the guns. The main ones were a Glock 40 with a silencer and a .357. The guns would be packaged up, placed on a semi truck, and delivered to Atlanta. Papi's nephew Suave did all of his big deliveries that crossed over state lines. They had instructions to call Papi the minute they made it back home.

"So what do you want to do in sunny Miami?" asked T Money.

"You already know - the hottest strip club in Florida. K.O.D.!" Cedez said, laughing and making her ass clap like a stripper. She was so damn goofy and T-Money loved that shit.

As soon as they walked in the strip club, all eyes were on them.

"Here, bae, go grab some ones," T-Money said as he handed Mercedez a stack of blue faces.

Mercedez had her eyes on the black stallion as she bounced her ass to "Cut Up" by Black Youngsta. T-Money knew Mercedez's type when it came down to strippers so he got the girl's attention, signaling for her to come in their area. By the time Mercedez came back with the ones, T-Money already had the stripper in their section putting on a show. T-Money patted the seat next to him for Cedez to sit down. She eyed the stripper with lustful eyes and handed T-Money the stack of ones. She admired the stripper's beauty off the rip. The girl was about 5'8" with black flawless skin and a very youthful face. She looked kind of reserved except for the fact that she was half naked.

"Damn," Mercedez said under her breath as she lightly ran her hands across the stripper's soft ass.

T-Money smirked as he watched his girl's face light up at the excitement. *I think my baby might be a lil gay*, he thought to himself, kind of liking the idea of it.

"So how you doin' tonight, ma?" the stripper said as she turned around, facing Mercedez with her titties directly in her face and wiggling her ass all at the same time.

"Shid, I'm great, baby, now that I'm in your presence," Mercedez replied.

T-Money just sat next to Cedez and enjoyed watching her have a good time. He had already put the stripper up on game to give Cedez all the attention. He tucked a couple ones in her panties as she and Cedez interacted. If Cedez had a dick, that shit would've been hard the way the girl was grinding all over her.

As Cedez continued to get her lap dance, T slid off to the DJ booth to request her favorite twerk song. "Aye brah, check it, could you spin "Twerkulator" by the City Girls?" he said as he placed $100 in the DJ's hand.

He wasn't expecting the D.J. to play the song next, but he did. As soon as the beat dropped, Cedez bounced up and down in her seat with her tongue out.

"Oh shit, oh shit…ayeee!" she yelled, the typical shit all black girls said when their song came on.

T-Money watched from afar, chuckling to himself. Anybody looking at him that didn't know what was going on would have thought he was crazy. He watched the show all the way back to his section. She stood over the young beauty, showering her with ones as she fucked it up. The girl didn't dance all ratchet. She had an elegant, polished way of moving her body. She twerked a little, but she swayed her hips very classily from side to side while popping her pussy in Mercedez's face.

She grabbed her right leg and held it straight up in the air while balancing on her left leg without bending her knee. She turned around and dropped in a split on Cedez's lap and jumped one cheek at a time. T-Money and Cedez were both in a trance. He was impressed with the way the girl twirled on her tippy toes.

Damn lil baby raw as fuck, T-Money thought to himself. He took a look at his time piece, being sure to keep track of the time since they had to hit the road soon. He glanced back up at Cedez and the stripper. *Man, this ma'fucka enjoying herself a lil too much. This bitch into girls or something and I 'on't know 'bout it,* T thought to himself. He examined Cedez a little more. He knew her so well that he could tell she was turned on big time. "Yeah, my baby gay," T said in a muffled voice, laughing to himself. Checking his watch again, he tapped Cedez's arm, signaling her that it was time to go.

"Aye ma, we 'bout to slide, but I really enjoyed your performance. I wanna get to know you a lil betta though. Wanna grab some air?" Cedez asked the girl.

T stepped up and passed the girl the rest of the ones. "I'ma go grab the wheels, baby."

"A'ight, bet," Cedez responded. "So what's your name?"

"Onyx," the girl answered with a soft, raspy, very feminine tone of voice.

"Damn, that name fits you well."

The girl's smile reached her cheeks. "Thanks, bae," Onyx said.

"Shid, dis yo' city, where you wanna go?"

"Let's go walk the beach. What? You're not from here or something?" Onyx asked.

"Nah, I'm from Orlando."

"Oh, okay, lemme go dress out real quick," Onyx responded.

They walked out together and made their way to the car.

"Man the fuck this ma'fucka got going on? She wild as fuck. I knew I was gonna have a threesome the minute I peeped she was into the chick," T said, rubbing his dick just before Cedez opened the door.

"Baby, let's hit the beach for a few, please. I want her to chill with us for a minute."

"Okay, cool," T replied, and the girls jumped in the Rover.

"By the way, this is Onyx, and Onyx, this my dude T-Money. Oh, and I'm Chantal, boo."

On the way to the beach, T-Money's mind wondered what Cedez had her mind on. She was so unpredictable. *Ain't no way Cedez gonna gimme a threesome on the beach, the fuck?* T thought.

After pulling up to the beach, they all jumped out. The waves were crashing against one another, splashing onto the rocks. The girls took off their shoes and walked in front of T. He couldn't help but admire the black Queens before him. "Shid, what they think, they all fancy and shit? I'ma take my shoes off too," T said to himself as he slipped out of his shoes.

The wind blew and whistled as the stars twinkled.

"Come up here with us, bae," Mercedez said.

T-Money joined them as they got to know each other.

"You don't seem like the type to be in a strip club dancing, sis. You're different...and it's something drawing me to you. No homo!" Cedez said with a little laugh.

Mm-hmm, not now at least, thought T with a little laugh of his own. T-Money kind of liked the girl's vibe because Mercedez wasn't the friendly type, so to see her actually interacting the way she was said a lot about Onyx.

"My real name is Celeste. Shid, strippin' not really my thing. I kind of just started actually. You know, just tryna get a bag real quick," Celeste said, not really getting into details about herself.

Mercedez studied her as she spoke, noticing a small tattoo on her right upper arm that read "Kaiden" with two baby feet next to it.

Automatically, Cedez knew she had a child, but she refrained from asking. If Onyx didn't bring it up, Cedez wasn't going to either.

They chopped it up for about a good hour, laughing, talking, and just vibin' before they hopped in the Rover and slid off.

They dropped Onyx off at a nearby apartment complex. Cedez made sure they exchanged numbers before departing.

CHAPTER SEVEN

"Welcome to Orlandooo!" Cedez screamed as they entered Orange County. She was instructed to meet the investigator at an office near Mr. Jameson's office. She trusted that the investigator wouldn't be on no funny shit since he was a friend of her mom's. He always helped Cedez out. He and Ms. Karen had been friends for years. Although they never really talked on a personal level Ms. Karen kept him close for the sake of her daughter.

"Hey Ma, I'm here," Cedez spoke into the phone, letting her mother know she'd made it safely and would be meeting with Mr. Nash in about twenty minutes.

They pulled up at their office and Mr. Nash was already inside waiting on her. T stayed in the car and peeped the surroundings, making sure there wasn't any funny shit at play.

"And we meet again, Ms. Smith." Mr. Nash extended his hand to greet her.

"Yes sir." Cedez nodded her head, hands sweating. She was nervous as hell about the info he had for her.

Mr. Nash took the seat behind his desk, pulled a laptop out of his briefcase, and popped a CD disk into the laptop. He adjusted his glasses on the top of his nose and motioned for Cedez to pull up a chair. The video played from beginning to end. The video showed Buddy Ro going into a hotel room with a thick red bitch walking directly behind him. The light-skinned bitch was the trick Cedez had put on to Buddy Ro. After about thirty minutes of Buddy Ro and the chick being in the room, next the video showed Mercedez going in. She stayed in the room for about five minutes and came back out with the chick. Only Mercedez could recognize herself. If you didn't know her, it was almost impossible to recognize her disguise.

Cedez felt like she was missing something, so she had Mr. Nash run the video back watching the video for the second time and she noticed much more. He ran it back to when Cedez first pulled up to the hotel.

"OMFG!" She jumped up, pounding her fist into her hand. She noticed a red Corvette parking in the parking lot, and she recognized the driver.

Mr. Nash sat back, opened his file cabinet and pulled out a picture of the red Corvette zoomed in on the person's face. He circled the driver of the vehicle. "Robert Douglas," was all Mr. Nash said. The room grew silent for a few moments. "Do you know him?" questioned Mr. Nash.

Cedez did not respond, so he asked again. She nodded her head. "I know exactly who that is," 'she replied.

"Well, that's who gave us your name. We have nothing on you except the eyewitness here."

She couldn't believe what she was hearing.

Mr. Nash continued. "We had no idea about this case until we got word from this guy."

She was devastated. She couldn't believe Snoop's ass was working. With all the shit he'd done and all the bodies he'd caught... Cedez's mind was blown. *Maybe he got caught up and tryna get off*, thought Cedez. She couldn't wait to tell T-Money, not only about the video, but also the fact that this fuck nigga was working with the crackas.

Mr. Nash just stared at her as she got her thoughts together. She rubbed her chin in deep thought. When she snapped out of it, she stood up and shook his hand. She thanked him for the info and made her exit.

"If there's anything else I can find out, I will contact Karen, but you stay low out there. You got me? And keep our visit discreet, as you already know"

"Oh, of course," Cedez replied. She was furious once she knew what was going on.

The door flung open as T-Money was rolling a blunt. "Damn, girl, I almost offed your ugly ass!" T said, reaching for his burna. "What happened?" he asked, knowing the visit must've gone left just by Cedez's body language.

She threw her head against the headrest and exhaled. Shaking her head, she began telling T how creepy Snoop really was, Snoop reporting the case, plus him being the only witness.

T was in disbelief, at a loss for words. When he was really mad, he didn't say much. All he could say was "A dead man can't talk."

Cedez phoned her lawyer to inform him that she was in town and would be stopping by.

"Hey there, Ms. Smith."

"Hey, I wanted to stop by."

"Well, I'm on my way out the door. If you could make it here quick, I'll see you."

"Okay, I'll be there in five minutes. I'm in the area."

When Cedez met with Mr. Jameson, he informed her of her warrant that was just put out.

"It's only for questioning right now though," said Mr. Jameson. Mr. Jameson didn't appear to be worried at all.

She let him in on the info she found out about Snoop being a witness against her.

"Petty case, no evidence. I got you, Ms. Smith, don't worry."

At that point, Cedez wasn't worried at all. The only thing she was worried bout was touching Snoop. She just couldn't understand why in the hell Snoop would roll on her. What was his purpose?

She hopped back in the Rover and they made their way to Ms. Karen's house. The ride to her mom's house was silent. Both T-Money and Cedez were deep in thought and more than likely, they were thinking the same thing: killing Snoop. When they finally made it to Ms. Karen's house, both of them went inside

Ms. Karen loved her some Tevin. He'd been in the family for some years and he'd done so much for her as well as her daughter. The Benz truck parked in her driveway was a Mother's Day gift from him to her years ago, and that wasn't even the half of things he'd done for her.

As soon as they walked in, Ms. Karen came walking down the hallway wrapped up in a house robe. "Hey babyyyy!" she said excitedly. She greeted T-Money first,

He leaned down, kissed her forehead and pulled her in for a gentle hug. "Hey Mama, how you doin'?" he replied, showing every diamond in his mouth.

"I'm alright, baby, hanging in there," she responded. She stepped back, examining her daughter from head to toe. Grabbing her arm, she embraced her with a big hug. "You got my hair turning gray." She laughed. She loved her some Cedez, but Lord knew she kept Ms. Karen worried

"What you cooked, Ma?" Cedez questioned as she strutted to the kitchen, lifting the lids off the pots that were on the stove. There were certain things she missed about being home, and her mother's cooking was definitely one of them.

They stayed over for a little while and chit-chatted before hopping back on the road to head to Georgia, trying to head out before Orlando traffic got hectic.

Smoking blunt after blunt and sipping a little bit of Rosé they jammed Moneybagg Yo damn near the whole ride. By the time they made it back, it was almost midnight and neither of them were in the mood to sleep. T immediately hit Papi up, giving him the okay to send Suave with the package. Suave made it to Atlanta in no time.

T got excited as he watched the semi-truck backing into his driveway. T and Cedez went outside and helped Suave unload the package. The main gun T-Money was waiting for was the 40. with the silencer. With the way Snoop moved, it most definitely would have to be a silent murder. That ma'fucka killed people for a living, so he moved real low-key, but at the same time, T-Money wasn't shit to be fucked with either.

They got all the guns inside the house. After T played around with them a little bit, he stashed them away until it was time for him to bring them out. He tried calling Snoop again and still there was no answer.

Five minutes later he received a text from him that read, "Taking care of some shit, I'll hit u up in a few."

T was trying to see exactly where Snoop's head was. He thought to himself, *Well, he responding, so he must not be on beat about me knowing he was riding by my shit.* T-Money knew Snoop pretty well

- at least he thought he did. T played everything cool, shooting a quick text back. "Okay bet bruh 100." It would only be a matter of time before he handled Snoop's ass.

Cedez laid back in the bed, staring at the ceiling.

"Here, baby, roll up." T threw her an ounce of that Zah Zah and a Backwood.

She rolled the blunt while he hopped in the shower. Draco, the biggest pitbull of the three, laid down by Cedez's feet, rubbing his nose on her toes. Being at Tevin's spot was certainly her comfort zone.

Later that night Mercedez received a call from an unknown number. She never answered unknown numbers but with all the drama in her life, she couldn't afford to screen nobody. Ain't no telling who was calling and what info they might have for her.

"Hello?" she answered in her proper voice.

"Aye, why you tryna sound white? This B.J." The man laughed.

Mercedez caught his voice before he even stated his name. It was her older brother Brian. Mercedez laughed. "Ohhh shid, boy, I ain't know who dis was. You change numbers more than you change your drawls," she joked. "Wassup though, bruh?" She hadn't talked to him in a while and whenever he called, he either needed to hold something or he had some street tea for her.

"I'm just chillin, sis. I called 'cause Mama told me 'bout da shit dat's goin on and word on da streets is, some nigga named Snoop from the A that deals with T-Money is supposed to be workin wit' dem boys to get his brother time knocked down."

Cedez's eyes grew larger than golf balls. "Say, you swear, B.J.?" she replied in disbelief.

"Hand to God, I wouldn't lie to you, sis." Majority of the time whatever tea B.J. had, 9 times out of 10 it was accurate.

They stayed on the phone for a while and B.J. told Cedez everything he'd heard.

She couldn't wait to drop the bomb on T about Snoop. He definitely had to go. He knew way too much and there was no way they could allow him to live.

The bathroom door swung open. "Bae, I was trying to wait until you got out of the shower, but I couldn't." T was tuned in. "So B.J. told me Snoop has a brother that's in the feds that's trying to give his time back so that's why Snoop turnin' state!" Cedez rushed it out in one breath.

T couldn't believe Snoop was moving like that, but the way the streets were set up, you can't trust nobody. Snoop had failed to return T-Money's call and at that point, T didn't even give a fuck. "The only thing I wanna do is rock Snoop's bitch ass to sleep, dawg!" T said through clenched teeth.

Cedez sat down on the toilet while T finished showering. "I wonder if the nigga caught a vibe when he seen you that day, or did he feel like I knew he was riding pass my shit?" T said to Cedez.

"Shit, all I can say is a guilty pig gon' squeal but da nigga don't know if we up on game or not so he walking light," Cedez mentioned.

"Yeah, sounds about right, ma."

Later that night they rode past a few spots that Snoop was known to hang out at. They were still sliding in the rental so they remained low-key. Snoop had no idea what they were riding in. It was still a Rover, just a newer model.

There was no luck. They rode around for hours to not even find Snoop's ass.

The next day Cedez went to the hair salon in the city where she always went while she was in Atlanta. A girl named Nay-Nay that was known for slaying celebrities' hair was Mercedez's stylist. She enjoyed going to Nay-Nay's shop. It was very chill and it always had good vibes. Nay-Nay was a close friend of T-Money's. He invested a lot of money into Nay-Nays salon.

Cedez sipped a little wine while Nay-Nay did a bad-ass frontal ponytail in her hair. As she was getting her hair done, she noticed a very familiar car ride by. *What the fuck?* Cedez thought to herself, focusing her attention on the red Corvette that parallel parked directly in front of Nay-Nay's salon, knowing it was the same exact car Snoop had been riding in, Mercedez was confused as fuck when the beautiful woman stepped out of the driver's seat. Mercedez's eyes followed the woman all the way in. She was about 5 feet, dark-skinned with a nice short cut. She had a Coke bottle shape, pretty white teeth, and a very sophisticated look about herself. *Dang her butt big! Can't call her a stallion though; she's too short. Ole My Little Pony-ass bitch. She cute though*, Mercedez thought to herself as the woman entered the building.

"Hey Nay-Nay, is Keisha here yet?" the lady asked.

"Hey Nicole, she right back there." Nay-Nay smiled and pointed to the back where Keisha's work station was.

Cedez sat there trying to put two and two together. She knew for a fact that was the same car Snoop had been driving, but who was this bitch. She was way too pretty to be his ole lady driving it, but who else could she be to him? Only women that fucked with boss niggas came to Nay-Nay's salon, or of course celebrities. Mercedez watched her surroundings the whole time Nay-Nay did her hair.

She listened closely to everything she heard Nicole say, which wasn't much of nothing. Mercedez got up to use the vending machine, which was located by the shampoo bowls where Nicole happened to be getting her hair conditioned. Mercedez put her dark shades on and examined Nicole, trying to be discreet as possible. She ran her eyes from head to toe. As soon as her eyes landed on Nicole's chest piece, she spotted a tattoo that read "Robert". It was big as hell. She couldn't help but notice it. And boom! A diamond ring on her marriage finger. *Ding ding!* Cedez thought. *A-ha! This bitch got to be his wife.* She instantly remembered the paper work at Mr. Nash's office with Snoop's government name on it.

Mercedez's adrenaline began to rush. She was ready to run out the door to get T-Money on the line. Keisha did plaits and rope twists, so Cedez knew Nicole would be there for a while getting serviced.

Cedez grabbed her Pepsi and Skittles from the vending machine, paid Nay-Nay for her hair, and quickly made her way out the door. Sitting in the driver's seat of her vehicle, she took a deep breath, let down her sun visor mirror, and took a quick glance at her new hairstyle. Nay-Nay always stepped every time she did Mercedez's hair.

"Okay, okay where my phone?" Cedez said to herself, reaching in her purse. As soon as she found it, she shot T-Money a text advising him to meet her at the nearest McDonald's. He made it to the McDonalds within seconds. He must have already been in the area. When he pulled up, he hopped out of his car, jumping in the passenger seat of Mercedez's ride.

"So wassup, baby, you miss a nigga or something, or you gotta run some shit by me?" he joked.

Mercedez mushed T-Money in the back of the head. "Both, nigga!" she flirted.

"So holla at me. What's good?"

Mercedez began telling him about Nicole. Snoop was so low-key, T had no idea the nigga even had a wife.

"I'ma hit Nay up and see what I can get out of her," T-Money said after getting the run down about Nicole. Nay-Nay knew pretty much everything about the bitches that came into her shop just by them sitting up gossiping or simply venting to the stylist. T called Nay-Nay up. She was almost like a sister to him. He knew that there wasn't anything she wouldn't tell him.

"Wassup, bruh," she answered on the first ring.

"Shid, ain't nun, sis. I was wondering who drove that red Corvette in front of ya shop." He got straight to the point.

Nay-Nay stepped outside and looked at the car. "Oh, that's a chick named Nicole's car." Off rip, Nay-Nay assumed T-Money was trying to holla at Nicole. "That's her ole man's car though, bruh," she continued.

T-Money got silent for a second. "Oh yeah, sis? Who her ole man?" he asked as if he actually wanted Nicole.

Nay-Nay and T were so close she was willing to put him in with other hoes knowing damn well she fucked with Mercedez the long way, but her loyalty lies with T. She began telling it all. "Oh, his name is Snoop. He got a lil change. They're married. He an ugly-ass nigga though." Nay laughed.

T-Money soaked in all the info Nay gave him. "Oh naw, I'm good, sis, I ain't tryna fuck with a married woman," T replied. They stayed on the phone for a few more minutes. She told T that Cedez had just left and how good she looked, not even knowing Cedez was sitting right next to him.

When their call ended T hopped back in his car and they trailed each other home so they could park T's car and ride together in the rental.

They bent a couple blocks around Nay-Nay's salon and parked where they were still able to have a good view of the salon. The red Corvette was still parked outside. They staked out for a good two hours until they saw Nicole walking out with her fresh long booty plaits, getting into her vehicle. Easing into traffic, they trailed behind her, leaving a couple cars between them, being sure not to make shit obvious, but making sure they stayed right up on her ass.

T-Money drove while Cedez was clutching.

"Bae, chill, man we just scopin' shit out." T laughed.

Nicole was heading in the direction of one of T-Money's other spots. She pulled into a driveway where two of her cars were parked. T kept driving right past the house and sat at a stop sign at the end of the street. He watched Nicole through the rearview mirror as she got out of the car and checked the mailbox. Clearly that was their home.

"Damn, this ma'fucka sneaky. I ride down this road every day and never knew he lived this close," T-Money thought out loud.

They watched Nicole as she unlocked the door and disappeared inside the house, then they slowly pulled away. From that point on, T knew the play was a go.

"A lil progress made, baby," Cedez said, leaning over to the driver's seat, kissing T-Money's neck.

Now they knew exactly where Snoop and his bitch laid their heads at.

Le'Monica Jackson

CHAPTER EIGHT

T had been silent from the time They'd pulled off from the stop sign watching Nicole. He had so much on his mind and Cedez could sense that he was tight. Cedez had always been very nonchalant about almost everything and that pissed Tevin off even more. Cedez was kicked back with her feet on the dashboard, playing Candy Crush.

"No, bitch, you know I was trying to swoop the green one and not the blue one, y'all stay cheating," Mercedez said, referring to her game.

T huffed and puffed. "Bruh, so you really playing a game right now and we supposed to be scoping?" questioned T.

"Boy shut up, I know how to multitask! I got three eyes. I saw da hoe check da mailbox and go inside," Mercedez responded without taking her eyes off the game.

"Yeah, a'ight," was all T could say because she definitely was on point. Bitch thinks she Wonder Woman or somebody, T thought to himself.

"Just chill, lil daddy." She really wanted T to relax. She placed her phone down and sat straight up in her seat. Reaching over, she rubbed this temple. "Don't we always come out on top, baby?" she asked, reminding T that he was in control and everything was gonna work out in their favor. T nodded his head. Mercedez continued "And don't you have the trealest bitch on ya team?"

"Mannn, bye, you think you Trina or something?" T-Money laughed. She knew him so well. She always could make him smile

They began laughing together. "Aye, bae, call B.J. back," T instructed Cedez.

She dialed his number, then handed T the phone.

"Yo, wassup bruh, this T. So you know da nigga name who in the feds?" T-Money and B.J. had dealt with each other before - nothing major though because B.J. was a working man. He sold a little weed here and there, but that was it. For some reason, he always knew what the streets were whispering about. It was crazy because he wasn't even a street nigga, but he knew everyone and everyone had a lot of love for him, mainly off Mercedez's face.

"Ummm…umm…damn, bruh, if I'm not mistaken… His name is Rodger Douglas. Call 'em Hot-Rod."

Cedez got on her laptop and looked up Rodger Douglas on the federal prison website. There he was, looking just like Snoop's ugly ass except he didn't have those big nasty-ass dreads. She read his charges aloud to T.

"Baby, this nigga got thirty years for repeated offender for trafficking heroin."

T glanced at the photo and just shook his head. "Dumb-ass street niggas be catchin mo' years than they even lived." T laughed. He could not believe Snoop was really playing police games. *It's all good though, the only thing he is playing is his damn self*, T thought to himself, T was about a lot of shit, but that jail life was not one of them.

The only thing Cedez was thinking about was a homicide

T sat back in his seat, looking up at the clouds turning gray. "Let's get home before the rain starts."

Cedez laid across the bed, looking out the window as the waterfall drizzled into the twelve foot pool. She was scoping out everything she could possibly scope on social media. She was not a social media type of bitch so she often logged on Tonya's page to get information she needed. She was searching through all of Tonya's Facebook friends. Tonya added everyone on social media, including people she didn't know.

"Hmph! Nicole 'So Pretty' Douglas!" Cedez clicked on the profile picture and it definitely was the bitch. Cedez was a pro at her investigation skills. Her heart was racing as she scrolled down Nicole's page, reading every single post Nicole had posted in the last three months. She noticed Nicole also had an Instagram.

Tonya didn't have I.G. so Mercedez created a fake page using pictures of some model bitch. As soon as she gained a few followers, she sent Nicole a request to follow her. Of course, like most girls, they just wanted them followers to go up. She allowed the fake page to follow her.

"Perfect! Now I can keep tabs on this bitch," Mercedez said aloud.

Closing out of the app, she went out to the patio, joining T-Money, telling him about the whole social media thing. He inhaled the smoke coming from his Backwood and nodded his head as Cedez spoke. She told him what she'd done and planned on doing. They put another blunt in rotation as they chilled on the patio.

Tapping into her fake page, noticing that Nicole had uploaded a new picture, Mercedez clicked on it and read the caption "Bae-Cation in Puerto Rico". She noticed Nicole's hair was in the plaits she'd just got done and she was on an airplane. Mercedez clicked back onto Nicole's main page. "And dis hoe got her location on? Oh yeah spot 'em got 'em! I'm on them!" Mercedez said in excitement. She passed T-Money her iPhone, tapping on the screen with her long fingernails, showing him that she had access to see Nicole's every move. She was ready to get down to business. T nodded his head in agreement to whatever it was Cedez wanted to do.

He didn't say much. He let his girl do all the planning and he just went along with it. This wouldn't be the first time she put a play together for them and plus her plays always played out perfectly. She continued watching Nicole's page for three days.

Every single thing Nicole posted, it alerted Mercedez's phone. The last post was a picture of her and Snoop with their luggage, standing in front of a black Escalade truck. The caption read "P.R. was lit, but back home we go, #Anniversary!" Their location placed them at the airport in Puerto Rico.

Mercedez and T hopped in one of the low-low cars, which were used for dirty work only, and once the cars were hot they got rid of them. They loaded up the guns and ammo and got ready to handle shit. T knew for a fact Snoop wasn't strapped since he was on a flight and had to be searched before getting on the plane. The way Snoop was set up, though, you just never knew what to expect.

Cedez continued keeping tabs on their flight, checking how close they were to landing back in Georgia. They drove over to Snoop's home, parking their low-low blocks away from Snoop's home. They wore normal clothing and got out of the car, walking to Snoop's house. Good thing he had no neighbors and there was hardly any traffic in his neighborhood. When they finally made it in the yard of Snoop's home, T-Money instantly clipped the power from the outside of the house, causing all of the electricity to go out.

Mercedez peeped the surroundings, making sure the coast was clear while T poked the back window with a glass poker. It shattered silently. He gently pushed the window in with black gloves on, careful not to cut himself.

He looked back and waved for Mercedez to follow him in. He crawled through the window of Snoop's home. It was beautiful!

They walked around the house with their guns, peeking around every corner. Cedez stayed close behind T, ready to let go of any mothafucka in sight. They checked every room, making sure nobody was in the house. They began rambling through all of their personal belongings. Between cash, drugs, and jewelry they collected well over the bands that Snoop had bucked T for.

After two hours of rambling and tearing up Snoop's home, Mercedez checked their location, seeing how close to home they were. "Baby, we have about thirty minutes and they should be back in Georgia." She showed T where the locator placed them at.

His nerves were so bad he lit up one of Snoop's Newports that were on the kitchen counter, and he didn't even smoke cigarettes. Mook boy said it best: "Call dat nigga Febreze 'cause he gon' spray." T-Money was on go.

They waited patiently for the couple to arrive, literally chilling on the sofa in complete silence as if it was their own home. Cedez pulled out a little baggie of blow and lined it up along the edge of the center table in Snoop's living room. Plugging her right nostril, she sniffed the line with her left nostril. She pulled out another baggie from her bra and prepared a line for T-Money to toot up with her. Blow definitely was not their choice of drug, but when it was time to go to war, they snorted a line or two just to get them in their zone. They rubbed their noses and gave each other that look.

"Baby, their location shows that they're five minutes away."

T-Money jumped up on that high man shit. He reached for his .40, holding thirty rounds, standing behind the front door he whispered to Cedez.

"Bae, go in the hallway closet, but leave it cracked open."

She did as she was told. No later than T said that, he peeked out the front window and whispered, "They're here." He stood with his back against the wall, pulling the .40 from his waist line.

Snoop grabbed a couple bags, putting his key in the front door, unlocking it to let himself in. "Bae, open the trunk! I'm coming back out to get the rest——"

Wham!

He was caught off guard. T-Money pistol whipped Snoop and kicked the front door closed, causing him to fall on his back.

"Bitch-ass nigga!" T said between clenched teeth. He stood over Snoop as Snoop looked T-Money in his eyes, bleeding from his forehead, confused as fuck.

"Bruh, what you got going on? I——"

Before Snoop could utter another word, T-Money kicked him in his side, causing him to gag and moan.

Nicole walked through the front door, arms full of bags, only to find her husband laid out in their own home. She turned to run when Cedez jumped out of the closet and shot her in the leg, stopping her. Nicole fell face first and started crawling.

"Aye, get her in the house and close the door," T-Money said forcefully.

"Neva mind, I got her ass. Just watch this nigga." Cedez aimed her fye at Snoop.

T grabbed Nicole by the hair and dragged her into the house as she kicked and screamed. "Sooo, Robert's the name, huh?" Cedez said, laughing an evil laugh.

She gave him the most pitiful look ever. Snoop's eyes were laced with confusion. He wondered how they knew his real name.

"Fuck-ass nigga, so you bucked my man for a couple bands and told them crackas on me?"

All Snoop could do was shake his head.

"Not only did you flip about the murder, but you were paid to kill the nigga and you didn't even do that," said T.

"No, bae, he wanna get his pussy-ass brotha out the feds, remember?" said Cedez.

T walked circles around Nicole. "I'm not even about to talk and play wit' ya ass, bruh. We don't got shit to talk about. I know everything," T informed Snoop. "Now look ya wife in her eyes and tell her you a fuck nigga and you the reason she dying today."

"T, come on, man, she don't have shit to do with this. Let her go. She solid. She won't say shit if you let her live," Snoop pleaded.

"Yeah, solid like you, right? Shid, birds of a feather flock together," said Cedez

"Yeah, bruh, that shit ain't happening. No witness, no case," said T.

Cedez was looking at T waiting for the okay. After a slight nod of his head, Cedez put three holes in Nicole's body, two in the chest and one directly in between the eyes. Her lifeless body dropped next to her husband. Blood spilled from every hole in her body with her eyes wide open.

Snoop stared at her laying there dead as if she wasn't just full of life moments ago. "Lemme explain, man!" cried Snoop.

"Shut up, police-ass nigga," said T.

Snoop was about to shit himself. T never saw that side of him. *Shid, this nigga supposed to be a hit man. Bitch ass*, T thought to himself. "So baby, what should we do with him?"

Cedez bent down and rubbed Snoop's head as if she had a little sympathy for him. Snoop's eyes pleaded for mercy. Before Mercedez could stand all the way back up, T leaned over Snoop, sending two slugs at the nigga's dome. Cedez stepped back, wiping blood from her cheek that splattered from Snoop's face.

T let off four more shots just to be sure the nigga was dead. Blood sprayed the wall and floor. Snoop's eyes were slightly open, but he had no pulse or any signs of life left in him. Nicole and Snoop were indeed together until death did them apart.

The whole scene was tragic. Cedez pulled her arm bag over her head and quickly pulled out a wig and two jogger outfits for them to change their appearances. They quickly removed their clothes, stuffed them in the bag and put on their jogger fits. Mercedez took one last look of the bodies on the floor and smiled, feeling relieved their mission was accomplished.

Le'Monica Jackson

CHAPTER NINE

"Come on, baby, let's slide." T grabbed Cedez's hand. They made sure there was no one in sight and began jogging a couple blocks as if they were just getting some exercise in. They made it to the low-low car and smoothly pulled off as if they hadn't just killed two damn people.

T-Money drove as Cedez laid back in the passenger seat, grinding her teeth. She was geeked up from the blow and most definitely in her zone. "Set it Off" by Lil Boosie was blasting through the speakers. Cedez sang along, chewing her winterfresh gum.

"Damn, you chewing that gum hard as fuck," T-Money said, looking out the corner of his eye at Mercedez. She was too high for all that funny shit though.

T-Money got off on the next exit in the direction of his personal chop shop, where he dropped off his dirty vehicles to get them stripped and rebuilt. Cedez was rolling good off that coke. "Baby, you like how it played out, huh?"

She turned the music down a little and began rubbing T's chest. He knew she was feeling good and was ready to fuck, but unfortunately, there were still things that had to be done before they could completely chill. T laughed and glanced over at her, looking her up and down as he bit his bottom lip. He gently caressed her pussy.

"Girl, you know you my rider, right?" He was so fucked up about how gangsta she was but so classy at the same time.

They pulled up to the chop shop, dropped off the low-low. T-Money had a car already there that he'd been getting worked on for the past five months.

"Damn, I love it!" T-Money said as he pulled into the garage chop shop where his homie, Lil Juney kept all of the cars that he rebuilt. T knew exactly which car was his: the all-black spaceship-looking car. He didn't even know the name of the car. He just knew that it looked foreign as fuck. Lil Juney definitely knew T-Money's style. Lil Juney was a young Italian boy in his early 20's that T-

Money had met at a car lot years prior. He was good people, He damn near lived in that garage, fixing up cars, making shit disappear, and drinking Coronas back to back.

"My boy! So which one is mine?" T-Money walked up to Lil Juney, dapping him up on some gangsta shit. Everybody he was affiliated with were Blood gang members.

"Yo, what's good, Blood?" Lil Juney was smiling from ear to ear just like everyone else. He loved seeing T-Money. "This is all yours right here!" Lil Juney rubbed the hood of the spaceship-looking build. He was so confident in his work.

They stood around and held small conversations as Cedez took their personal belongings out of the low-low car and put them into the new car. Lil Juney's was the spot for anyone in the streets. He didn't just strip and fix cars. He also got rid of guns, bodies, clothes, etc., anything that would cover up a crime. It was a Candyland or strip club for real niggas that were gooning in real life.

"Aye bruh, I'ma need to get rid of some fye and clothes," T-Money whispered in a very low tone.

Lil Juney barely heard him. "Say no mo'. I gotcha. Meet me in the dungeon." Lil Juney was already heading that way.

"Cedez, bring ya peanut head ass in and grab the bag out the truck!" T shouted out to his girl.

Cedez didn't even reply. She was so used to him trying to crack jokes. "Nigga think he a damn comedian or something, meatball head ass. I ain't even gone say shit. Nigga gon' wanna act like he on battle of the comedians or something all day," Cedez mumbled to herself under her breath as she grabbed the bag and headed into the dungeon.

The room was pitch black with only black lights and a tub of acid. They opened the bag, emptying everything inside. Standing there, they watched the items dissolve down to nothing. One thing about them: they were never sloppy when they handled business. They handled everything and then headed back home, where they could actually sit back and analyze how the whole day played out.

The day was coming to an end and they'd finally made it home safe. They got in the shower, bathing each other and talking about everything that happened. As they got out of the shower, Cedez laid on T's chest in bed and began juggling his balls with one hand. His dick was rock hard. Under covers, ass naked, body to body, enjoying each other's bodies... She slowly climbed on top of him face down. T-Money pulled the hood of her clit back and began sucking on her clit, flicking it with his tongue in a fast motion.

It was feeling way too good. Mercedez's body began jerking as she came all over his mouth. He laid her down and took control, throwing her legs way back to the headboard with his knees planted in the mattress. He dived in her opening, giving her dick for days. After an hour of pleasing each other, they fell into a deep sleep.

Cedez woke up about 9:00 a.m. to a few missed calls and unread messages.

"Fuck that, where da gas at?" She muffled in her morning voice. The only thing she was concerned about was logging into social media to see if there was anyone posting about the homicides. She rolled herself a blunt, sat on the toilet smoking, and scoped Facebook from Tonya's page. Clicking on Nicole's profile, the first post was from @Flygirl Thomas and it read, "God how could you take my only sister away from me? Rest in peace Coley. You'll forever be missed."

Cedez read it aloud to herself. One of her legs began to shake and her heart pounded. She'd come down from her high so she was completely in her right state of mind and clearly aware that just the day before, she and T-Money had killed Snoop and his wife right in their own home.

She quickly finished using the restroom and normally she would hop in the shower, but this specific morning it was mandatory that she wake T up and turn the news on.

"Baby." She gently rubbed T's back.

He turned over with his sleepy voice, looking up to see Cedez standing over him. "What's up, bae? What's wrong?"

Cedez sat on the edge of the bed and grabbed the remote from the night stand, turning the news on. T sat up in the bed rubbing his eyes to wake himself up. The news channel was on commercial. Cedez looked over at T and smiled. "Baby, you were sleeping so good, but you know we gotta see what the lick read on the news. People already makin' posts on Facebook."

No sooner had Cedez said that, the news reporter spoke loud and clear through the surround sound hooked up to the 72 inch flat screen T.V. mounted on the bedroom wall. "Married couple found dead in their home after their five year anniversary vacation. Shot to death, Robert and Nicole Douglas were murdered, leaving behind two children. We have no suspects leading up to their death as of right now. If you have any information, please call our crime line…"

T grabbed the remote and turned the TV off. "Shit, that's all we need to know, baby," he said. This type of shit was normal to them.

Cedez was on Facebook almost all day reading the normal shit everybody posted when a bitch died, the typical shit like "Gone but never forgotten". Then eventually they forget about ya.

"So what's next, baby?" Cedez looked up at T, waiting for his response.

"Shit, what do you mean what's next? We live like ain't shit happened. You ain't new to this," he replied, as calm as can be.

She loved how calm his spirit was. Even in situations where he should be worked up, he remained calm, which kept her leveled out as well.

CHAPTER TEN

Weeks had passed and still no word on who killed the Douglases, which was a good thing. T and Cedez had no worries.

It was a Sunday morning, almost noon, and Cedez had a lot on her mind. She hadn't heard from Mr. Nash or Mr. Jameson, which was good too, but she wanted to know something. At least they were aware that the witness on the case had been killed. T knew Cedez like a book. He could tell she was tight. He threw her two stacks of money wrapped in rubber bands, straight blue faces.

"Here, go shoppin', ma, get ya mind off the bullshit." He knew shopping was her escape from real life.

Cedez stashed the money in her purse and got dressed. She put on a skintight white Louis Vuitton dress and a pair of red bottom designer pumps and headed out the door. She already knew exactly what store she was going in first: her favorite boutique, Fas Galore Boutique. It was a small boutique owned by a young Chinese girl. Cedez was known in that store.

The doorbell went off as Cedez entered the store. The store owner's face lit up at the sight of Cedez. She knew Cedez came to spend big money on that expensive-ass shit in her store that most bitches complained about the prices. Some of the shit was real designer while other shit in there just looked good as hell and you couldn't find anywhere else because it was custom made.

"Say-Deez!" The Chinese girl came from the back of the store, getting Cedez's attention with her strong accent.

"Hey Tina! How are you?" Cedez replied.

"I no see you long time, girl. You no like my shit no more?" Tina rubbed Cedez's arm as she laughed along with her. "I got new things for you. You like, Say-deez!" Tina walked her to the center of the store, where she had brand new two pieces that she had just put out on the floor a few minutes prior to Cedez walking in.

She was the only person in the boutique, buying just about every damn piece in the store. The doorbell went off again. Tina greeted the tall Hispanic-looking guy that walked in. Cedez looked back, smiled, and continued shopping. She went in the dressing room and tried on a few outfits. She was definitely buying everything she picked up.

The Hispanic guy was having a small conversation with Tina about a black dress as Cedez waited at the counter for her until she finished helping her customer.

Cedez had never seen a man inside of Tina's boutique. "Hmmmm he must be picking his girl up something. He got good taste," she said to herself.

The man decided on the black dress and proceeded to the counter to purchase it.

"You find everything you want, Say-Deez?" Tina said as she rang up the items. "$1675.73," she told Cedez.

Mercedez reached in her big Gucci bag and pulled out her cash. The tall Hispanic man removed his pitch black glasses from off his face, setting them on top of his head. He pulled out a silver and gold badge with a star on it that was hooked to his necklace that he had tucked under his shirt.

"Mercedez Smith, you're under arrest for an out of state warrant. Put your hands behind your back!" The man grabbed her arms, placing them behind her back.

"No, no sir! This is a mistake you're making. My name is Chantal Jackson!" Cedez yelled as she tried to squirm out of the grip the man had on her.

Tina stood behind the counter speechless. Cedez dropped her head in disbelief. Everything happened so fast. Before she knew it, she was being walked out by two officers to an unmarked Chevy Impala. There were people out in the plaza shopping at other stores watching as she was being walked out in cuffs.

"Oh wow, she must was trying to steal out Tina's boutique," Cedez heard one girl tell another girl she was with.

Any other time Cedez would've put a bitch in their place for even speaking of her, but at that moment, she was wishing she caught petty-ass charges for stealing compared to what she was really being arrested for.

Tina stood at the door watching as everyone else did while the officers drove away with Cedez in their backseat.

T-Money was blowing Cedez's phone up. His nerves were so bad. He was thinking the absolute worst.

"Man, fuck! Phone steady going to voicemail. I wonder what the fuck going on?" he spoke out loud to himself. His mind was racing. He couldn't even think clearly.

He pulled out his phone and began calling every hospital in the area.

Le'Monica Jackson

CHAPTER ELEVEN

"Hello, is there any possibility y'all have any patients by the name of Mercedez Smith or Chantal Jackson?" T-Money was distraught.

"One moment, sir," the lady on the other end of the phone said.

He calmed down a little bit hoping they'd just say yes so at least he could know where she was. Seconds later, the lady got back on the phone.

"No sir, we have no one by those names, sorry."

T-Money slammed the phone down. He grabbed his keys and went to all the stores he knew she shopped at. The first store that came to mind was the boutique. Tina knew T from him coming in the store with Cedez.

As soon as He entered the store, Tina ran up to him, barely able to utter a word out

"Teeeee, the police came. They took Say-Deez. She did nothing wrong!" Tina was waving her arms around, trying to explain what happened."

"Calm down, Tina. What you're telling me is Mercedez went to jail?" T grabbed Tina's hand, trying to get her to relax.

"Yesss, Tee! She do nothing. Me know no why they took her. She spent good money with me."

He knew exactly why she had been arrested. He got as much info as he could from Tina and immediately jumped in his truck and contacted Ms. Karen, letting her know they needed to contact Mr. Jameson, the lawyer, ASAP. He pulled off, heading back to his spot. He had to think of something quick.

"What the fuck, brah! I should've just kept her here with me!"

The police impounded Mercedez's car. Good thing the car was in Tonya's name. T-Money paid Tonya to pick the car up and keep it parked at her house for the time being. He went online to see if Cedez had already been booked, as there was no Mercedez Smith in the system. In the middle of him searching for her, he received a call from Mr. Jameson.

"Hello, Tevin, I was informed about Mercedez's arrest. No worries though. They have her booked under Chantal Jackson and they can't seem to find her fingerprints to match Mercedez Smith," he said.

T-Money was pacing back and forth as he took in everything the lawyer was telling him. "Okay sir, so are they extraditing her? And are you good with all the money? Do I need to bring you anything?" T had a thousand questions.

"Everything is good on the money. Karen brought me the full payment, and yes, she'll be extradited, but I'll have her out as soon as I can."

T felt a lot better after talking to Mr. Jameson. He knew he always made shit happen when it came down to Mercedez and that was off the love he had for Ms. Karen as well. Plus Cedez was a well-paying client, which meant he always got full payment up front.

***

Cedez sat in the holding cell, waiting for her name to be called for medical intake. Her stomach was tied in a knot. She hadn't spoken to T-Money, her mom, or the lawyer. She had one more thing to do in booking before she could make her free call, and that was seeing the nurse. Mercedez was feeling nauseous. She didn't have a chance to grab a bite to eat before they arrested her. She was feeling sick to her stomach nervous as fuck and some more shit, but she knew she couldn't show it in front of the police. As far as she was concerned, she wasn't even the person they were looking for. She washed her face with cold water as she heard the nurse calling to get her vitals and shit done.

"Chantal Jackson!" the nurse yelled out with a very squeaky, immature voice, she looked to be no more than twenty-one years old at the most.

Cedez dried her face with her blue uniform shirt as she stepped out of the cell. "I'm coming!" She slid her feet into her jail Crocs and headed to room number three, where the short fat girl stuffed into a medical uniform sat behind the desk waiting for her.

"Are you Chantal Jackson?" The nurse looked up from her glasses, glancing at Mercedez, then back down at her charts that laid in front of her.

"Yes ma'am." Cedez pulled out a chair and took a seat on the opposite side of the desk.

The girl began asking Cedez the typical questions you're asked in medical intake, checking off boxes on the paper as Cedez answered each question. "Last menstrual?" The nurse pulled a calendar from the pocket of her uniform shirt.

"Ummm, damn, I'm not sure." Cedez rubbed her chin, trying to think back on when her last period was. It hadn't even dawned on her that she hadn't had her period.

"Is there a possibility you could be pregnant?" The nurse put her pen down and searched Cedez's face for answers.

"Naw, I don't think so," she said, not sounding too sure.

"How about I just give you a pregnancy test?" she insisted.

"Um, okay, that's fine," Cedez replied, shrugging her shoulders. She had been fucking T-Money unprotected for years and she'd never gotten pregnant, so that was the least of her concerns.

The nurse handed Cedez a cup and pointed to the nearest bathroom. "Step in there and fill the cup up as much as you can." she said.

Cedez went to the restroom and handled her business, came out, and placed the cup of urine on the nurse's desk. "Here you go, ma'am."

The girl opened a cabinet, pulling out a pregnancy test kit. She busted open the plastic wrapper with a pregnancy test stick inside of it. She removed the stick and placed the end of it inside the cup for about five seconds. She set the stick on a napkin and began making small talk with Mercedez as they waited for the results. "So are you bonding out?" she asked, clearly just trying to find something to talk about, because Cedez knew the nurse could care less whether she went home or not.

"Mm-hmm." Cedez just said anything to shut the girl up.

The girl looked down at the test. "Well, Ms. Jackson, you have two very dark blue lines here. You're definitely pregnant."

Cedez went from not concerned at all to very concerned. "Uh, no, that can't be accurate, ma'am." Cedez scratched her head in obvious frustration.

The nurse said nothing. She held the pregnancy stick up, showing her the results. The timing was definitely fucked up because of the predicament she was in.

The nurse signed a couple forms and put "X" everywhere Mercedez had to sign. She almost forgot her name was Chantal Jackson. She was about to sign Mercedez Smith, but then it dawned on her. She was tripping. She had to get in the habit of being Chantal Jackson.

She got up and waited in the holding cell for her free call, her mind was going 100 miles per hour. She didn't know who to call first and if she wanted to break the news about her being pregnant or just talk about the case. Mercedez dropped a tear. She was so overwhelmed. There was way too much going on at one time. Wiping her eyes, she looked at herself in the small blurry mirror, giving herself a pep talk. "Tighten up, Mercedez. You're a soldier; you're strong. Girl, this small shit to a giant." She wasn't sure if she was crying about the pregnancy or the situation she was in. It usually took a lot for her to break down or even shed a tear. But this was a bit much.

It was a very busy day inside the jail and the booking area was packed. There was a slim chance she would even get the chance to make her free calls. She was scheduled to see the judge first thing in the morning and of course be extradited to Florida the following day, and there she would be informed if she was eligible to post bail or not. The fact that she had to stay in jail overnight really pissed her off. She was so used to being able to bond out immediately and fight her charges from the outside.

Hours passed and her name still had not been called for the phone. She had no idea what time it was or if it was even still daylight because the cell had no windows. She held her shirt up, looking down at her belly, still in disbelief. "You gotta be fucking kidding me," she said to herself.

She was all alone with nothing but time to think. After hours of thinking, she drifted off into a deep sleep.

She hadn't even realized she'd slept that long. It was a new day and she still hadn't talked to anyone. She saw the judge, got her charges read, and went on about the day waiting to be extradited. She didn't even bother to bring it to the judge's attention that her name was Chantal Jackson, but she was booked on charges for Mercedez Smith. It didn't matter because it wasn't the judge who signed off on the warrant. She had to go back to Orlando, Florida to court and see what they had over there before anything could be done. She was worried if anyone even knew where she was.

Cedez finally made it to Florida, riding in a blackout van for seven hours with two other inmates. She was uncomfortable as fuck. They arrived at the jail around 10:00 a.m., so she would be seeing the judge the following morning.

The first thing she did after being booked was call T-Money.

"This is a collect call from…Chantal…at the Orange County Jail," the operator spoke loud and clear.

T-Money repeatedly pressed one, before the operator could even say, press one to accept this call. "Baby, before you even start speaking, I've talked to your lawyer, and everything good. I'm on my way to Florida right now, so you'll be out ASAP, baby."

Cedez couldn't get a word in. T-Money was answering every question she was about to ask him. As soon as he gave her a chance to talk, she spoke without thinking twice. "I'm pregnant, T!"

The phone instantly got silent. "Say you swear!" He was in disbelief. He had never heard a woman speak that kind of language to him. As much pussy as he got, he never had gotten anyone pregnant before. She caught him off guard with that one.

"I'm dead serious, baby. The test came back positive while I was in intake in Georgia."

T-Money was lost for words. "Um, okay then, well, we'll talk about it as soon as you are released. My main concern right now is getting you out of there."

She knew he loved kids and shit, but she never imagined him with his own, especially sharing one with her. They'd done everything together besides bring a child into the world.

"Mr. Jameson will be there at your court date with me, you don't have a bond as of right now, but you'll have one once you see the judge." He told her everything Mr. Jameson had told him. "You gon' be fine, baby. Do you ever sit in jail?"

"No, baby," she answered in a soft immature voice.

"Okay then! So just sit tight and you'll be out in no time."

She felt a load lifted off of her shoulders just hearing him assure her that she would be out soon.

The fifteen minute free call ended. She was tired and in desperate need of rest. Although she was anxious to tell her mom she was pregnant, she figured it would be a better idea to give her that kind of news in person. She went to sleep and woke up for court the next morning.

"State of Florida vs. Mercedez Smith," Judge Gatson addressed her case.

Cedez wasn't sure if she should acknowledge the fact she was being called Mercedez Smith' since technically her name was Chantal Jackson. She shot her lawyer a look of confusion. He nodded at her, giving her the okay to remain seated. She smiled, glancing over in the audience, noticing T-Money and her mom present for her support.

"Your honor, we have Chantal Jackson here in custody for charges for a Mercedez Smith, however, Ms. Jackson's fingerprints do not even match the fingerprints of Mercedez Smith. I'm convinced you have the wrong person, which leaves me to believe she has to be released until further notice." Mr. Jameson stood at the podium and spoke with great authority.

The judge looked at the state.

Oh my gosh, I know this damn girl, Cedez thought to herself. The girl representing the state glanced at Mercedez, knowing for a fact she was indeed Mercedez Smith.

There was an awkward silence in the courtroom as the state attorneys skimmed through their documents. The state couldn't find anything to keep her in custody.

"No objection, Your Honor." The young girl representing the state appeared to be overpowered. You could tell by the look on her face that she felt defeated. "Chantal Jackson, sorry for your time. Release her ASAP!"

The judge seemed to be agitated. Mercedez was escorted to the holding cell located in the back of the courtroom beyond the double doors. She had to wait to be taken back to the jail to be released.

T-Money shook Mr. Jameson's hand and met him outside of the courtroom to chop it up with him. Ms. Karen was relieved.

The only thing Cedez could think about was how the fuck she was going to keep the state attorney on her side. She went to school with the girl. As a matter of fact, they were in the same Algebra class in ninth grade. Ashley Simpson, the state prosecutor, knew Mercedez Smith personally. Mercedez couldn't wait to be released to give T-Money the run down about this state attorney bitch. The only thing she had in mind was paying Ashley off to not look deeper into the fact that she was actually Mercedez Smith.

She sat in the holding cell back at the jail, patiently waiting for her name to be called to be released. It was busy at the jail, and almost every officer was familiar with her from doing time before, so that alone had her nervous as hell. All it took was for one officer to say the wrong shit that could cause her release to be delayed.

"Hey Ms. Smith, what are you here for now?" An officer came around to do her fifteen minute cell check.

Mercedez just looked up and grinned, pretending she was out of her mind. There was no way she was answering to Ms. Smith when clearly her paperwork read Chantal Jackson. She had to get out of there in a hurry.

Le'Monica Jackson

CHAPTER TWELVE

T-Money decided to chill with Ms. Karen until Mercedez called to be picked up. They went out to eat at the finest diner in Orlando, Ruth Chris, and of course, he treated, per usual.

"Ma, Cedez broke some news to me when she called from jail." T-Money and Ms. Karen were very close. He could talk to her about anything.

She cut into her $80.00 steak with the fancy eating utensils. "Oooh, this steak juicy, thank you, Tevin. You've always been good to our family and most of all my baby." She unintentionally ignored the fact that he had some tea to tell her.

"Y'all have always been like family to me." He rubbed Ms. Karen's back.

"Yeah, baby. Now tell me what is it that Cedez told you when she called." She was focused on her food as she spoke. There was an awkward silence. Ms. Karen put her utensils down when she realized it might be a little more serious than she thought. Looking T-Money in the eyes, she suddenly became worried. "What is it, T, what's the news?"

He didn't know if he should go ahead and tell her or allow Cedez to tell her. "Well, um, you know I love Cedez, right? She my best friend, the love of my life, my everything." He paused, waiting for Ms. Karen to agree that she knew these things.

"Yes, of course, Tevin." She had a look of worry on her face. She had no idea where the conversation was going.

"Well, uh…now she's about to be the mother of my child."

"Yesss, Lord!" Ms. Karen jumped to her feet in excitement. She hugged T-Money tightly around his neck, screaming, causing the whole restaurant to turn their heads to see what the hype was all about. He laughed as Ms. Karen sashayed around his chair. "I'm 'bout to have a grandbaby!" she sang. She was a little hood but that was fine because she was more classy than anything. "What?" She looked around, noticing everyone was focused on her. "My baby is having a baby!" she said.

The people returned their attention back to their own tables.

Ms. Karen was very outspoken. She and Tevin talked all about parenthood and how excited Ms. Karen was. They finished eating right in time. As soon as T pulled out his wallet to pay for the tab, Mercedez was calling.

"Baby, I'm ready, I'm released." She was relieved to finally be out.

"Okay bae, me and Ma will be there shortly."

T did the dash to the jail house to pick his girl up. Ms. Karen couldn't wait to talk about the pregnancy with her daughter. T was excited as well but kind of over the edge about it too because it caught him off guard and he really had no plans on being a father anytime soon. He knew they would make great parents together, but he had a hidden secret that Mercedez had no idea about and he didn't know how he would break the news to her. He knew he'd eventually have to tell her.

They pulled up to the jail and Cedez was standing there in the same clothes T had last seen her in. She was beautiful, of course. She jogged to the car and hopped in the backseat like a kid getting picked up from school. She was just glad to be out. It could have turned out really bad, since the officers and state prosecutor knew her. She told her mama and T all about the officers and State knowing her.

Ms. Karen was just happy to be in the presence of her daughter and not having to see her through a glass, especially the fact that she was now pregnant. "Sooo, Cedez, is there something you need to tell Mama, girl?" Ms. Karen turned all the way around in the passenger seat, looking Mercedez directly in her eyes. If Ms. Karen didn't love anything else in her life, she was crazy about her grandchildren, and Mercedez's baby would make grandchild number five for her.

"What is it you want to know, Mama?" She had no idea T-Money had already broken the news to her mama. He leaned over on the armrest looking at Mercedez through the rearview mirror, rubbing his beard with his right hand.

All Cedez could do was smile. He looked so good smirking at Cedez and licking his lips. All she could focus on was his big Rolex watch and his 24K pinky ring reflection in the rearview. She had a feeling he must have broken the news just by the way he was looking at her.

Ms. Karen looked down at Mercedez's belly and burst out laughing. "Girl, I'm excited!" She clapped her hands and laughed dramatically with her tongue all out like she did whenever she was excited about good news.

Mercedez laughed along with her mama. "Ma! Oh my gosh!" She mushed T-Money in the back of his head "He told you!"

"Damn right he did!" Ms. Karen was happier than Cedez and T-Money, which wasn't surprising. She had been waiting for Cedez to bear her a grandchild in hopes that a baby would slow her down.

They talked about the baby the whole ride to drop Ms. Karen off as if Mercedez hadn't just got out free on a murder charge. She and T had a lot to talk about, that was for sure. The whole situation still hung over Mercedez's head.

They dropped Ms. Karen off and headed to meet with Mr. Jameson and Mr. Nash together. Before Cedez could inform the lawyer and detective about the officers and state prosecutor recognizing her, Mr. Jameson, the lawyer, was already telling her he got a call right after court from the State mentioning they knew that the person in custody was in fact Mercedez Smith. Mr. Jameson placed his hand on her shoulder.

"Calm down, Ms. Smith. Since the State knows you personally, she has to withdraw from the case because it's a conflict of interest and without a witness to point you out, they can not charge you because there is lack of evidence. Like I've stated before, without Robert Douglas, the State has nothing."

From that point on, Cedez knew she was good. T-Money shook the lawyer's and Mr. Nash's hands.

"Okay, we'll contact you if we hear anything else. Until then, stay out the way and stay out of trouble with the law."

T-Money thanked them and they got in the car, filled up on gas, and jumped on the highway to head back to Georgia.

"So baby, how you feel about having a baby?" Cedez was driving while T lay back in the passenger seat. He was tired from all the driving and handling business for the past two days. He could finally relax his mind now that Cedez was there and back in his presence again.

"Shit, I really don't know how to feel, bae. I'm happy, but look at the lifestyle we are living."

Cedez felt a little burn in her throat since there was a "but" after him saying he was happy. She just sat there silent with her eyes fixed on the road. He could tell his response had her feeling some type of way. He rubbed her cheek with his knuckles.

"We'll book you an appointment as soon as we get back to Georgia."

Cedez nodded her head, but remained silent. He really didn't know what else to say. Her mind was all over the place. There was no doubt he would be a good father, because he took care of everybody connected to him, so she could only imagine how spoiled their child would be. Her main concern was would a baby change the great relationship they had, even though what they had never held an actual title? Cedez and T-Money were in love. They never even talked about being in a relationship because the bond they shared didn't even require titles.

Mercedez was in one of her moods. She turned on her girly music. Of course some slow shit - all girls loved slow R&B when they were in their feelings. Monica's "Should've Known Better" was quaking throughout the car. T-Money had dozed off and Cedez was kind of glad so she could think to herself without worrying about if he was trying to read her mind. He knew her so well.

His phone was vibrating back to back, and for some reason, Cedez wanted to grab his phone out of curiosity. "Nooo, I've never done that and I'm not starting now. Don't start the crazy baby mama shit, Mercedez, tighten up." She had to give herself a mental pep talk in her head. Her womanly instinct caused her to just glance over just to see what name was popping up on his phone and it read "Alexus" with a heart and a lock emoji. Cedez fucked around and said it out loud.

T-Money opened his eyes and looked at her. "What's wrong, baby?" He didn't hear exactly what she said.

"Oh, nothing, I was singing," she lied.

He closed his eyes, rubbing her thigh and drifting back off to sleep.

She never cared who and what T was doing but she'd never thought in a million years he would have a bitch saved in his phone with emojis next to their name. *The bitch must have had his phone to save her own number because T ain't no mushy-ass nigga to be putting emojis by a bitch name, and if she had his phone, she must be important. I've been around for years and I know one thing he don't play about is somebody fucking with his phone.* Mercedez's inner bitch was talking to her. If T was awoken to see her facial expression, he would've known there was a whole conversation going on in her mind.

She instantly turned the music from R&B to some crunk shit. She wasn't feeling the vibes she was catching. It may have been her hormones and the changes her body was going through. This was all new to her. There was so much she wanted to say to T-Money, but she knew it would be just speaking out of anger.

They made it back to Georgia. The majority of the ride, T had slept, and the other half they didn't say much to each other, they just vibed to the music.

Mercedez called and made a doctor appointment. She didn't know whether to use Mercedez Smith or what so she went with her first mind and scheduled the appointment under Chantal Jackson. The last thing she needed was anything leading up to her being Mercedez Smith since she had already been arrested as Chantal Jackson.

***

The tall young white nurse peeped her head out into the lobby, calling for Cedez to be seen. Cedez and T-Money walked to the room they were directed to. The nurse started by asking Cedez a ton of questions and then did an ultrasound. The smile on T's face was priceless when the nurse squeezed the clear gel on Cedez's belly and put the monitor to her stomach and he heard his baby's heartbeat for the first time.

"Well, Mom and Dad, there seems to be two in there and you seem to be almost seven weeks along."

Cedez and T couldn't believe their ears. "TWO!" Cedez sat up on the table looking at the screen of the two things she'd never seen before inside of her stomach.

T rubbed his beard and grabbed her hand. "Relax, baby," he said, trying to program the fact that he was about to be a father to not one, but two children.

The nurse gave Cedez a folder full of papers giving instructions on how to be pregnant and carry the babies without difficulties. She definitely had no idea on how to even be a pregnant woman. She stayed on the go and her life was way too fast to be pregnant, but she had to face the fact that she was sharing her body with two other people now. Reality hadn't kicked in yet that she was about to be a mother in eight more months.

Cedez rolled a blunt and rode home in the passenger seat, pulling on the blunt as if she didn't have two other hearts beating inside of her. T-Money didn't stop her either. He'd seen pregnant women smoke weed and it never affected their baby, and besides, he could only imagine what Mercedez was feeling mentally and emotionally, so he let her enjoy her high. That's the only thing that seemed normal at that moment.

She was waiting to break the news to Tonya and everyone else even though she knew her mama had probably already told the whole world. Ms. Karen couldn't hold water when it came to those kinds of teas.

CHAPTER THIRTEEN

It had been almost three weeks since T and Cedez had killed Nicole and Snoop. Cedez checked social media frequently and watched the news daily. There was nothing being said. People were still grieving on social media and the only thing Cedez could think about was being pregnant with twins and she had just taken a mother away from her kids. She knew karma was real and she couldn't imagine something happening to her and leaving her babies without a mama. Her conscience was eating at her, but it was either Snoop and Nicole had to go or she would have been having her twins in prison and leaving someone else to raise them.

T-Money didn't even have a family. His mama died when he was twelve years old. She was murdered by her boyfriend. T-Money and his two sisters were split up into different homes that the state placed them in. He never had a father or even knew of one so he had no form of a father figure and had no idea how to even be one. He only knew what he saw on T.V Cedez's family was the closest thing to a real family for him. There was way too much going on at one time for him. He was in desperate need of a vacation to just relax and organize his thoughts.

Cedez made herself a bubble bath, dimmed the bathroom lights, and relaxed in the tub, listening to the new Rod Wave album on her iPhone. She closed her eyes and laid her head back on the rim of the tub. All kinds of thoughts ran through her head. She went in a daze picturing how life would be as a mother, then her mind drifted to the whole murder scene with Snoop and Nicole. She opened her eyes, trying to shake the thought of being arrested for their murders and being taken away from her children. She was almost positive though that they didn't leave any trace behind. As far as the streets knew, T was going to get the nigga that was responsible for his dawg's and his wife's murders.

Cedez was about to yell for T to bring her a bottle of water because she was dehydrated from the steam in the bathroom until she heard him talking on his phone as if he was trying to whisper.

"Yeah, baby, I sent it to you, check your Cash App."

Cedez turned down the music on her iPhone, leaning over the tub, trying to hear T's conversation.

"I miss you too, girl. I'm gon' buy my ticket this week. I'll see you this weekend. I love you too."

Cedez knew she had not just heard those words coming out of his mouth. She never knew he had it in him to talk to another girl like that besides her. She repeated his words to herself. "I'll see you this weekend? I love you too?" She was disturbed and questioned if she heard that correctly. As bad as she wanted to say something, she knew she couldn't just bring it to him like that, so she decided she'd wait for the weekend to see where exactly he was buying a ticket to go to. She only knew for him to fly out when he had to handle business.

She waited until she knew he was off the phone and yelled out for him to bring her a bottle of water. T came in the bathroom and sat on the sink counter, opening the water bottle for Cedez. She acted as normal as possible like she didn't just hear him sweet talking on his phone. *Everything that happens in the dark comes to the light*, she thought. She instantly shook that thought, knowing she'd done so much in the dark and if it ever came to the light, she and T-Money could possibly never see daylight again.

T-Money started a conversation with Cedez. He noticed her attitude without her even saying a word. The last thing he thought was that she'd heard his phone conversation. "Baby, you ain't saw nothing new on social media or nothing, have you?" He ran his fingers through her hair while she sat up in the tub, tapping her nails along the edge of the tub.

"No, there's nothing new. Anything new with you?" Mercedez said sarcastically.

"New with me? Naw, ain't nothing new except the fact I'm 'bout to have two kids!" T-Money responded with sarcasm as well.

She smirked and remained silent. She could not do the most without any accurate information. She'd always been the type to do her research first and pin the tail on the donkey before she mentioned anything.

T knew something was up with Cedez because her whole demeanor was totally different. He just couldn't put his finger on it. He left the bathroom and laid across the bed as she got dressed. She threw on her pink Victoria's Secret house robe, tied her inches up in a bun, and sat on the side of the bed opposite of T and lotioned her feet. The name Alexus kept running through her head. It would only be a matter of time before she found out who Alexus was to him. She began wondering if Alexus was the same girl he would be seeing this weekend and that he'd just told he loved her.

Friday was slowly approaching and Cedez was patiently waiting to see what story he was going to come up with about where he was flying out to. She was downstairs on her laptop in the sitting room, Googling different things about pregnancy and babies. She heard his footsteps coming down the stairs but she kept her focus on the laptop. She knew he was coming to see what she was up to. He had been on her trail heavy this past couple of days trying to peep her vibe, trying to figure out exactly what was wrong with her. He eased his way next to her and sat on the loveseat, caressing her thighs.

"So what's really up, Cedez? You've been out of jail. Is it something you not tellin' me?"

Little did T-Money know the last thing on her mind was jail and shit. "No, baby, I told you everything that happened. I don't keep anything from you - never have, never will!" She couldn't help but be sarcastic every time she talked to him.

"Oh yeah? You kept it away from me when you killed Buddy Ro," T joked, trying to make her laugh, but she didn't find anything funny. "Well shit, while you on the laptop, could you book me a flight to leave out Friday morning or Thursday night to go to California?"

Mercedez nodded her head yes. "What's in Cali, baby?" She knew exactly what she was doing: trying to get answers out of him.

"Oh, I'm gonna leave you a nice sack for the weekend, but I got to link up with a couple of my partnas in Cali. We trying to put something in motion. I'll be back Sunday night or first thing Monday morning."

At that moment, she knew for a fact he was lying to her. *It'll all unfold*, she thought. She did just as he had told her and booked the flight, informing him what time and date his flight was scheduled for. She closed her laptop and remained calm. *What if he's going to Cali to see this Alexus girl that keeps blowing his phone up? What if he's going to see this girl he said he loved on the phone? What if it's all the same girl?* Mercedez had a thousand questions that she was determined to find answers to. There was so much happening in her life at one time. Funny how things could change so drastically in a matter of days. She had three bodies on her hands she had to worry about, now babies on the way, and the fact that T-Money wasn't keeping it all the way G-Code with her. She felt like he really tried her like she was an average bitch by even saying he'd leave her a sack - as if she needed his money, like she ain't have big bank herself. She did what was smart and just went with the flow. She wasn't sure exactly how she would find out what she needed to know, but she was certainly putting a plan together.

T-Money's flight was taking off in less than 24 hours. She knew he'd be tapping in on the cameras to see what she was doing at the house while he was away, not because he didn't trust her, but more so that he wanted to make sure nothing happened to her while he was gone. Cedez helped T-Money get his shit together for his flight. She played everything off perfectly. Little did he know she'd booked herself the same flight at a later time and she had programmed his location to come straight to her phone. She could not believe she was going so low to try to track him down but at this point, she didn't care. She was desperate to know what was really going on with her soon-to-be kids' father. She'd never imagine herself being those same hoes she talked down on for chasin a nigga or being on a nigga's trail.

"Baby, while you're gone, I'm going back to Florida to chill with Ma. We have a lot to talk about face to face and I didn't really have the time when you picked me up from jail. It was too much going on at one time that day. So I'll be back in Georgia Monday as well, if not sooner." Mercedez had her plan put together.

"Okay, cool, baby, just be safe and try not to be on the scene too much. You know them crackas still gone be on ya ass for a while." T-Money had no idea she was going to Cali right behind his ass.

T-Money's flight landed and he already had a rental car waiting at the airport for him. He went to the hotel room that was already booked.

Cedez was keeping up with his every move. *I know for a fact he doesn't get rooms in his own name*, she said to herself. She got ready for her flight to take off to Cali. Her phone was going on airplane mode, which made the flight the worst ever since she couldn't keep up with where he was until the plane landed. Her stomach was feeling weak as soon as the airplane took off. It kept slipping her mind that she was carrying babies. She got up from her seat and made her way down the aisle to the restroom. She began throwing up uncontrollably. She hadn't thrown up since right after she'd found out she was pregnant. She'd read on Google it was all normal though. She rinsed her face with cold water and made her way back to her seat.

"You okay, sista?" A black lady that looked to be in her early 50 sitting in front of Cedez looked back as Cedez sighed.

"Yes, I'm okay, thank you." She forced the fakest smile ever.

"Okay, just checking, God bless." The lady was definitely a different type of breed from what Cedez was used to women around her being.

Cedez just closed her eyes and got as much rest as she could before her flight landed. She had to brace herself for whatever it was she was about to find out.

The flight finally landed. That had to be one of the longest flights she'd ever been on. As she got up from her seat to exit the plane, the same lady who was sitting in front of her handed her a card with a bible verse on it. "Enjoy the rest of your day, sister," she said.

Mercedez smiled. "Thank you." She stuffed the card in her bra without even reading it. She immediately took her phone off airplane mode, grabbing her one suitcase. She sat on a bench and skimmed through her phone, trying to gather her thoughts. She texted T-Money's phone. "Hey bae hope you had a safe flight. I love you."

He responded within seconds. "Fa sho. I love you too."

She then checked his location and it showed him to be at the Westin Resorts. Mercedez was very familiar with that hotel. She ordered an Uber to take her straight there. Her heart was beating out of her chest. She didn't know what she was walking into and all she could think about was what if T saw her snooping on him? What would he think of her?

The Uber arrived. Mercedez grabbed her belongings, getting in the back of the 2017 Jeep. Another girl sat in the back of the Uber, obviously getting dropped off to the same place as Mercedez or either somewhere close along the way. Mercedez wasn't friendly, so she sat down without saying a word.

The girl glanced at Cedez, then looked back down at her phone. They looked to be around the same age, although the girl appeared to be more on the "good girl" side, but these days you couldn't tell because as fine as Cedez was, no one would have even expected her to be out there committing homicides.

The Uber was slowly pulling up to the Westin Resort. The girl tapped the back of the driver's seat. "You can stop here, sir."

Mercedez was daydreaming about her next move not even realizing she was at her destination. Mercedez and the girl both exited the vehicle, Mercedez grabbing her small suitcase while the girl grabbed just a Birkin bag. Mercedez put on her sunglasses and proceeded to the entrance of the hotel. The other girl disappeared through the hotel, obviously going to her room. Mercedez stood at the sliding doors, not even sure what she should say to the front desk clerk because she was sure the room wasn't in T's name. She went with her first mind. Tevin's last name is Carter so she figured she'd say she needed the room number to someone with the last name Carter.

"Hello, ma'am, how can I help you?"

Mercedez's face had to be beet red because her anxiety was through the roof. She hesitated. "Umm, can I have the room number for Alexus Carter." *Fuck!* Mercedez thought. *What the fuck did I just say?* She stood there mad at herself for even saying that. She had that name Alexus on her mind since she saw the text message. The fact that the clerk pulled out her binder and looked for that name made her feel she could have a heart attack right then and there.

She had no intention of saying what came out of her mouth, but she was glad she did. The clerk replied, "That would be room number 2119, right up the elevator to the second floor, should be the last room on your left."

Mercedez's babies had to be feeling everything she was feeling because her stomach was literally doing back flips. She inhaled some fresh air and made her way to the elevator, feeling like she was floating. Being the only person in the elevator, her eyes began to get heavy at the thought of T-Money even giving his last name to another woman. She had been down to ride for so many years she couldn't imagine him doing that to her.

The elevator stopped on the second floor. Mercedez swallowed hard, feeling like a golf ball was stuck in her throat. She stepped off the elevator and prepared herself for the worst. It was way too ironic that an Alexus texted T-Money's phone, now a hotel room that he was apparently staying at for a whole weekend was booked under not only Alexus, but Alexus Carter. Cedez was a lot of things, but dumb was not one.

"2116...2117...2118..." Cedez read the room numbers while slowing down her pace as she got closer to room 2119. She felt so out of place creeping up on T-Money, especially without her burner on her. She never slipped like that, especially walking up on some shit she had no clue about.

Mercedez stood in front of room 2119. She covered the peep hole and put her ear to the door to see if she could hear any irregular noises coming from inside the room or T's voice. To her surprise, her heart dropped and a tear fell from her eyes.

Le'Monica Jackson

CHAPTER FOURTEEN

"Damn, Lex, I missed you, baby. Throw that ass back on daddy!"

She heard T's voice, it was more affectionate than she'd ever heard him be. She could not believe this was really happening. True enough, she knew he fucked other bitches and did his thing, but she'd never think it would come to her in such a way. Even though they shared no title – well, besides the fact that she was now his baby mama - she never expected there to be a woman in his life other than her. He always told her, "A bond means more than a title."

Mercedez layed her head against the door for a second just listening to T not fucking, but clearly making love to this woman that she had yet to put a face to.

"Ahh, ahh, yes, Tevin, go deeper, daddy," the woman who was obviously Alexus moaned softly, but loud enough that Cedez could hear it.

A part of her wanted to just leave and fall off the face of the earth, leaving T-Money clueless. The other part wanted to kick the door in and empty a clip on both of their asses. Making her next move without thinking, Cedez knocked on the door as hard as she could. The room immediately grew silent. She knew T so well, it's like she could see him through the door grabbing his gun. She heard him cock the hammer back and at that point, she was in rage and ready for whatever took place next.

"Who is it!" T called out. She could tell he was standing close to the door. Knowing him, he was probably ducked behind a wall ready to shoot whoever walked in.

Cedez had to think quickly. She changed her accent as if she was from the Islands. "It's housekeeping! I have to come in and switch your shower curtains out, deh last person bring deh own and left dem behind, deh not belong to us, this will be quick, my apologies." Mercedez didn't even make sense to her damn self; she just said whatever came to mind at that moment.

"Coming!" Alexus responded.

Cedez knew T-Money hadn't caught her voice. He sent Alexus to open the door while he low-key was still clutching on his gun just to be on the safe side. T had used Cedez as bait so many times to knock niggas off. He always thought if he got caught slipping it would be a bitch his enemy would send at him so he didn't sleep on shit.

As soon as Alexus opened the door, Cedez barged her way in with her eyes fixed directly on T. He jumped up from the edge of the bed, walking towards Mercedez.

"Man, what you got goin' on, Cedez?" He put his gun down, confused as fuck, wondering how the hell she ended up way in California.

Alexus stood to the side in her robe, pussy still dripping. She was speechless, looking at Mercedez as she was yelling at the top of her lungs.

Cedez hadn't even got a good look at Alexus yet. All she wanted was answers from T-Money. He punched the wall, busting a hole in it, causing the whole room to come to complete silence. Cedez and Lexus stood there staring each other down from head to toe. They looked real familiar to one another. Cedez couldn't put her finger on it. Alexus pulled her hair up in a sloppy bun and it all came back to Cedez why she looked so familiar.

"Wait a minute! Weren't you just in the Uber with me?" Cedez tapped on her temple, trying to put it all together.

Alexus replied, "Yes I was, but right now I need to know who you are. Because I'm Alexus Carter, the wife of Tevin Carter." She pointed at T as if Cedez didn't know who the fuck Tevin Carter was.

T-Money didn't say a word. All he could do was drop his head. He was embarrassed as fuck. This was not the way he wanted the secret to be revealed.

Cedez's mouth dropped in disbelief. "Really, T? So you're married?" Before he could say anything, Cedez jumped straight to the point. "Well, I'm the mother of your husband's children."

The room grew silent. Cedez refused to be the only bitch standing there looking crazy.

"Mercedez, come on, baby, can't we handle this another way?" T-Money was trying to diffuse the situation.

"Mercedez? Cedez Smith?" Alexus yelled.

Cedez was definitely confused. "Yes, I'm Mercedez Smith! And how the fuck do you know me?" She was ready for all the smoke. She wanted to know who the fuck this bitch was that was married to her soon-to-be kids' father calling her by her first and last name.

Alexus burst out crying hysterically. "Whyyy, Tevin, why?" You a dirty dog, T, you dirty as fuck!" Alexus was definitely losing it so to calm her down he began explaining himself.

"Lexus, please, baby, I'm sorry, just let me explain."

Cedez watched him comfort his wife right in front of her as if she wasn't hurting as well. Alexus ran to the bathroom. She couldn't stand to be in T's presence at the moment. All she could do was cry. It was like Cedez was feeling her own pain and Alexus's pain too. She suddenly felt bad for even going about the situation in the manner that she did. She walked over to T sitting on the edge of the bed and nudged his shoulder.

"So that's what this is? You been livin' a double life?"

He was so caught up, he didn't utter a word. He didn't do well with confrontation.

Cedez was still curious how Alexus knew her name. She made her way to the bathroom to find Alexus sitting on the bathroom counter crying, listening to "Woman to Woman" by Ashanti featuring Keyshia Cole.

"Sooo, uh, you wanna go ahead and tell me how you know me?"

Alexus wiped her eyes and turned the music off. Facing Mercedez, she looked her straight in the eyes and began. "Cedez, do you remember years ago when you first met Tevin on that website?"

Cedez was instantly tuned in. She hopped up on the counter and sat next to her. "Uh huh, I remember." She was anxious for Alexus to just spit it out already.

Alexus went on, "So the name Alexus doesn't ring a bell?"

Mercedez was clueless. She had no idea what Alexus was talking about.

"You know, Cedez, Lil Lexi…remember?" Mercedez was deep in thought as Alexus continued, "Lil Lexi, the girl who T would always take on dates with the Johns off of the damn website!"

Cedez jumped up. "Ohhh! Yeah, I remember Lil Lexi. What about her though? He told me she ran off with some pimp one day and never came back."

"No, no, no, Cedez!" Alexus interrupted. "I am Lil Lexi!"

The room came to an awkward silence.

"I've grown up, Cedez. She got down from the counter and opened her robe, exposing her body to Cedez. "Tevin got me some work done on my body, put me through school, and he married me six years ago."

T was listening to the whole conversation but he didn't interrupt because there was nothing he could say. He loved both of them and couldn't stand to see either of them hurting knowing he was the one to blame.

Cedez was baffled, looking at Alexus's body from head to toe. She looked totally different from what she'd remembered. That's what happens when you go from a paid nigga's hoe to their wife. Alexus was always pretty but she was finer than a mothafucka now. All those years Cedez was thinking Alexus just disappeared and T had stopped tricking hoes after she ran off. Meanwhile, he'd hidden the hoe, changed the bitch's life, and married her. Lexus was one year older than Cedez and they'd been around each other several times, but they were on two totally different levels.

Cedez had never been too friendly so she never engaged in a conversation with Alexus while Lexi was really out there fuckin the Johns. Mercedez was a jack girl, setting up dates just to rob their asses. They'd both grown so much over the years. Alexus was about an inch taller than Cedez with a nice round high booty that T-Money had paid for. She had a caramel complexion with nice pretty white teeth to compliment her nice smooth skin. She carried herself very well and just by looking at her, Cedez could tell Alexus had really bossed her life the fuck up. The same bitch she was disgusted with how many nigga she was sleeping with was now the same bitch married to the man of her dreams.

Alexus gave Cedez the whole run down as tears slowly ran down Mercedez's face. She listened to Alexus brag on the fact that she was now a social worker and had a degree in Psychology, she was now living well without committing any crimes. Alexus had no kids and was happily married while T paid every bill she had. They had a home in Hawaii that was paid for. Alexus had no idea Mercedez was still in his life. T had pretty much taken Alexus out of the tricking game and turned her green to all the street shit. Granted, she knew he was still a drug lord, but they also owned businesses together that her name was on as well as his. T-Money was definitely living a double life and kept it hidden for so long.

Mercedez was sick to her stomach listening to Alexus go on and on, thinking to herself, *Never underestimate the bitch you think is beneath you, 'cause the tables can turn right before your eyes.* Cedez accepted everything she was learning about T-Money. She waited patiently for Alexus, his wife, to finish so she could give her the rundown about where she stood in his life. By the time Alexus was done, Mercedez's make-up was smeared all over her cheeks from all the tears she had cried. The pain she felt was something she never felt before. Mercedez felt betrayed, played, and most of all, stupid.

The bathroom grew silent for a split second as Alexus waited for Mercedez to begin to spill the beans. Clearing her throat, Mercedez began, "Well, Alexus, it's clear we both were in the blind about each other. You thought I disappeared and I was told you did too. I first of all think you should know I'm almost three months pregnant with Tevin's twins. Although we never held a title over all these years, me and T still handle business together. I have keys to almost everything he owns."

Alexus interrupted, "No, you have keys to not even half of what he owns."

Mercedez gave Alexus a look that said shut the fuck up

"Okay, let me finish!" Before Mercedez could begin speaking again, Alexus continued snickering. "Let me guess: you have keys to the spot in Georgia? And probably the minor shit like the cars in Georgia?" Alexus was asking but kind of informing Mercedez that she really did not have shit because that was basic shit compared to what she and Tevin actually shared.

Mercedez was sensing a little attitude coming from Alexus and the last thing she wanted to do was have to pounce on the bitch like a loose pitbull since Alexus did know exactly who she was. Mercedez handled the situation very well. She stayed calm until Alexus shut the fuck up and allowed her to finish.

"Like I said! Me and Tevin never lost each other since the day I came into his life." Mercedez got a little snappy herself, but still remained calm.

"Let me guess: you're still his lil jack girl. He got you workin' those tricks now?" Alexus laughed as if she found something amusing. Clearly she had forgotten where she came from.

T-Money had this hoe feeling like she was on top of the world. She even talked different, all proper and shit as if she wasn't just a young, dumb, uneducated trick just years ago. Mercedez cleared her throat and popped her tongue extra loud. She tried to refrain from taking it there with Alexus, but at this point, the bitch had to be brought off her high horse and back down to reality.

"Check this out, Alexus. Obviously you forgot you was just the same bitch that turned tricks just to keep a roof over ya head and to clear the air. I've never tricked and you know that ain't even my style, but you, on the other hand, done fucked more niggas than you can ever count. But we not gon' talk about all that. You either gon' listen to what I have to say, or I can leave the door open for you to figure it all out, 'cause this shit deeper than what you think. Just know your husband - my babies' daddy - will ALWAYS fuck with me. But you and I have always known that, right?"

Mercedez slammed the bathroom door, leaving Alexus standing there looking dumb as she made her way out the door, pulling herself together. She walked right past T-Money, not even acknowledging him standing there.

"Cedez...Cedez! Let me talk to you!"

The door slammed. She was out. Mercedez called an Uber and booked a room at a different location for the night. She planned to fly out to Georgia the next day. T-Money and Alexus had their issues to deal with because in all reality, Cedez owed neither one of them a fucking thing. They made vows to each other, not Mercedez.

***

Alexus stood in front of T-Money with tears rolling down her face. He couldn't even look her in the eyes.

"So when were you going to tell me you had kids with Mercedez? Why did you marry me, Tevin, if you knew you were not really committed?"

Before Alexus could go any further, Tevin stood up, pacing the room back and forth. "Listen, Alexus, I love you. I'd be lying if I say I didn't. But you knew what type of nigga I was before you said 'I do'. Understand that I need you because I love you. I don't love you because I need you. You needed me - remember that! And I care about you so I saved your life and changed your life. In this life I live, a nigga needs Mercedez and I love her too. So I couldn't just let her go, and if I would've let you go, your ass would've been dead or on drugs somewhere by now. You know what you came from, Lexi, and it takes a real man to know who you was and still love you through it, and most of all, accept you. I married you so if something ever happened to me, by you being my wife, you'd always be straight. Mercedez is straight without me, Alexus. She's street smart and book smart. No cap, she's my backbone."

Alexus couldn't believe what she thought was so real and genuine didn't seem so real after all. She knew T-Money didn't trick hoes anymore and she knew for a fact with the mentality Cedez had she would never fall for that type of fuckery anyway. Alexus knew there were actual real feelings T-Money had for Mercedez. Her heart was shattered into pieces.

"So what you telling me, Tevin, is that you pretty much married me because you felt sorry for me?"

"No, Alexus! I married you because I love you, girl, and I fell in love with the woman you've become, but I also love Mercedez and I'd be lying if I told you that I'm just gonna leave her. Cedez and I share secrets and things that me and you could never even discuss with each other."

"Secrets?" Alexus was getting angry listening to T-Money express his emotions about Mercedez. "So the main secret was these babies I knew nothing about. You mean to tell me there's more secrets, Tevin?"

"We just found out about the pregnancy, Alexus, and understand my kids would never be a secret to anyone. I was trying to find the right words to let you know I had kids on the way. It's not like you can have any kids, so we shouldn't even be having a conversation about someone having my babies."

"How could you throw that shit in my motherfucking face, Tevin!" T-Money knew he'd hit a sensitive spot by bringing up the fact she couldn't have kids. He had a bad habit of bringing up her past when he got upset. Alexus went insane on his ass. "Nigga, don't fuckin' forget I was able to have children before you manipulated me and had me trickin' for you and let me go on a date and them niggas raped and beat me!

"Let you?" T laughed. "No, bitch, if you wasn't trying to trick on ya own instead of listening to what a nigga tell you, you would have never got raped. Remember, you ran away and thought you could make money on your own, only to find yourself running back to me after three days of being out there alone. You let yourself get raped and beat. But because of me, them niggas ain't livin to tell the story."

Their argument was getting out of control. He was the only person that could actually hit a nerve with Alexus because he knew who she was before the degree and body work. T-Money hated for Alexus to try and blame him for the fact that she couldn't bear any children and never gave him credit for the fact that he was the reason she lived a better life. Even though he didn't care to have children, he always knew someday he wanted to leave his seeds behind to carry out his name and legacy. Alexus felt some type of way knowing she could never give him that. Although life was great for her, her past still haunted her. T-Money immediately felt bad for saying what he'd said, but he knew at that moment an apology wasn't fixing shit.

Alexus cried uncontrollably. T-Money had never talked so harshly to her before, not even when she was just his hoe. He'd always talked to her with plenty of respect. The fact that he was dead ass wrong and seemed to be angrier than her really threw her for a loop. What was supposed to be a good vacation turned out to be the worst day ever.

Le'Monica Jackson

CHAPTER FIFTEEN

Mercedez felt betrayed since Tevin didn't even attempt to stop her from walking out. She felt like a bottom of the barrel-ass bitch. She sat on the balcony of the hotel suite she'd checked into and smoked a blunt of loud, gazing over the city of California, trying to clear her mind as best as she could. The scene of Alexus just standing there showing off how good her body looked kept replaying in her head. Tears ran down her face. She'd never felt so low in her whole life. The shit had her questioning her fuckin' worth. That was the main thing a woman should never have to do. Queen Naija-Karma was on repeat as Cedez contemplated on whether or not she should shoot him a text. The sad part was she didn't even know what to say to him. It was like damn, did she even really know this nigga? How could he have had something so serious for so long?

Mercedez was driving herself crazy with her thoughts. She desperately needed someone to talk to but her closest friend besides T-Money was her sister Tonya. There was no way she could tell Tonya something like this, especially when she stayed in Tonya's ear about no good-ass niggas. Tevin's secret had become her secret. Mercedez had an image to uphold and T-Money being married to a well-known hoe would definitely affect that. Mercedez couldn't wait until the next morning to get on her fight and leave California. She wished she never found out all this shit. *True statement: when you go looking for things, you find it*, she thought.

For some odd reason, the lady from the airplane that gave Mercedez that card randomly popped up in Mercedez's head. She reached in her bra, pulling out the card. It was a pink and purple business card with white letters that read "Vengeance is mine, says the Lord." And the words "Women Empowerment" was in big lettering across the back of the card. Mercedez kept repeating the scripture on the card. It was as if God was talking to her at that specific moment. She wanted revenge so bad, but she knew for a fact if she got revenge, someone was going to die, and it wasn't going to be her.

Mercedez finally got up from the balcony chair after hours of crying, thinking, and breaking herself down. Within just a couple hours, she felt like her body had been to hell and back so she decided to run herself a warm bath. One thing about a heartbreak though: it's a whole different kind of pain your body experiences. It drains you physically, mentally, emotionally, and most of all, spiritually. Even if you aren't a spiritual person, heartbreaks tend to kill your spirit from within.

Mercedez laid down and drifted into a sleep that was very much needed. She had to be up by 10:00 a.m. to catch her flight back to Georgia. As soon as she woke up, she checked her phone. It was 8:33 a.m. and she had 63 missed calls: 60 from T-Money and three private calls rather than the 60 from Tevin. "Who TF would be calling me private?" Mercedez rubbed her eyes, trying to wake all the way up. The private calls were all a minute after three of Tevin's calls. Mercedez assumed it was T calling private, but the way things were going, it could've been anyone. She had so much on her mind and was not going to start her morning off with more worries than the day before.

While making herself a cup of coffee, she wondered if she should return T-Money's calls. He didn't send any text messages, which she was hoping he did so she would know what he wanted and decide if she would respond or not. Mercedez rolled herself a blunt and began getting her things together for her flight. She was so unsure about what exactly her next moves were. All she knew was her next move was going to be her very best move. The thought of bringing children into the world motivated her even more to jump in her bag and secure it, which meant she had to some way, somehow, turn all of her dirty money into legit money. She tried her best to block out all the real life things she was facing. She needed to change her vibe.

She loved to listen to City Girls to simply boost her ego. She played their whole album as she got dressed. "Fuck, fuck that nigga," she sang along as she bounced her ass to the beat. JT and Young Miami couldn't have said it any better. Every song that came on reminded her of the bad bitch that she was and confirmed that niggas truly ain't shit. Listening to the City Girls sliding on the beat definitely changed her whole mood. She put on her Balenciaga shades, tied her wig up in a tight knot, and turned up a little bit. She was feeling herself. She wore a white T-Strap shirt with cut-up jean booty shorts, and her D&B slides. She wanted to be comfortable for the flight. She looked in the mirror and checked herself out from every angle. She wasn't showing yet and had not one flaw. Mercedez tooted her lips up and quoted a line from one of the City Girls songs "You tried it, hoe, but it ain't work." She giggled to herself, hit the bathroom light switch, and decided she was going to really try to leave the hurt bitch that she became right in California with the bullshit she came there for. Eventually, she would have to talk to T-Money. It might not be anytime soon, but there was no way she would let their issues get in the way of being in his children's lives and besides, T wouldn't go for that shit anyways. On another note, they still had things to worry about together as far as Snoop and Nicole's murder.

She just needed time to put her big girl panties on and really sit down and talk about everything with Tevin. A part of her wished she could just cut him completely off, but her feelings for him would never allow that to happen. They'd been through hell and high water together.

Mercedez's flight was ready for take-off. She prepared herself for the sickness that she knew would come at any given time. As soon as the flight took off, she dozed off and happened to sleep the entire flight.

"Ma'am, we've landed." The flight attendant softly tapped Mercedez's shoulder.

"Damn, I slept the whole ride!" She squinted her eyes, blinded by the bright light, exiting the plane. She was hoping T-Money would decide to stay in Cali a little longer or maybe go to one of his other spots. Hell, he could even take his ass to his home in Hawaii that he shared with his wife. She didn't want him in her presence no time soon, and her going back to Florida wasn't an option. Right now she wanted to kick it at their spot in Georgia in hopes that he would just stay away for a while. Since she was already under investigation for Buddy Ro's murder, there was no way she was going to be prancing around in Florida.

Pulling up to the house, the only thing Cedez wanted to do was rest. Her first trimester was really taking a toll on her. The thought alone of being pregnant was draining her.

Mercedez walked in the house up the stairs to find T-Money sitting on the bed. He had rose petals leading to the Jacuzzi tub with candles lit all around the room and "I'm sorry" cards laid out all over the bed.

Mercedez was in total shock to see that he'd made it back before her. "Wow! Shouldn't you still be in Cali laid up wit' ya wife?" She acted very nonchalant about the whole cute little setup he'd done for her. It was way too soon for the "I'm sorry" bullshit. A situation as serious as this one required time.

"Cedez, as a man, I take full responsibility for the shit I held from you for so many years."

"Yeah, hmph, now you do! Now that yo' ass got caught! I'll be damned, you're a whole fuckin' married man – to Alexus, at that! How could you keep that away from me, T? We are way better than that!" She set her purse down on the nightstand, standing in front of him, and stared into his soul.

As he sat on the bed, he held her hands, squeezing them as she looked down at him, searching his face for answers. Before T could even try to defend his case, she slipped out of his grip and collapsed on her knees with her face buried in his lap. She lay there letting out all the tears she thought she'd cried out in California. Mercedez had always been the type to hide her pain. She never let nobody see her weakness. In every situation, she appeared to be so strong but this situation was unbearable.

"Whyyy, Tevin, why would you do this to me, man?" She was a mess, snot was running from her nose and her eyes were swollen from crying.

"Mercedez, please, baby, let me just right my wrongs!" Tevin felt like his heart had been ripped out of his chest and run over by a semi truck as he heard her break down and fall apart right before his eyes, knowing that he caused her to experience the worst pain she'd ever felt. He stood up, pulling Cedez up with him. She was like dead weight in his arms. He held onto her, bear hugging her as she buried her face in his chest. There was nothing he could say in that moment to ease the pain that not only she was feeling, but he was feeling as well. All he could do was hold her. Curling his bottom lip in, he was trying to fight away his own tears.

Mercedez had never seen a weak side of him, but seeing her hurting was definitely exposing his weakness. His weakness was her. As bad as he tried to stop the tears from falling, blinking long and hard so they would disappear, they were only replaced with heavier ones. The tears began running down his cheeks, each one falling on top of Mercedez's head as he held her close.

"I'm sorry," he whispered over and over until Mercedez's hysterical sobbing became light weeping. She knew she would forgive him someday. She just wasn't sure if she'd ever trust him...

***

"Good morning, baby." Alexus yawned, turning over in bed, still in the hotel suite. She realized she was in bed alone. She was in such a deep sleep she didn't even feel T-Money get up.

"W-W-What the fuck!" Alexus jumped up butt naked, threw on her robe, and noticed all of T-Money's shit was gone. "Did this nigga really leave without even saying shit?" she said to herself. She was confused as fuck. Grabbing her phone, she dialed T-Money's number over and over, only to get the voicemail each time. "He must've put me on the block list." Alexus was in disbelief. She couldn't even bring herself to cry over the shit. "And I'm supposed to be his wife." Granted, Alexus loved T-Money, but they never shared the bond that he and Cedez shared. While Cedez was genuinely in love with him and not for what he had to offer, Alexus loved him, but was more so in love with what he could do for her. She was simply playing her part to get where she needed to be in life. Alexus was more content and comfortable with T-Money because that was all she knew. The fact that he knew the real her made it hard for her to ever take him seriously. Before marriage came up, Tevin knew her to be a hoe, so she couldn't understand why in the world he would even want to marry someone like her anyway. She did grow to love him as her man and not just her pimp, but she always kept a mental note that he was in fact her pimp before anything. She could never put on in front of him as if her past didn't exist. She loved being around people, especially men who didn't know her history. She could put on and act however she wanted to without them judging her past.

Days passed and Alexus had yet to hear from T and at that point, she was becoming worried. He'd never pulled no shit like that before. She tried not to put too much thought into the fact that she'd learned her husband had twins on the way. Alexus never doubted the fact he wasn't being faithful, but to actually bring children into their marriage was a bit much. She returned to her normal schedule, trying to focus on her job assignments. A part of her wanted to be on some evil-ass cutthroat shit and get T-Money for everything he owned, including his children he had on the way, while the other half of her was telling her she'd come too far in life to let anyone be a distraction of her success. Alexus wanted children badly and the thought of T-Money getting Mercedez pregnant made her sick to her stomach. *If only he didn't allow me to get raped I could have had as many babies as I liked*, she thought.

Alexus was in her office when she got a call on her desk phone.

"Hello Mrs. Carter, we have your husband Tevin Carter here at the hospital in Atlanta Georgia. He was stabbed three times in his chest. You were on his emergency contact list."

Alexus slammed the phone down, jumped in her 2020 Tesla, and headed to the airport, hopping on the first flight heading to Georgia. At that moment it hit her how much she really did love her husband. "Lord, please Lord! Don't let my husband die on me," she prayed. She was thinking the absolute worst.

CHAPTER SIXTEEN

Cedez stripped the bed she and Tevin had slept in the past few months. His blood was everywhere. She'd let her emotions get the best of her. Mercedez waited until T-Money was sleeping, and when she got up to use the restroom, she went through his phone and read old message threads between him and Alexus until she couldn't stand it. She took a twelve inch butcher knife, stood over T, and stabbed him three times. Before she realized what she'd done, Tevin was lying there holding his chest as blood gushed out. He couldn't get a full sentence out as he tried to speak

"Cedez, w-wha——" was all she heard before she picked up the phone and dialed 911 for help.

She had no intention of hurting him or trying to kill him. She could have simply emptied a clip on him, but she'd blacked out and stabbed him.

***

Alexus made it to the hospital within hours. She ran through the double door and stood at the front desk. "Tevin Carter, please!" Alexus was anxious for the young white boy behind the desk to give her a room number.

"And you are?" The boy looked up from the desk.

"His fuckin' wife, dammit!" She didn't have the patience for the bullshit.

"Ma'am, ma'am, take the elevator up to the fifth floor. He's in ICU in room 503."

She ran through the hospital, not giving a fuck who she ran into. Alexus was trying to get to her husband ASAP. The fact that he'd been stabbed and not shot was throwing her for a loop. *Now what nigga would stab a nigg like T and not just simply shoot him?* she thought. Alexus had all kind of questions running through her head.

She walked into the room to see him hooked up to all kinds of machines and an oxygen machine on his face. He looked normal with the exception of bandages all over his chest. She calmed down a little to see that he was still alive.

A nurse stood next to his bed with a stack of folders in her hand. "You must be Mrs. Carter?"

"I am," Alexus responded. "Could you tell me what happened to my husband please?" Alexus sat in the chair by the head of T-Money's bed and held his hand. He was on so many heavy medications that put him in a deep sleep he didn't even know Alexus was there.

"He was picked up in the ambulance around 6:00 a.m. Paramedics said they got a call from his sister stating she'd walked in the house and found him in a pool of blood. He'd been stabbed in his chest. She rode on the ambulance with him and left maybe thirty minutes ago. She gave us your number out of his phone, informing us that you were his wife. As of right now we have no information as far as who stabbed him, but when Mr. Carter wakes up, there will be a detective in here to speak with him."

Alexus rubbed T-Money's hand. "You gonna be alright, baby," she whispered. "Ma'am, how long will he be hospitalized and is he going to be okay?" Alexus stopped the nurse as she was getting ready to leave the room.

"Yes, yes, he'll be fine Mrs. Carter. He was stabbed pretty deep, a couple inches away from his heart, but he's strong. He will be out within two weeks max."

Alexus felt relieved. Now she was desperate to know who was responsible for stabbing him. "Ma'am, one more thing. My husband doesn't have any family. I'm all he's got, so there's no way his 'sister' was here."

The nurse seemed to be a little irritated. "Well, Mrs. Carter, a woman by the name of Chantal Jackson was here and I can only tell you what I was told." The nurse left the room. Clearly she had more work to do.

Alexus had never heard of Chantal Jackson, she knew T-Money had a sister, but he had no dealings with her. He hadn't seen her since they were kids. She wanted to know who Chantal Jackson was badly. The fact that T-Money had just left her hanging for

Mercedez was so irrelevant to her at that moment. The only thing Alexus was concerned about was being by her man's side.

"Yeah, where is Cedez now?" she spoke out loud, knowing T-Money was out of it and couldn't hear a word she said.

Alexus stayed by his side and stuck by him like a wife was supposed to. After an hour of sitting at the hospital, T finally woke up. Alexus wasted no time before she began with the bullshit.

"So you leave me at the suite for another bitch and now yo' ass laid up in this hospital stabbed up and shit and look who's by your side!" She poked herself in the chest with her long diamond cut stiletto nails.

T-Money didn't have enough strength to go back and forth with her. He totally ignored her bullshit. Even though Mercedez stabbed him, that was the only person he wanted to wake up to. He shook his head, not saying a word, and began looking around the room for his phone. He reached for his phone. It was sitting on the table next to his bed. Thank God Alexus didn't know his password, otherwise she would have had space and opportunity to go through his shit knowing that medication had him out of it. He scrolled to Mercedez's name, hesitating to text her. He sent a message off before putting too much thought into it. "I love you Mercedez" the message read. He knew she had only acted out of anger Had she been anyone else, she would've been a dead bitch walking. He couldn't seem to leave Cedez alone though, especially now that she was carrying his babies. She was his best friend, the woman he truly loved, and now his baby mama.

Alexus wanted to turn up on his ass so bad. She was trying not to be a bitch with the situation he was in, but deep down inside, she wanted to cuss his ass out.

Alexus stayed every night with him at the hospital until he was released. T hadn't said much to her the whole time and every time she brought up the whole ordeal with Mercedez, he shot the shit down. He ended up going to Hawaii to their home, allowing Alexus to care for him until he fully healed. Each day that passed, he got better and better. Mercedez had never returned his text.

Alexus worked through the day from home while waiting on T-Money hand and foot. He always took care of her, so it wouldn't hurt for once in life if she took care of him. T-Money couldn't seem to get Mercedez off his mind though. While T was healing, money still had to be made and with him and Mercedez going through it, it left him no choice but to have Alexus handle certain shit for him.

Weeks went by and he was completely healed, Alexus prayed that things would remain just as they were with T-Money staying in Hawaii with her and forgetting that Mercedez existed. She wanted the companionship more than anything. T-Money refused to tell her that Mercedez was in fact responsible for him being stabbed. Alexus assumed they'd fallen out for good after Cedez found out about T being married to her. Alexus never mentioned anything to T about the nurse mentioning someone by the name of Chantal Jackson. She didn't want to do anything to piss T off, so she decided she'd do her own personal investigation on that.

Eventually Alexus had to get back to her job working her normal hours and coming home every day to do her wifely duties. Everything was just how she always wanted it between her and T. She felt like she'd proved her love to him by being by his side when no other bitch was. Alexus decided she wanted to do something special for him.

She waited until T stepped out one day to go to his storage spot he had out in Hawaii. She set up a romantic scene for him. Alexus was bringing her "A" game, being sure to keep her man around. Candles were lit all the way from the front door going upstairs to the third floor where their master bedroom was. She put on a nice red lingerie piece that exposed her clit and her nipples and she wore six inch red bottom heels. Alexus planned on showing out for her husband. She stood in the mirror twerking and winding her hips to Yung Blue's new song ft. Brooklyn Love, "Don't Wanna Lose". Alexus was getting ready to shut shit down for T-Money as soon as he walked in.

It was 8:05 p.m. and he still hadn't made it back home, he had been gone over three hours after promising Alexus he'd be right back. She began blowing his phone up. It went straight to voicemail each time without even ringing. She instantly became worried as hell. He'd just been stabbed not even two months ago and she still had no idea who did it. With all the shit going on, Alexus didn't know what to think when he never returned.

***

T-Money's flight was taking off in thirty minutes. He had to return back to Georgia.

Le'Monica Jackson

CHAPTER SEVENTEEN

The weather was great out in Hawaii and although T-Money appreciated his wife stepping up and taking care of him as he went through the healing process, he had to get back to Mercedez, where his heart belonged. If they weren't right, nothing seemed right. Even after the incident, T still had mad love for Mercedez. There was nothing she could do to change the way he felt about her.

Besides, she'd only acted out of anger and hurt. It had been months since the last time they'd seen each other and T-Money was willing to risk losing Alexus to make sure the relationship he and Mercedez shared was secured.

T-Money's flight had just landed. Taking his phone off of airplane mode, he shot Mercedez a text.

"Cedez I know I fucked up but a nigga ain't mean for shit to play out the way it did back in Cali. I'm fully recovered and I'm back in Georgia. A nigga desperately wanna see you. I'm not mad at you for stabbing me we can get past all that shit. Stop tripping and hit me back Cedez, I love you."

It was early in the morning when Mercedez woke up to the message from T-Money she definitely wasn't expecting. After disappearing, she'd made no attempt to contact him, knowing if she ever ran into him again she'd probably have to go ahead and take him out before he took her out. Tevin was the type of nigga that stuck by the street code, which meant if you attempted to kill him, then you may as well go ahead and proceed with it because he was definitely going to get you. "Damn, I wasn't expectin' to hear from him. The fuck he want anyways?" Mercedez yawned as she read the message.

She had gotten herself a nice two-bedroom city view loft right in the middle of Atlanta. With the bullshit going on in Orlando, she refused to lay her head there. There was no way she was going to be living under the same roof as T-Money either though. However, she would much rather risk running into T-Money in Atlanta versus having to duck and dodge them crackas back home for the death of Buddy Ro. It was bad enough they'd already picked her up for the shit. That alone was enough to keep her ass the fuck out of Florida. Honestly, she regretted ever putting that knife through T's chest because his spot was in fact her comfort zone, but her emotions had gotten the best of her that night. She missed him dearly, but she had to think smart, and going around him just didn't seem like the brightest idea.

Mercedez pulled her blinds open, allowing the morning sunlight to beam straight through her skyscraper loft that she lived in alone. Mercedez's ass jiggled in her purple boy shorts as she walked to the kitchen to pour herself a glass of water to take with her prenatal vitamins. She had finally begun going through the changes. Her breasts were sitting extra plump while her ass and hips were spreading by the day. She was getting used to sharing her body with her babies.

Mercedez's phone went off, reminding her she had a doctor's appointment in less than two hours. "Oh shit! I forgot all about that," she said to herself. She would be finding out the sex of the twins at the appointment and never imagined having to experience one of the best days of her life alone.

She thought about giving in and responding to T's text message, but that thought quickly vanished upon thinking about him hurting their babies in her stomach. Although she doubted he would do that, her motherly instinct wouldn't allow her to take a chance like that.

Yung bleu ft. Noby "Come by at 12" was blasting through Mercedez's house as she showered and got ready for the appointment. She considered hitting her sister up, but decided she'd be just fine going alone. The only person she really wanted there was her baby daddy. Even though she was alone, she hadn't felt alone since she learned she was pregnant and actually heard their heartbeats. Her twins made her feel like they were all she needed.

Mercedez put on a comfortable sun dress she'd ordered off of Fashion Nova and a pair of Versace slides that color coordinated perfectly with her dress. She pulled her jet black frontal wig up into a messy bun, making sure her baby edges were laid. She wore a pair of Versace sunglasses and a Versace bag to match. Two babies weren't stopping a fucking thing. Mercedez wore her pregnancy very well and she was still making major moves in the streets, pushing big weight. She was still supplying damn near the whole west Orlando with everything.

Mercedez locked up her spot and headed to the doctor's office in her 2019 Maserati she'd just bought off the lot. The whole ride, she contemplated on whether or not she should at least hit T-Money up to inform him about the appointment.

I'll just text him when I find out the sex, she thought to herself. Cedez didn't even want him knowing she was still in Georgia. It still hurt finding out that he was married to Alexus, but she was more worried about going around after she'd stabbed him. Had she not done that, being in his presence wouldn't be that big of an issue.

CHAPTER EIGHTEEN

Arriving at the doctor's office, Mercedez signed in under her alias and waited to be seen. She glanced around the room, and seeing all the other pregnant women and women that had car seats with newborn babies in them instantly warmed her heart.

Damn this is really about to be me real soon, she thought as she looked at the woman in front of her whose titties had popped out. She had a beautiful baby girl with a head full of hair sucking on that tit for dear life.

"Chantal Jackson." An older black nurse who looked to be in her late 50s-early 60s peeked her head into the waiting room, calling for Mercedez to be seen.

Mercedez grabbed her purse and followed the lady to the back down the hall, where she would be finding out the sex of her unborn babies.

"Hello, my name is Nurse Douglas and I'll be doing your ultrasound today, Ms. Jackson."

Mercedez's heart dropped upon hearing the nurse's name. The first thought that came to mind was Robert and Nicole Douglas. "Okay." Mercedez smiled, trying not to make it obvious that she was paranoid.

"I need you to go ahead and remove your dress and put on the paper gown please. I'm going to step out while you undress and put the paper gown on."

Mercedez lay back on the reclining bed and closed her eyes and waited for the nurse to return.

"Knock knock, are you ready?" Nurse Douglas entered the room, pulling a cart behind her with everything on it that she needed to do the ultrasound.

Mercedez sat up, smiling. "Yes ma'am, I'm ready."

"Okay, go ahead and lay back down, cover your lower area with this towel, and I'm going to get started."

The nurse handed Cedez a throw towel and turned the unit on. Squeezing a clear gel onto Mercedez's belly, she used a white remote control looking instrument to view the inside of Mercedez's stomach. A black and white image appeared on the screen of the monitor. Mercedez could see clearly there were two babies in her belly unlike her first ultrasound when they were only the size of a sweet pea. She could hear their heart beats, and it sounded like horses galloping in a race. That was the most beautiful thing she had ever heard. Mercedez was in love listening to the life growing inside of her.

"Hmmm, well, you look to be a little over 18 weeks, their heart beats sound great. Are you ready to know what you're having?" said Nurse Douglas.

Mercedez was nervous. "Yes. I hope it's two boys. Lord knows a little girl would be payback for me." She laughed.

The nurse slid the remote-like instrument across Cedez's belly in search of the baby's genitals. "Here we have baby number one! He's definitely a boy!" The nurse turned the screen in the direction of Cedez, pointing at the baby's penis standing straight up.

Well, he sure get that from his daddy. Mercedez laid on the table for about another twenty minutes, holding conversation with the nurse as she played hide and seek with baby number two.

"Is this your first pregnancy?" Nurse Douglas asked.

"Yes ma'am, and probably my last since it's two." Cedez chuckled.

"I remember having mine. Girl, that was years ago," Nurse Douglas replied with a chuckle as well.

"How many do you have?"

"Well honey, I have three, one girl and two boys."

Cedez was kind of digging Nurse Douglas's vibe. She reminded her a lot of her own mother a little bit: a nice humble black woman.

Nurse Douglas continued, "Yeah, baby, my daughter just had a baby boy and one of my sons is in the feds, and my baby boy…uhhh…" She swallowed hard and paused for a second. "He, uh…was murdered a few months ago."

Mercedez's heart dropped to the pit of her stomach. "Ohhh, I'm so sorry to hear that." She was instantly ready for the appointment to be over. God forbid the nice sweet lady doing her ultrasound was the mother of the nigga Snoop.

"Yeah, my baby was killed, but I'm a strong woman. I thought I was gonna lose my mind but God kept me sane through it all and he blessed me with my grandson exactly a month after his death." Nurse Douglas sighed.

Mercedez remained silent and just listened as the nurse vented about her loss.

"Uh oh, Mommy, looks like baby number two is finally exposing the genitals. Welp, I should've known. It's a little girl! Girls are usually stubborn." She laughed.

"Oh my gosh! A girl?" Cedez screamed, cupping her hands over her eyes. She didn't want a girl but what more could she have asked for than being blessed with both sexes at one time? She was ready to call her mom and sisters to spill the tea. Ms. Karen was hoping for two girls.

The nurse cleaned Mercedez's belly off and gathered her cart together. She stepped out of the room, giving Mercedez privacy to get dressed.

"Okay, Ms. Jackson, congrats on your bundles of joy. You can go ahead and get dressed. Meet me in my office right across the hall when you're finished so we can get your next appointment scheduled and your ultrasound printed out."

"Okay, thank you."

Cedez quickly got dressed, grabbed her purse, and made her way to the nurse's office.

Nurse Douglas sat behind her desk stapling the sonograms to a package of papers with Mercedez's next appointment date and time on them. Her office was set up real nice. It was obvious she loved designer things and was family-oriented just like Mercedez. She had cute little designer ceramics and family pictures all over her desk.

Mercedez stood on the other side of her desk skimming across all of the family photos as she waited for her paperwork. She saw a picture she assumed was Nurse Douglas's daughter and grandbaby. The girl was dark-skinned with beautiful melanin popping skin just like Nurse Douglas. The baby was a chubby little newborn baby boy with similar features to the woman holding him. The next photo that her eyes landed on caught her by surprise. It was Nurse Douglas standing next to Nicole and Snoop dressed in wedding attire.

The nurse wasn't handing over the papers fast enough. Cedez could actually hear her heart thumping. She had a lump in her throat, making it hard for her to swallow. She was ready to haul ass up out that damn office. She didn't regret taking Snoop out since he did some creep-ass hit, but it was ironic as fuck that his mother happened to be the nurse giving Mercedez the best news of her life.

The nurse finally handed Mercedez the papers. She smiled and scurried out of the office.

"Thanks again, Nurse Douglas," she said and waved goodbye.

"See ya later, sweetheart." Nurse Douglas stood up and yelled out as she watched Mercedez exit through the double glass sliding doors.

Cedez jumped in her Maserati, turned her A.C. to the max, and just sat there for a second trying to gather her thoughts before pulling off. She was sweating bullets. Seeing Snoop's picture fucked her head up. She couldn't stand the fact knowing the nurse who was just so sweet and kind to her was suffering the loss of her child and it was because of her.

Mercedez swallowed her pride and shot T-Money a quick text message before she shared the news with anyone else.

"Tevin you're having a son and daughter, I had a doctor's appt this morning. The babies are healthy.

Bye."

She kept the message short and simple. It took everything in her to put her pride to the side and text him, but it was only right that he knew the sex of his children.

T-Money must've been staring at the phone all morning waiting for her to respond to his message. No sooner had she sent the text than he was calling her on Facetime. She quickly ended the Facetime and called him straight through. He answered on the first ring.

"Damn, Cedez, it's like dat, huh? I want to see ya face, man, why you ain't answer da Facetime? We gotta get past dat shit, man.

And why you ain't let me know about the appointment so I could've came?" He seemed to be really mature about the whole situation.

"Yeah right, Tevin, I know you better than you know ya damn self. You ain't 'bout to kill me so you and ya lil wife can play house with my kids," Mercedez responded, being sarcastic as fuck but low-key she was being dead ass serious.

"You trippin' for real, Cedez, I would never do nothing to physically hurt you. Yeah, you stabbed me and shit, but I'm the same nigga who taught you to never spare a nigga 'bout yo' respect."

"Uh huh...and you da same nigga disrespected me too and I ain't spare yo black ass." She laughed.

"I'm gon' make it up to you, man. I really need to see ya face. I miss my baby mama,"

"Boy don't try to use dat baby mama card." Mercedez burst into laughter and banged on his ass. She had to end the call before she ended up giving in to his ass as she definitely had butterflies after hearing his voice. T-Money was truly the love of her life. A part of her wanted to pull up and jump into his arms and another part of her wanted to open his stab wounds back up. She couldn't give in so quickly but she still opted out of going around him because she wanted to make sure he felt her pain first.

***

Meanwhile, Alexus desperately wanted T-Money back home in Hawaii with her. She had no choice but to believe he'd taken off to run after Mercedez. He'd been avoiding her calls for weeks as if she'd done him dirty when in reality it was vice versa. He was trapped in a love cycle. Alexus loved him dearly but it was more so her respect she was fighting for. She refused to feel like a bitch had one up on her. She'd called every hospital and jail in the state of Georgia checking to see if he was there, but obviously he was just simply avoiding her,

"How could he do this to me after I stopped everything I was doing to nurture his bitch ass back to health?" Alexus cried.

Sitting on her private deck, she admired the beautiful view of the lake before her. Lexus began thinking of a master plan. She wanted Mercedez completely out of the picture. She had to get revenge someway, somehow. Alexus was an evil-ass bitch and she was willing to do anything to win T over. Going against Mercedez was certainly a challenge though.

Suddenly a bright idea came to Alexus's mind. She pulled her iPhone out from her titties and logged into her Facebook. Since she couldn't get to T-Money, she as going to shoot her shot at the closest nigga to him, and that was Honcho.

Alexus clicked on Honcho's profile picture and jumped head first into his inbox.

"Wassup Honcho. I've had my eyes on you for a while. Now I'm sure you know who I am. If you can keep a secret, let's link up and get to know each other." She put the wet emoji at the end so he would know the play off rip. Alexus was playing a dangerous-ass game. God forbid Honcho ran his mouth to T-Money. That could possibly cost Alexus her life.

T-Money had so much pride and his ego was so big he would never allow a nigga to have the ups on him by having any dealings with a bitch he felt belonged to him, especially the hoe he gave his last name to. Even though Alexus had changed, she still had hoe tendencies and now was the time for her to reactivate her hoe powers. Let's be real; every bitch got a lil hoe buried deep inside of them. She always thought Honcho was sexy as fuck and she'd caught him watching her on several occasions as well, but knew he would never go as far as disrespecting T-Money by trying to holla at her. She definitely was going to have to make the first move if anything was going to get started between them.

Alexus went inside of her home and stretched out across the king-sized bed she slept in alone and waited for Honcho to respond. His page showed that he was online so Alexus liked a few pictures to get his attention. Surprised he was already responding to her message, she got a notification shortly after.

"Hey sexy what's good, a nigga know exactly who you is, bang my line baby I don't really fuck w/fb like dat 678-555-6831."

"Ahhh!" Alexus stuck her tongue out, raising her hips off the bed, and popped her pussy in the air as she laid on her back. The bitch was so dramatic. She had a strong feeling her plan was going to work out well.

Le'Monica Jackson

CHAPTER NINETEEN

Alexus saved Honcho's number in her phone, but she wanted to wait a day or so before calling him. In the meantime, she just responded to his Facebook message with the 100 emoji. She had to play her cards right and be discreet with the way she moved. Alexus tossed her phone across the bed and stepped out of her house coat. Walking around her bedroom naked, she picked up a photo of her and T-Money kissing on the beach. Alexus stared at the picture for a second and thought back to the times where they actually were somewhat happy together before sending the frame crashing into the wall. Glass was everywhere and Alexus was an emotional wreck. She didn't even bother picking up the pieces "Fuck him!" she screamed. Pouring herself a glass of Ducè, she turned her Bluetooth box on to the max as K-Michelle's "Cry" blasted through her home. She often kept music playing or the TV on because the silence of her home often fucked with her mental.

She ran herself a hot bath and tried to free her mind of the bullshit. Ever since she'd written Honcho, he kept randomly running through her mind. Alexus was so easy when it came to men. She couldn't wait to give him the pussy knowing a young nigga like him would be fucked up about her the first time she gave it to him.

She eased her body into the steaming water. Her ass cheeks were stinging like a mothafucka, but she was loving the sensation. When she got used to the water temperature, she laid her head back against the rim of the tub and relaxed. Her bathroom ceiling was made of mirrors so she could look up and see her reflection.

She often used the mirror to pleasure herself. Her body was in need of sexual healing. Pulling her knees back to her chest, she spread her legs wide, busting her pussy wide open, admiring her pink juicy insides. Spitting on her index finger, she began rubbing her clit in a circular motion, causing her body to buck. Her pussy was throbbing as she inserted two fingers inside of herself. She pinched her nipples with one hand and finger fucked herself with the other. She moved her hips to the beat of the music until she came all over her hand.

"Ahh yeah, fuck!" she moaned as her legs quivered uncontrollably. Alexus knew exactly how to please herself. Most women do though. The crazy thing about it was she thought about Honcho the whole time she was fucking herself, which caused her to cum faster than she usually would. She laughed to herself at the fact she had come so fast off of a nigga she never even fucked before. That hoe shit was just a part of who she was.

***

Mercedez was the total opposite, if it wasn't T-Money dicking her down, she could care less about busting a nut. Her head was so far in her bag the last thing on her mind was some dick and lately her only concern was preparing herself to be a mother. That meant getting out the game first. She wanted to make things right between her and her baby daddy and start a real business together for the sake of the twins. Getting T-Money out the game was not going to be easy because that's all he knew, but Cedez figured since they were a great team doing illegal business together, they would certainly prosper flipping their money to open up some legit shit together.

Mercedez had to run a few errands and totally forgot to call her mama to let her know what she was having. Traffic was backed up and Cedez was stuck in the same spot as she headed to grab herself a bite to eat. *There must have been an accident*, she thought to herself as she reached in her purse to call her moms up.

Her face lit up instantly as Ms. Karen's face appeared on the screen of her iPhone. She was, in fact, a mama's girl. "Heyyy baby!" Ms. Karen said with her phone propped up on her bathroom counter as she put her hair rollers on.

"Hey Mama, how you doin'?"

"I'm alright, baby, I been waitin to hear from you all day."

"I know, Mama, I'm sorry. I had got caught up handling business. I got good news for you though, lady!"

Ms. Karen put the hair roller down and picked her phone up, bringing it close to her face. "What you waiting on, child? Tell me!"

"Welllll, Mama...I got one girl for you!"

Before Cedez could finish telling her, Ms. Karen had put the phone back down, doing a silly-ass dance. "Yes Lord! I got a girl!"

"Mamaaaa," Cedez whined as she died laughing watching her mama cut up on Facetime. "I have a boy for you too, Mama."

Ms. Karen was overly excited. She was crying happy tears. Mercedez just smiled as her mother had her moment

"Did you tell ya sistas yet?" said Ms. Karen in between sniffs.

"Stop crying, Mama." Cedez laughed. "And no, I haven't told them yet."

Ms. Karen was ready to tell the good news. She rushed Cedez off the phone.

"Alright, I'll call you back. I'm gon' call Tonya and Janicka right now." She didn't give Cedez a chance to say another word before she ended the Facetime.

Cedez burst out laughing, tossing her phone into the passenger seat. Her smile quickly disappeared as thoughts of Nurse Douglas instantly came back to mind.

Trying to shake the thought, she turned her radio up to the max, jamming the Woop Nation album. She was fucked up about the local rappers from her city. Orlando was up next when it came to the rap game and that was no doubt.

Mercedez was feeling herself. She made a Snapchat video jamming to the music and that was something she never did. She actually forgot she had a Snapchat account because she never used the shit.

Mercedez sang along and flexed for Snap, zooming her camera on her steering wheel, showing off the fact that she had snapped on the new Maserati. She wasn't a show-off type of bitch, but it wouldn't hurt to flex just for once and shit on all the broke hoes who was gettin chump change. They did it all the time, so why not? Cedez thought. Since she and T weren't vibin' how they usually did, she had been doing a lot of shit she didn't usually do.

210 people had watched her Snap within three minutes. Mercedez was a hot commodity. She could be social media famous if she posted daily how most bitches did, but that just was not the

type of shit she was on. Mercedez was bossed up in real life and didn't have time to be tryna convince some irrelevant-ass niggas and hoes who sat on social media 24/7 and probably didn't have a dime to their names. She watched her video. That bitch was raw! Never tooting her own horn, but she knew without a doubt she was stepping way harder than the average bitch and everybody else knew it too.

"What da fuck!" Mercedez said as she checked her notifications. Someone had screenshotted her Snap.

She immediately realized who the nigga was that did it. She recognized him from Bankhead. He was a jit that copped drugs from T.

"The fuck he screenshottin' my shit for?" She blocked his ass off rip.

CHAPTER TWENTY

Mercedez pulled into the parking garage for her loft, swung into her parking spot, and quickly made her way inside. It had been a very busy day for a bitch carrying twins. Cedez was ready to kick back, relax, and bust down on the hibachi she'd picked up on her way home.

Three text messages came through back to back before she could even make it inside.

"Well damn," she said as she tossed her stuff on the love seat in her living room. Doing the pee pee dance, she shot straight to the bathroom. She had to piss like a mothafucka and trying to hold it wasn't even an option with them babies sitting right on her bladder.

"Whoever textin' me back to back gon' have to wait," Cedez said to herself. She threw her dress right above her ass and relieved herself. Good thing she wasn't wearing any panties, because she would've pissed on herself trying to get them down.

***

T-Money was in the lab cookin up. He had been working on flooding the streets with his new work he'd gotten when he received a screenshot of Mercedez looking good as fuck driving a Maserati. Blaze, T-Money's worker, had sent him the picture. All of his homeboys knew Mercedez was his girl and wouldn't dare step on his toes.

T-Money read the message attached with the picture

Ain't dis ya old lady, Blood?

"Aye, finish this up for me, lil dawg. Don't fuck my shit up either, jit." T-Money tossed the fork he was using to whip his shit up to his right hand man, Honcho. Even though Honcho was a lot younger than T-Money, he was on his shit when it came to keeping the streets laced up. He was T-Money's strongest worker.

"Bet, big homie, I gotcha." Honcho grabbed the fork and beat the pack out.

T-Money pulled a chair out and shot Cedez a text.

"Aye man I know I fucked up but all that extra shit moving all reckless posting Snapchat videos trying to be seen gon' make a nigga spaz out fa real fa real! Take that shit down, Mercedez. We got too much goin on and you know better. Come on baby you movin real sloppy right now tryna piss a nigga off but you really bout to have a nigga body some shit! Got my young niggas sending me screenshots of you and shit."

Mercedez knew just how to get under his skin without even trying. Clenching his jaws, T-Money shot Blaze a simple text message, the one hundred emoji followed by the gun and big X emoji, clearly letting Blaze know that was in fact his girl and he'd bust his ass about her, even though he knew Cedez would never give Blaze the time of day. She was a boss, and Blaze was a worker. Cedez wouldn't dare!

T-Money walked in the kitchen as Honcho was finishing up. Honcho peeped the play and could sense that T-Money was pissed about something.

"Damn, brah, you good?" he asked.

He'd already seen Mercedez's snapchat but he didn't bother running it by T-Money because he didn't have time for T-Money to be thinking he was watching his bitch.

"Yeah, I'm straight. Let me see how the shit turned out."

T-Money grabbed the Pyrex bowl and gave Honcho a thumbs up. He rolled a joint and got back to work, packing up different shit that had to be shipped out. Cedez was totally distracting him. He had to get his mind right and stop allowing what she had going on interfere with his money moves.

***

Mercedez was sitting on the sofa watching her favorite show, *Queen*, and going in on her plate when she finally read the messages T-Money had sent her. She immediately burst out laughing, seeing how easy that nigga got in his feelings when it came to her.

This nigga just scared another nigga might catch my attention. Too bad I'll never dick ride another nigga. Bet he wish his wife could say the same.

Mercedez shot him a quick text back

"#1 tell ya broke ass homie to get his bread up and stay off my shit screenshotting my shit sending it to you. I'm grown ASF! #2 you sound a lil pressed BABY DADDY. I'm not ya wife. These niggas don't impress me. I was bored and just made a video. I don't think I should be explaining a damn thing. You wasn't trying to explain shit to me when I busted you with your wife! You made sure you explained shit to her tho? Right! FUCK OUTTA HERE NIGGA!"

Mercedez went from finding the shit funny to pissed the fuck off. Every time she thought about the fact that Tevin was married to Alexus, she got mad all over again. She threw her phone to the other end of the sofa and began flipping through the channels. "Nigga got me so fucked up." She devoured a juicy-ass piece of hibachi steak. The twins had her eating like crazy, as if every meal she ate would be her last.

Her phone rang.

"Damn, a bitch can't even eat in peace. Oh shit, this Tonya!" Cedez said, smiling, answering her Facetime.

"Hey, fat girl!" Tonya said as Cedez's face popped up on her screen.

Mercedez's nose was beginning to spread and her face was getting a little chunky. She was holding the babies mostly in her breasts though, going from a C-cup to a DD-cup fast.

"Hey sis, wassup!" Cedez laughed in between chewing her food.

"Well, I'm sure you know Mama called me. So I'm having a niece and nephew! Me and Janicka want to get together and plan your baby shower. I talked to her earlier." Janicka was Mercedez's oldest sister. They were close, but not as close as Mercedez and Tonya.

"Okay, girl. I still can't believe I'm having kids…"

"Me either, sis, but I know you and T gon' be some good-ass parents."

Mercedez rolled her eyes upon hearing his name.

"Why you rollin' your eyes, girl? You know that man gon' be a great father!" Tonya laughed.

Mercedez wanted to vent to Tonya so bad about the whole Alexus bullshit, but she wouldn't dare tell her big sister no shit like that. Tonya's whole outlook on Tevin would change when it came down to her little sister.

"Oh, nothing, sis, I guess these pregnancy hormones just been fucking wit' me 'cause I can't stand his black ass," Mercedez said.

"Oh yeah, that's how it be, sis, that's normal. Them babies gon' come out looking just like his ass. You know what they say: ya baby come out looking just like the person you couldn't stand the most during your pregnancy."

Mercedez didn't want to complain about T since Tonya had lost her kids' father and she could never imagine being in her sister's shoes, so she just laughed at Tonya's statement. She didn't mind her kids coming out looking just like Tevin. Shid, he was fine as fuck with some nice-ass features.

Mercedez and Tonya chopped it up on Facetime for a little while longer. They gossiped, laughed, and did all the normal shit sisters do. Tonya and Janicka knew her better than she knew herself, so she could only imagine how amazing her baby shower was going to turn out. That was one less thing she had to worry about when it came to this whole pregnancy thing. She knew her sisters were going to step hard for the shower.

CHAPTER TWENTY-ONE

Sitting at the round table in the lab, Honcho felt a tug in his chest as he re-read the Facebook message Alexus sent him. He wanted to run it by T-Money, but it was too late because he'd already responded. Typical nigga, thinking with the head on his dick instead of the one on his shoulders. He figured he'd just see what was up with Alexus Hell, he knew she fucked with T-Money, but the only person Honcho ever heard him talk about was Mercedez, and he would never try T with her. Honcho was a young fly-ass nigga and even though he was used to fucking with model bitches, it was just something about Alexus that made him want to see about her. *It's bros before hoes. Shid, T-Money would understand if he ever found out*, Honcho figured.

He shrugged his shoulders and closed out the Facebook app.

***

"Damn, brah, a nigga havin' a son and a daughter soon." T-Money finally told someone about his twins.

Honcho's eyes got so big. "Naw!" he said, automatically thinking Alexus was up to some creep shit. "A son and a daughter?" he asked.

"Yeah, man, at da same damn time," T-Money responded, rubbing his hands together, appearing to be a little stressed out.

"Damn, T, I'm tryna be like you, brah, two bitches having my babies at the same time," Honcho joked.

"Oh naw, lil dawg you trippin', it's one bitch having two babies," T-Money corrected him.

The first thought that came to Honcho's mind was that Mercedez and Alexus were both pregnant. He noticed T-Money and Mercedez were going through it, but he knew not to ask T anything about his personal business, especially about Mercedez. Any nigga he brought around Mercedez had a very clear understanding that he would put a bullet in their ass for her and about her. He loved the ground that bitch walked on and that was no secret. The only person that didn't seem to know that was Alexus.

"Oh, okay, man, I was about to say, you ain't playin' out'chea. Congrats though, my nigga." Honcho dapped T-Money up. The fact that T-Money seemed a little stressed out had Honcho curious about which bitch was actually pregnant, Alexus or Cedez. He damn sure wasn't asking that question though. He planned on just waiting for Alexus to hit him up and see what she had to say. Hell, he wasn't trying to do nothing more than smash the bitch anyway. She'd already proved what type of bitch she was by even hitting him up knowing he was T-Money's Ace Boon goon.

Ring! Ring!

"Who da fuck?" Honcho said. He looked at the screen of his phone, not recognizing the number, assuming it was Alexus. He answered and spoke first

"Lemme bang ya back later, I'm handling something"

"Okay, daddy," the woman on the other end of the phone said in a sexy soft voice and then hung up.

Honcho stuffed his phone back in the pocket of his True Religion jeans. He was damn near done in the lab with T-Money and he'd planned to call the number back as soon as he hopped in his ride.

T-Money had plans on running Mercedez down his damn self. A bitch is always a nigga's main distraction. Little did T-Money know that while he was trying to fix shit with his baby mama, his lil homie Honcho was gon' by trying to get in his wife Alexus's guts.

Honcho had no idea T-Money was married to that thot. As far as he knew, Alexus was just a lil piece T-Money had on the side. From the outside looking in, you'd think Mercedez was the wife. She was the bitch all his niggas knew about. True statement when they say a real street nigga keeps the wife put away. He kept Mercedez on his side like he kept his banger on his side. She should've been the one wearing the big rock on her finger, but unfortunately, that wasn't how shit played out. Now he was paying for it, and it was stressing him out beyond measure.

"Fuck! I gotta get my bitch back." T-Money bit down on his bottom lip, doing the dash in his mobbed-out Range Rover.

T-Money and Honcho had gone their separate ways. T-Money was on a mission to get Mercedez back and dodge Alexus at the same time. He had only one missed call from Alexus all day which was weird as fuck because she was blowing his shit up all day every day since he'd hauled ass and left her in Hawaii at the home they owned together.

***

"Damn, he sounded so sexy," Alexus said, licking her lips seductively. She couldn't even wait a full day before calling Honcho after she'd come so quickly fantasizing about him. She couldn't resist hearing his voice. The plan was to get close to him to get to Tevin at first, but now she was really considering getting far away with him and making him her man. Crazy, because she didn't even know him like that.

Alexus's thoughts were disturbed by the ringing of her phone. Her head was pounding out of her chest and she thought about screening the call, but instead she put her sexy voice on, amazed that he'd returned her call so urgently. "Hello," she said.

"Yo, wassup Alexus, it's Honcho."

"I'm just chillin'. Wassup wit' you?"

There was an awkward silence. Alexus was nervous as hell. She hadn't completely thought out her plan and she didn't realize it until they were actually on the phone. However, she was going to just go with the flow and let the conversation come naturally.

"I mean, shit, not much, ma. What's on ya mind, what made you hit me up?"

Alexus was laid across her bed, legs crossed, twirling her hair like a high school girl talking to her puppy love boyfriend.

"I've been wanting to holla at you, but you know…uh…"

"Know what? That you fuck with T-Money?" Honcho interrupted.

Alexus blinked long and hard before responding. "Yeah, we have a lot going on right now and I get lonely, baby." Alexus pouted.

Honcho smiled, thinking to himself, *Oh dis hoe just wanna get fucked.*

"Yeah, I feel you, ma. So what you saying is you tryna fill the void with my company?" Honcho pulled the hair on his goatee as he swerved in and out of the busy traffic of Atlanta, trying to process the fact that his main man's bitch was coming onto him and he was falling into the fuckery slowly but surely.

"Not exactly fill the void, but yes, I would love your company. The only problem is I'm way out in Hawaii.

"Hawaii?" That threw Honcho for a loop. *Man, what that bitch got goin' on? How she expect a nigga's company and she way in Hawaii?* he thought.

"I live in Hawaii, but if you ever wanted to, I could easily buy you a plane ticket or I could buy one and fly out to Atlanta."

Honcho laughed, thinking to himself, *Oh, she think she J.T. or Young Miami tryna get a nigga flewed out.* He was confused as fuck as to why Alexus was willing to do all that just to see him. He had to get off the phone with her and let everything she was saying marinate on his brain. "Shit, that sounds good, ma. I got a few things to handle and I'll hit you back a lil later and we'll talk more about it, a'ight?"

"Okay, baby, I'll be waiting," Alexus responded before hanging up on him. She was nervous the entire time they talked but she felt a lot better after the five minute conversation they held.

Honcho set his phone down on his lap next to his 9mm and grabbed the already rolled Backwood of that zah from the ashtray right beneath his radio. Turning up his music to the max, Lucci-wet blasted throughout his 2017 Maxima as he put fire to the Backwood. He sparked that shit up and inhaled the smoke, bopping his head to the music. He thought about hopping on a plane for the first time to go see exactly what Alexus was about.

CHAPTER TWENTY-TWO

Shit was making sense now as to why T-Money flew out to Hawaii a couple times a year. *This nigga got a whole bitch out in Hawaii*, Honcho laughed to himself. He really looked up to T-Money. He admired how swiftly he moved. T-Money was definitely Honcho's role model. He couldn't understand why a bitch that fucked with T would want to downgrade and fuck with him. Not that he wasn't just as good-looking, but he was nowhere near on his level when it came to his lifestyle. Honcho was still living with his grandma in the projects. It was not that he couldn't afford his own place .It was more so because Ms. Gladys was too stubborn to get out of her comfort zone. She'd lived in the projects since Honcho was a baby. He refused to let her live alone in the hood with all the hot shit he'd done over the years. Meanwhile, T-Money had options when it came to where he laid his head. Each spot was exclusive and not in the hood. Honcho had a long way to go before he even came close to being on T-Money's level. Honcho knew that as long as T-Money had breath in his body, he would never come up beyond T-Money. T was the real head honcho in charge and was the reason niggas from Georgia to Miami all the way to Orlando were eating. T-Money was far from an average basic-ass drug dealer. The Jitterbug in Honcho got a thrill out of knowing that T-Money's bitch wanted to jump on his dick. He was blinded to the point where he couldn't see that Alexus was on some creep shit. All he could see was blue faces and a bad bitch. Honcho was still very young and hot headed. If shit went left, he had no problem taking her out. He was going to let her set up everything for him to link up. Shit what's there to lose, he thought to himself.

***

T-Money drove around for hours, thinking about how badly he'd fucked up everything with Mercedez. He knew she was in Georgia, but had no idea where to begin to look for her. The fact that she was so close but yet so far away was killing him. He had no control over this situation and that was very unusual. The only place he could think of where he had any chance of running into her was the doctor's office. Pulling out his phone, he immediately Googled the doctor's office to get her next appointment.

"Shit, that's a whole month from now," T-Money murmured to himself. He had to see Mercedez before then, but she was stubborn as hell. She had left him no choice. He'd hire the private investigator that he used to locate his enemies. Now he had to hire him to locate his baby mama. All kinds of crazy thoughts were running through his head. *What if she's with another nigga?* he thought. That thought instantly left his mind when he remembered Cedez wasn't Lexi. Cedez didn't even get down like that. That wasn't her style to be entertaining another nigga, being pregnant and all. "Plus she knows I'll break my foot off in that ass," T said aloud to himself.

T-Money was going crazy without her. It really fucked with his mental in the worst way. With all the shit that happened in the last few months, he really needed his best friend to keep him level-headed. More than anything, he didn't want to miss another second of her pregnancy. Just knowing he had a double blessing, a little King and Queen, filled him with so much joy. He wanted to begin connecting and creating a bond while they were in the womb. T-Money would never be a dead beat. He knew the feeling all too well growing up in a foster home. On top of that, the real nigga in him wouldn't allow him to turn his back on his seed. *How long she gonna make a nigga suffer?* he thought, pinching the bridge of his nose, shaking his head. He was stressed beyond measure.

***

Mercedez spent most of her days shopping online for the twins, distributing drugs throughout the city and trying her hardest to avoid Tevin. She was getting low on product and needed new shit. T-Money was flooding the streets, but she refused to give in. After she got rid of everything she had, she figured that would be the start of a new beginning. She planned on leaving the game alone. She was a mother-to-be and the dope game and streets don't give a damn about her or her children. She'd made a name and earned her reputation. It was time to put up her gloves. Mercedez had saved up enough money for her and the twins to survive for at least five years even if she never made another penny. She wasn't the type to just sit on her ass though. It would only be a matter of time before she had her hands in some shit. She could've been opened numerous businesses, but her mind wasn't on that. Mercedez was just living her life without a care in the world, until she got pregnant. Reality hit and she knew she had to tighten up and do better.

"Oooh, I like that." Cedez sat at her kitchen bar wrapped in a silk blanket, scrolling on her laptop, ready to put her card into it. "Damn, this is a really nice twin bassinet set." She grabbed her card, ready to purchase the twins things, when a text came through on her phone.

"Hey sis, please don't go buying everything for the twins, me and Tonya are throwing you a big-ass baby shower. So see what gifts people bring you first before you go to spend all that money, girl."

Cedez smiled as she read the text message from her sister Janicka. Everyone seemed very excited, which really made her feel so good.

"Okay, sis, I was just about to order this really pretty bassinet set but I guess I'll just umm…LOL. I love you chick."

Cedez was trying to do everything to keep her mind off T. Shopping was definitely her escape and most certainly an addiction. She already had a room full of shit for the babies from diapers to bags, shoes, clothes, and toys. She was new to this shit and all she knew was her kids weren't gonna want for a damn thing.

"Maybe I should give this lady a call," Cedez said to herself as she was putting her card back in her wallet.

The business card she received from the lady on the airplane was just standing out. She'd had the lady's card for a few months and kept making mental notes to call, but it kept slipping her mind. With all the bullshit going on, a little spiritual guidance would be nice. She retrieved the card, contemplating on whether or not she should call. She dialed the number but still hesitated. Before she knew it, the phone was ringing. She went to end the call, but before she could hang up, a voice spoke from the other end on the phone.

"Hello, this is Patricia Hogan. What can I do for you?"

Mercedez was stuck. "H-Hi-hi, I, uh, my name is Mercedez Smith."

"I'm sorry, baby, you're breaking up, could you repeat that please?"

She mentally kicked herself for using her real name. "This is Chantal. You gave me your card a few months ago."

"My, my, my, God is good, I tell you, since I saw you on the flight, my spirit had been telling me I'd be hearing from you. I'm just a woman of God that stands strong on his word and enjoy empowering our young people, especially women to seek God!"

Mercedez instantly felt the energy through the phone, Ms. Hogan had a spirit that screamed "God-fearing woman".

Ms. Hogan's service had nothing to do with money, even though Cedez would pay a fortune to have that type of happiness in her life. Ms. Hogan was simply in the business of empowering women and counseling out of the kindness of her heart.

"Well, ma'am, I was wondering, would you mind saying a quick prayer for me? Nothing's wrong. I just need a little Jesus in my life." Mercedez chuckled.

"Oh, of course, baby! Anything specific you want me to pray for?"

"No, ma'am, just need a little prayer sent up to my daddy."

"Umm, okay, close your eyes as I pray for you and with you. While I pray, you talk to God silently. I don't need to hear it. The Lord knows what you need. Okay, dear father God, I come to you as humble as I know how, first off thanking you for Chantel, Lord. I thank you for using me to pray for her. I don't know what led her to call me, Father, but you do! Whatever is going on in her life that makes her want to seek you, I pray you work it all out in her favor. I pray that you manifest in this young lady's life, and help her to keep you first in all that she does. I pray all these things in your son Jesus' name. Amen."

Mercedez opened her eyes, not even realizing tears were slowly rolling down her cheeks. "Thank you so much," Cedez said, almost holding her breath, trying not to let Ms. Hogan hear the hurt in her voice.

"No problem. This is the main reason I gave you my card. Never hesitate to use my number. I'm available 24/7 for prayer or anything else."

Mercedez didn't understand why she felt such a strong connection to a woman she didn't know from a can of paint. As soon as Ms. Hogan began her prayer, Cedez could feel her load getting lighter by each word that came out of her mouth. She knew that change that she was seeking would need way more than just one prayer. "Okay, I'll definitely be keeping in touch with you."

"Okay. God bless you."

Mercedez ended the call and laughed to herself, realizing that the lady had just prayed by the name of Chantal. *Hell, God knows exactly what's going on. He knows I'm Chantal on certain occasions*, she thought. There was something authentic about Ms. Hogan, but Cedez couldn't put her finger on it. What she did know was that little prayer was very much needed. She put the card in a safe compartment in her wallet and saved Ms. Hogan's phone number with the praying hands emoji next to her name.

Days passed and Mercedez was spending a lot of time soul searching. She wanted to genuinely forgive Tevin. Every morning there was a daily inspirational text message from Ms. Hogan. She was shocked by the fact that they were very powerful and actually helped her get through each day. She was slowly but surely beginning to open up and confide in Ms. Hogan. She told her bits and pieces of all the shit she was going through as far as Tevin, even though Mercedez wasn't completely giving her the whole rundown with the little she'd already told her. Ms. Hogan definitely made it a lot easier to deal with. As each day passed, Cedez felt herself becoming the strong black Queen she knew she was. Ms. Hogan had to be her angel.

Le'Monica Jackson

CHAPTER TWENTY-THREE

T-Money's private investigator was on his shit he'd tracked down Cedez. He was amused that Cedez was right under his nose the whole time not even thirty minutes away. He got a thrill out of knowing when and where she was at, at all times.

"I definitely thought she'd run outta state. I raised a bad one. That's my baby. I would've done the same damn thing." T said out loud. "You are a reflection of me," T-Money sang twice in his head. He had an address, but refused to just pop up at her crib on some stalker shit. He wasn't on no jittybug shit. He was a boss at all times. He decided he'd just chill until she was ready to see him. It felt good to finally be able to focus on his paper and not worry about Cedez's whereabouts.

While Mercedez was soul searching, Tevin was busy flooding the street with grade-A everything and secretly running her down. Shit was going great for him and his team, everybody was eating, everyone was a boss, no one was left out. T-Money was about to recruit more niggas to push his weight and be his shooters.

It was a Saturday afternoon and he'd called for a meeting with his young niggas in the lab. T-Money was seated at the round table with Honcho to his right - his right hand man, the one that was up next. Blaze sat directly across from him along with two others that were brothers named Quan and Quay. T-Money had just taken them under his wing. He kept his circle small; his shit was more like a dot. Between his four lil homies his product was gonna boom all over the city. Quan and Quay were simple corner store boys that were ready to be men when T-Money first met them. Now they are coming up in the game and making a name for themselves.

"Alright, I'ma bless all y'all with a lil something. I wanna see how quick you can make this new shit bump in the city. If it's doin' numbers and y'all got my money back by next week - umm, Friday, let's say - then we gonna go to a whole new level, my G's." T-Money spoke with so much authority, just like the boss he was.

"Hell yeah, fuck yeah!" Everyone around the table was ready to prove to T-Money that they could do it.

They all chopped it up for a while and when T-Money was done busting down the pack, he supplied everyone with a nice amount of work to start getting off.

"Alright, young niggas, get out there and put in work." He dapped up his whole crew followed by the hood arm lock before departing.

"Aye boss man, I need to holla at you on some one on one shit," Blaze said as everyone else headed out the door.

T-Money closed the door of the meeting room and pulled his chair back, taking a seat. "Aye, before you start, I don't want to hear about no social media shit, lil dawg." T-Money rubbed his chin, curious as to what Blaze had to tell.

"Oh hell naw, boss, I'on be on that hoe shit. It ain't nothing about that."

"A'ight, so wassup?"

"Shit, I got a nigga named Truck that's in the feds and I've been lacing the nigga up with lil shit, and he been doing his thang. He's from Baton Rouge. He 'bout to jump soon and I think he'll be a good candidate."

T-Money was tuned in, liking what he was hearing and where the conversation was going. "Hmm, Truck? Baton Rouge? Nigga sounds familiar as hell. That's where I grew up at." T-Money was in and out of foster homes growing up and the last family he was with, he had a little brother by the name of Truck. Last he heard the nigga did go to the feds. The shit was too on point. It had to be him. T had not heard from him because he ended up going up the road himself. They just ended up going their own ways and time had divided them. Shit, he wasn't his real brother, not by blood, so it wasn't nothing to forget about the nigga. He had stopped getting attached to people in them foster homes. The minute he did something, they were ready to get rid of him anyways. He and Truck actually clicked from day one though. They'd both lost their mothers to domestic violence and were left for the state to deal with them.

"Okay, Blaze, I'll tell you what. Shoot the nigga my number to my burna phone. Lemme see where his head at and we'll go from there."

"A'ight, bet, say less."

The meeting was over, T jumped in his whip, hoping to hear from Truck sooner rather than later. His gut told him that was his lil bro. He could really use a nigga up the road to flood the feds and make triple the money. Prices were way more behind them walls with the inmates. Guaranteed they weren't getting the shit T-Money had to offer. He kept the best shit the street had to offer. It was only a matter of time that anybody who wasn't copping from him wouldn't be able to make a dime at all. T had the streets on lock and if he liked the way the nigga Truck was talking, He'd have the prison on lock as well. Money was the least of his worries, He was facing problems with love. Alexus went from calling ten times a day to once a day or maybe every other day.

If only just one of those calls was from Mercedez... T thought he loved Alexus, but she'd never have the effect on him that Mercedez had. Cedez pulled on his heart strings. There's a big difference between loving someone and being in love with someone just as there's a thin line between love and hate.

***

Alexus loved T-Money, but her love for him was beginning to turn into hate because of the way he was treating her. The last thing she wanted to do was divorce him and give Mercedez the opportunity to have her title as the wife. She could file for a divorce and have damn near everything he owned. But at this point it wasn't about money. It was about revenge.

Alexus had played her cards right and everything was going great. Honcho was making it so easy to go through with her plans because he was already fine as fuck. She could tell he had a good vibe in real life. Alexus didn't have to force herself to fuck him or be around him. She was honestly attracted to him and vibing hard. *This is going to be easy*, she thought. She licked her lips and daydreamed about having Honcho laid up in the bed she sometimes shared with T-Money. She had no intentions on actually liking him, which made her a little skeptical. She found herself randomly going on his Facebook, skimming through his pictures. Honcho had hella pictures that he and T had taken together. She liked a few pictures, making sure he knew she was on his trail.

A text message came through Honcho's phone as he was sitting parked in his car in the projects right in front of his building. He looked around. "I gotta get her to move up out of this shit man," he said aloud. He hated what the surroundings looked like. Niggas was posted to his left and some ratchet hoes walked up the sidewalk with some thot slides on that looked like a stray animal. *Fuck is this?* he thought, grabbing his phone, grinning as he saw that it was Alexus texting him

"It was nice to hear your voice, daddy. Don't forget to lemme know what you wanna do. Either way I'll book the flight. I'd love to see you."

Honcho made his mind up already. He figured he'd let her come to him and just book a room for the week. Ms. Gladys damn sure wasn't letting no heffa shack up in her apartment with her grandson. Honcho didn't think flying out to Hawaii was a good idea. He was already pulling some foul shit for even entertaining the bitch. The last thing he needed was T-Money peeping game, especially knowing T trusted him more than any other nigga.

I could just kill him and I'm next up in the game. The streets would be mine. Honcho instantly shook that thought.

Funny how a bitch could have you even considering taking the nigga out who's responsible for you eating. Niggas always tend to bite the hand that feed them.

CHAPTER TWENTY-FOUR

T-Money had a call from an unknown number on his burna phone. "Who the fuck?" he said, frustrated as hell. Every time his phone went off, he was expecting it to be Mercedez. He thought about screening the call but when he realized it was a Georgia area code and it could possibly be important, he immediately answered.

"Talk to me."

"Yo, what up, this Truck."

"Wassup, Blood, holla at me." T-Money knew off rip the nigga was bleeding or else Blaze would've never plugged him in.

"Shit, a nigga got less than a year left up da road, but I got dis shit on lock, big homie."

"Uh-huh." T-Money was already tuned in to the lil niggas conversation.

"I mean, shit, I call shots in dis ma'fucka and my boy Hot-Rod gon' take this shit over when I jump. I'm gon' keep the work coming in consistently for him and he gon' flood dis ma'fucka."

"Hmph, that sounds like a go for me, Blood. I'll get with Blaze and make sure you straight in dat bih. So you say ya name Truck, huh?"

"Yeah, I go by Truck, I earned that name growing up. I been putting niggas on they neck since a jittybug." Truck laughed.

"Damn, sounds familiar, brah. You from Baton Rouge?"

"Hell yeah," Truck responded.

"Ya real name Antwan Cooper?" T-Money asked.

"Hell yeah, brah, where I know you from?" Truck asked suspiciously.

T-Money burst out laughing. "Man, nigga, this Tevin!"

"Man, naw! Brah, I thought a nigga would never hear from you again." Truck sounded so excited.

"Yeah, small-ass world, ain't it?"

Truck and T-Money talked longer than expected. They were, in fact, brothers in one of their foster homes. T-Money was ready to put everything in play for Truck. The link up was real!

It was a day before Thanksgiving and T-Money still hadn't heard much from Mercedez. She'd sent pics of her belly, but that was about it. He wanted so badly to go ahead and call Ms. Karen and vent to her, but he refused to make himself the bad guy in her eyes. That was the last thing he needed was for his baby mama's family to hate him for hurting her. Ms. Karen had sent him the text message she sent out to the family every year inviting him over for the family Thanksgiving dinner and it would definitely be out of the ordinary if he didn't show up. Besides, it was a tradition he'd been accustomed to for the past few years. He was going regardless of what he and Mercedez were going through. He knew she hadn't told her family about their issues because Ms. Karen's crazy ass would've called him jumping down his throat. On the flip side, he was excited he would finally be seeing Mercedez in less than 24 hours. The Thanksgiving gathering was being held in Orlando at Ms. Karen's house as it always was. T-Money was ready to see the people that he called family.

As he pulled into Ms. Karen's driveway, the yard was filled with cars and the first one he noticed was a Maserati that he assumed belonged to Mercedez, the one she was showing off on her Snapchat video. T-Money sighed, preparing himself to face Mercedez. Hopefully she held her composure and didn't ruin the gathering by showing out on him.

Upon entering the house, Ms. Karen greeted him at the door. "Hey baby, it's good to see you. Cedez told me you'd be here shortly. You know I was gon' feel some type of way had you not showed up."

Tevin kissed Ms. Karen on the cheek. "Oh, you know I wasn't gonna miss eating your good cooking, Mama. I just had to handle a few things before I jumped on the road."

T-Money walked around saying his hellos and dapping up Mercedez's brothers and all of her male cousins and uncles. Mercedez's brother B.J. and T-Money held a small conversation as everyone gathered around talking and laughing. It was nothing but good vibes, per usual.

T-Money felt someone staring at him. Of course it was Mercedez, standing there in the kitchen in a peach-colored sundress with her arms crossed tight over her belly, which was huge compared to the last time he'd seen her, where you couldn't even tell she was carrying babies. Her eyes were burning a hole straight through him. If looks could kill, he would've fallen dead on sight. T-Money was stuck. He didn't know if he should approach her or not. Thinking with his first mind, he excused himself from B.J.

"Aye, hold on, brah, I'll be right back." He made his way into the kitchen.

Mercedez turned her back to him the minute she saw him walking in her direction. He grabbed her waist, turning her around to face him. Good thing no one else was in the kitchen because now was the time for him to try and make things right.

"Man, Cedez, come on, bae, can we not make shit so obvious?" He lifted her head by her chin, forcing her to make eye contact with him.

She was so stubborn, looking past him, making sure he knew that she was still hurt and upset. She blinked long and hard, refusing to let a tear fall. "We good, Tevin," she said, keeping it nice and simple.

Tevin lifted his shirt up and revealed the scar on his chest where she had stabbed him. Grabbing her hand, he forced her to feel the wound. "I love you, Mercedez."

She cracked a smile, knowing she scarred him just like he'd scarred her heart.

"Crazy ass," T-Money said, laughing as he let this shirt down. Ironically, they were wearing the same colors as if they'd planned to dress alike.

Janicka walked up on them in the kitchen, catching both of them off guard.

"Let me get a picture of y'all."

On cue, Mercedez posed with one hand on her hip and Tevin jumped behind her, holding her belly. They looked so good together.

"Awww, y'all so cute! Couple goals, bitch!" Janicka boasted as he pulled them in to see the picture on her iPhone.

"I bet y'all gon get hella likes as soon as I post it!" Janicka was ready to kill the timeline on Facebook.

"Alright, now move over, boys!" She brushed past them, making her way to her mama's famous sweet potato pies.

Mercedez and T-Money went with the flow for the rest of the day. It had actually been a breath of fresh air to be back in his presence.

CHAPTER TWENTY-FIVE

"To the right, to the right, now kick, now kick…" .

"The Cupid Shuffle" was playing and Mercedez was doing her thing.

"Go sis!" Tonya yelled as she joined Mercedez, all attention was on them.

Janicka and B.J. had their phones out, making Snapchat videos. The whole family was there. Lorenzo and Kobe, her brothers that barely came around, were even there.

"Congrats, sis," said Lorenzo as he walked up and rubbed Mercedez's belly. It had been almost two years since she had spoken to him. They had fallen out about some money. Mercedez was slowly but surely becoming the mature woman she needed to be for her babies. She had vowed to never speak to Lorenzo as long as she lived, but there she was speaking to him.

"Thanks Lo." She hugged her lil brother, instantly putting their differences behind them.

"Mama said come eat!" Kobe, the youngest of Ms. Karen's children, yelled, causing everyone to stop what they were doing. He was a little on the heavy side so him making that announcement wasn't surprising at all.

Everyone made their way to the kitchen with the children lining up first. Ms. Karen made everybody's plate.

"Bae, make my plate." T-Money softly rubbed Mercedez's ass.

"Nigga, we still beefin'," Mercedez replied, rolling her eyes and smirking at him as she began making his plate.

It was shit like that, that turned him the fuck on.

Thanksgiving turned out nice. Ms. Karen put her foot in the food, as always. Mercedez had so many things to be thankful for and most of all, she was thankful for her mama's bustin'-ass collard greens. Everyone made extra plates, saran wrapped them, and said their good-byes.

"Cedez, me and Janicka will keep you posted about the baby shower once we're done planning it, okay? Love you," Tonya said as she was loading up her daughters to get on the road heading back to Georgia.

"Okay sis, love you too," Cedez replied.

The fact that Cedez had to drive back to Georgia alone instantly aggravated her especially after the good time she and T-Money had. She wished she was riding back with him. B.J., Lorenzo, and Kobe stayed over, helping their mama put up all the tables and chairs that were set up outside.

T-Money walked Mercedez to her car. "Ya ride clean, lil mama," he teased.

"Yeah, yeah, I know," she replied, being petty right along with him.

"Ya new nigga bought it for you, huh?" T-Money seemed to have all the jokes.

"As a matter of fact…"

Before Cedez could even joke along with him, he instantly got serious. "Stop trying' me!" he said between clenched teeth.

She burst out laughing, finding it so cute how easily he got in his feelings.

"Alright, bet! Meet me at your loft in the city on the eighth floor." T-Money stormed off and hopped in his truck.

"How do you know where I stay? Yo' crazy ass!" Mercedez yelled. She was dying laughing as she started her car and pulled out of the driveway. "Damn, how he knowwww?" she said to herself, really trying to figure out how the hell he found out where she lived. He had the floor number and all. She shook her head at the fact that T-Money had been on her ass the whole time while she thought she was laying low on his ass.

Mercedez put on SWV "Weak in the Knees" and sang along. That nigga really had her weak in the knees. Weaving in and out of lanes, she was keeping up with T-Money, tailing behind him. Each time she passed him in traffic, she did some petty shit like flicked him off or played songs that were dissin' niggas.

A notification came through on T-Money's phone. He unlocked his phone and noticed he had two missed calls from Alexus. "Man, a nigga ain't on this shit," he said to himself. Alexus had waited a few days without calling and she would pick the day he and Mercedez started back talking to try and call him. He was actually loving the fact she hadn't been calling. Hell, it ain't like he was answering anyways. T-Money knew he could never handle Mercedez the way he did Alexus. He had to go hard to get Cedez back to normal. The minute he came back around, Mercedez actually had morals and expectations.

***

"Fuck-ass nigga," Alexus said under her breath after calling T-Money's phone and getting the voicemail. She was at the airport waiting on her flight to take off for Georgia. She was kind of glad he was screening her call because she was going to Georgia to do her own thing, just like he was doing.

Honcho had booked them a hotel suite for four days and Alexus was desperately waiting to see him face to face and spend time with him. They had been texting and sexting the past couple days and getting to really know each other. Alexus was ready to find out if he was really about all that freaky shit he was hollerin' about over the phone because she sure as hell was ready for all the action. T-Money had one up on her, but not for long. Alexus was getting ready to take his man on the ride of his life. She put her ear buds in as the flight took off.

Honcho had been running around all day catching plays and handling business, trying to make sure he was in place when Alexus's flight landed so he could pick her up from the airport. Ms. Gladys had always told him, "First Impression is everything" and as crazy as it may sound, he actually wanted to make a good impression for her. Something about her had him more interested than he should be. Her conversation was everything and her personality was lit, plus she was pretty as fuck with a busting-ass body, according to the flicks she'd sent him. That pussy was fat and nicely groomed too, Honcho was just as ready as she was. The only thing was he had to be careful not to be seen with her. He planned to take her out, but it would definitely be on another side of town because the fact still remained that Alexus was T-Money's bitch whether they were going through it or not.

Alexus had yet to inform Honcho that she was his wife. She didn't go too far into details when she explained hers and T-Money's relationship either.

***

T-Money had put Alexus on the block list. The last thing he needed was for her to call and it pissed Mercedez off all over again.

Mercedez pulled out her key to get in her loft. T-Money followed her through the gate, hoping she wasn't going to be on the bullshit. Little did he know Mercedez was in heat and as bad as she didn't want to give in, her hormones were through the roof and she was ready for him to fuck the hell out of her. He was looking so good at the Thanksgiving gathering. If it wasn't for the respect she had for her mama, she would've let him bust her right there at the gathering.

"Damn, baby mama this how you do a nigga? Snapped on you a place, got it fully furnished and all…and don't even tell a nigga?" T-Money said, walking in her place, noticing all the expensive furniture and decorations she had.

Mercedez waved him off. "Stop calling me that. I obviously ain't have to tell you shit. Seems to me you already knew." She was trying so hard to have an attitude with him, which was the hardest thing in the world since their bond had always been so tight.

"You are my baby mama. What do you mean? And damn right I knew, and as long as you were carrying my jits, I got the right to know." T-Money walked up behind her as she was taking her jewelry off and placing it on her bedroom dresser.

Seeing him in the mirror standing behind her instantly made her pussy throb.

"Look at us, Mercedez. What we got is unbreakable, girl. A nigga love you, man," T-Money said as he pressed his dick up against her ass, planting soft kisses down her neck, going farther down to her back.

Mercedez cocked her head to the side, giving him the okay to continue. "Mm-hmm," Mercedez moaned as he continuously kissed her, pulling her dress off up over her head. She held her arms up and let him do all the work as she stood there still watching him in the mirror. She was so horny and the last thing on her mind was a bitch named Alexus.

The last conversation Mercedez had with Ms. Hogan was about the Lord restoring her broken relationships, and Cedez was standing on that. He was definitely restoring things with her and Tevin. Before she knew it, they were both ass naked. That make-up sex be the best.

"Damn, bae," T-Money whispered as he picked her up, sitting her on top of the dresser.

He slowly spread her legs as he stuck his tongue damn near down her throat, caressing her breasts with one hand and gripping his thick long dick in his other hand. He rubbed it up and down on her clit.

"Ahhh," Mercedez moaned softly. Her pussy had a whole damn heartbeat at that moment. That mothafucka was its own person. She hadn't had sex since she'd found out she was pregnant.

Mercedez was damn near scooting off the dresser trying to make him stick his dick inside of her. She dug her nails into his back and he pulled away, dropping to his knees. That nigga was getting ready to marry the pussy. Mercedez threw her legs over his shoulders as he dived in, spreading her pussy lips. T-Money was making love to her shit. He had a point to prove. Pushing the hood of her clit back, he flicked her clit with the tip of his tongue so fast, causing her to instantly cream all over his face. Her pussy was so wet and T-Money had her juices dripping from his beard. Mercedez had both her hands on his head, shoving his face further in her blossom.

"Damn, Tevin, fuck!" she hollered as she moved her hips, grinding her pussy in his face.

T-Money was loving that shit. "Arrrgh!" he roared, sounding like a lion. He lifted her from the dresser to the bed with her legs straddled around him, cuffing both her ass cheeks. He had to be careful with her. He'd never fucked a pregnant woman before. He didn't want to harm the babies.

Turning her over, ass up, face down, he spread both of her ass cheeks, admiring her cotton candy pink insides before he slid in. "Ahhh, Cedez, damn I missed this pussy," he said in between moans as he watched his rod disappear inside of her.

"Yesss, daddy!" Mercedez was throwing that shit back, matching his rhythm.

He missed the pussy so much they weren't even five minutes in before he felt his cum rising to the tip of his dick. He knew she was nowhere near ready for him to release, so he pulled out and began sucking the soul out of her again. Mercedez's body was bucking. She looked as if some exorcism shit was going on. She was literally going crazy, cumming back to back.

After T-Money made her cum three times, it was his turn to catch his. He had been holding back just for her. Turning Mercedez on her side towards the wall, he got behind her. Mercedez laid on her right side, which was more comfortable for her, holding her left ass cheek for him to get in. T-Money gripped her waist, getting about ten good strokes in. He came all inside of her.

CHAPTER TWENTY-SIX

T-Money and Cedez were taking things slow. They were back together but she felt it was best if they continued living in separate homes, at least until she found out exactly what he was going to do as far as his marriage.

Mercedez and Ms. Hogan were becoming damn near best friends. She had finally confided in Ms. Hogan, telling her all about T-Money and the situation she was in, being pregnant with twins and finding out he was married. She wanted to tell Ms. Hogan about Nurse Douglas too, but there was no way in hell she was putting her in her game room about murders she'd committed. Telling her about Nurse Douglas meant she had to tell about her and T-Money killing Snoop. Mercedez was no green-ass bitch by far. That type of stuff was shit she would only discuss with T-Money, and she hadn't even told him about Nurse Douglas yet. She decided to keep that to herself. The last thing she needed was for there to be tension when he went to doctor's appointments with her. The way T-Money was set up, he would've been ready to take Nurse Douglas out too just off the strength of her being the nigga's mama.

It was early in the morning and T-Money woke up alone in his own bed, feeling good knowing that he'd just got some pussy from his baby mama the night before. Even though she wouldn't allow him to stay the night, they were making progress. T-Money got out of bed, walked down stairs, and let his pitbulls out in the backyard to use the bathroom while he sparked up his morning blunt. T-Money's spot was ducked off so the only thing you could hear were birds chirping. Checking his phone, he saw that he had a missed call from Truck. Mercedez had really taken his energy away after they had sex and he made it home he fell straight to sleep.

"Damn, missed a call from Truck at 10:41 p.m.," he said to himself. T-Money had been waiting to hear back from him. He immediately returned the call and Truck answered on the first ring.

"Yo brah, I hit you up last night to let you holla at my boy Hot-Rod that I told you about. You got a minute?" said Truck.

"Yeah, a nigga was knocked out, brah, I didn't hear my phone. Lemme holla at him though," T-Money replied.

Truck removed the phone from his ear. "Aye Hot-Rod! Come to my cell, G!"

T-Money could hear all the commotion in the prison as he waited for Hot-Rod to get on the phone.

"Wassup, brah? Dis Rod."

"What up? My lil brotha told me you tryna come up in there and you still got a little time left to do, right?"

"Yeah, I still got a lil stretch, man. I got pulled in here though 'cause I been down a while already. Shit, I got family out there I'm still tryna feed while I'm behind these walls. If y'all can supply me wit' da product, we can all eat and I'll make sho' you got yo' bread up front." Hot-Rod was fast talking, trying to let T-Money know he really meant business

"Okay, okay, my nigga, sound like we got something goin' here." T-Money pulled at the hair of his goatee as he processed his thoughts. Hot-Rod was doing most of the talking

"Alright, cool. My brother was just talking about putting me on with a nigga he worked for, but somebody ended up slumpin' my brother before he got a chance to even put me on."

T-Money could hear the pain in Hot-Rod's voice. "Damn, shit crazy out'chea homie, I got you doe. You gon' eat fa sho' fucking with me. Every nigga on my team eating and off Truck's face, I got you. But who ya brotha was though? I just lost one of my niggas that worked for me," T-Money said.

"I appreciate it, big dawg, I'ma show you I can handle it up in here. But my brother's name is Snoop. He just got killed a couple months ago."

"Oh naw, I don't know brah, sorry fa ya loss though, man. Keep ya head up in there. I'ma look out fa you. Lemme holla at Truck."

"A'ight, bet. If you can, add somebody on my visit list that you can send out here. I already got an officer that's down. We can put her on a consistent payroll and she can do what's needed," Hot-Rod said

"Okay, say less.

Hot-Rod put Truck back on the phone.

"Aye Truck, it's a go. I'm fucking wit' 'em," T-Money said.

"I knew you would, brah. I'm still da same ole Truck you know. I always kept niggas round me that get a bag." Truck laughed.

"Yeah, lil nigga, you learned from me," T-Money joked.

"A'ight, brah, the crackas 'bout to walk in We'll chop it up later," Truck said.

"A'ight, love," T-Money said before hanging up, sparking his blunt back up that he had allowed to go out while he was talking. He began thinking hard

"What da fuck!" he yelled. T-Money was a swift-ass mothafucka. Hot-Rod was Rodger Douglas, the same nigga that had Snoop trying to swap Mercedez out for him to get out of prison.

"Small fucking world," he said to himself. Rodger probably had no idea about Mercedez or who she was, but T-Money knew exactly who Hot-Rod was. He planned to still go through with letting the nigga work for him. T-Money had already informed him that he didn't know Snoop and he was going to keep it that way. Hot-Rod had no idea the same nigga that popped his brother would be the same nigga supplying him.

T-Money needed to holla at Cedez face to face about that shit, but that would have to wait until later because he needed to call Honcho ASAP to make sure his product was selling like he was expecting it to. He scrolled to Honcho's name and made the call.

***

"Ahhh, mmm, damn, Lexus, suck that dick. Yeah, just like that, baby girl.

Honcho was sitting on the edge of the bed in the hotel suite enjoying every bit of the sloppy head he was receiving. Alexus was on her tippy toes squatting between Honcho's legs, sucking the skin off his dick.

"Mmm," she moaned as she sucked. Going down further, she began sucking on his balls, drooling all over them. She knew she was doing the damn thing when she looked down and saw his toes curling.

He grabbed a handful of Alexus' long jet black wet and wavy bundles. Honcho began moving his hips, forcing his dick further down her throat.

Honcho's phone was lying on the bed next to him, vibrating. Alexus leaned up and noticed the caller ID read T-Money. He would be calling right about now , Honcho thought. The head was so good there was no way he was answering. When Alexus realized it was T-Money calling she purposely started slurping even harder. Looking up at Honcho, Alexus winked, letting Honcho know she peeped the fact that he'd screened the call.

It had been two days already that Alexus had been in Georgia. She and Honcho were really hitting it off. They fucked the majority of the time and Honcho was loving it. He left her at the hotel one time to go and check on Ms. Gladys and for those couple of hours, he found himself rushing to get back to her.

Honcho wasn't a sucker for no bitch, especially a bitch that fucked with his homie, but there was just something about Alexus that he was really digging. They had two more days to spend with each other before Alexus' flight back to Hawaii, and they were already making plans for their next link up.

Alexus was really feeling Honcho as well. Her plan turned out to be a little more than she'd expected. Their vibe came so natural that Honcho was even in her raw, not even thinking about the fact that she was indeed T-Money's bitch so he could never take her too seriously. Although he was feeling the fuck out of her, somehow he had to control his feelings. Alexus had yet to explain her and T-Money's relationship and now she was thinking maybe it would be best if she did not even go into detail about them.

"If he don't ask, I'm not saying shit," she said to herself as she stepped out of her robe, getting in the shower to freshen up before going out to eat.

It had been a while since Alexus had been out on a date since T-Money didn't spend much of his time with her. She was going to make sure she looked her best. It would be their first date out together and she wanted to be flawless walking next to him.

Alexus stood under the shower, lathering up in her Dove body wash as Honcho stepped out of his Calvin Klein boxers to join her. He could not get enough of her. He'd planned to pull up on T-Money later, but at the moment, the only thing he was worried about was the thick fine ass bitch in his presence.

"Damn, you look even sexier lathered up, girl" Honcho said as he slapped her ass cheek.

"Oh yeah, daddy?" Alexus turned around to face him as she ran her nails down his chest.

Honcho bit down on his bottom lip and began to kiss her passionately. She could feel his dick pressing up against her stomach. He was rock hard and Alexus knew exactly what time it was. He slid two fingers inside her, causing her pussy to tighten. Honcho could feel her walls closing in. He turned her around, spreading her ass cheeks apart, and slid right in, holding one of her legs up. Alexus was taking the dick. You could hear her ass sounding off every time his balls slapped her ass from behind. Honcho was putting in work for the time T-Money should've been.

They got there quickly and got dressed for their special date. Alexus wore an off-white, almost cream-colored, strapless catsuit made by Chanel with a pair of tan red bottoms and a red clutch to go with it. She styled her hair in a top knot and laid her baby hairs to the gods. Honcho had copped a new Armani Exchange outfit and a fresh pair of the new Jordan releases. He put his chain on, his diamond Rolex by Johnny Dane, and topped it off with his pinky ring. They actually looked really good together. Alexus wanted to take pictures with him and post them on her Facebook so badly, but she knew that was a no-no off rip. They really made a fly-ass couple though.

Honcho and Alexus cruised through the city, heading to the other side of town, looking for the perfect place to dine. Alexus sat in the passenger seat with her legs crossed, looking good as fuck. She kept looking at Honcho, thinking to herself *Damn, he looks good. It's the dreads for me.* She caught him continuously glancing at her from the corner of his eyes. He couldn't even keep his eyes off her either. Having a bitch like her riding on side of him had him really feeling like the mothafuckin' man. He had that Boosie and Webbie "Smokin On Purple" playing as he pulled on his blunt, switching lanes. He sang and bopped to the music while Alexus had her phone out making Snap videos. She did the typical shit bitches do on Snap, playing in her hair, batting her mink lashes, and putting the camera on Honcho's body, but being sure not to get his face. It was the simple shit like that bitches got one million likes for. All they needed was a bad-ass frontal on, some lashes, a face beat, and that alone made bitches go viral.

They finally made it to the restaurant. It was a fancy upscale place that had a variety of different kinds of food, from pastas to seafood to soul food.

"Table for two please," Honcho said when they met the waitress at the door.

Alexus was definitely pleased at how hard he was going for her. Every little thing about him had her head in the clouds. They engaged in conversation, sharing things about themselves as they waited for the waitress to help them. The topic that Alexus tried to avoid finally came about. She knew it would be coming sooner or later.

"So baby, what exactly do you and T-Money got going on? 'Cause I'm actually feeling you and I don't want it to be no pressure," Honcho said.

Alexus closed the menu and gave Honcho her undivided attention. "Well, bae, it's complicated. We 'were' a thing, and then I found out he had a girl named Mercedez pregnant, so you know, I kinda just removed myself." Alexus was partially telling the truth, but leaving the real facts out. She refused to tell him they were married. With the way they were hitting it off, she definitely wasn't mentioning anything to make him want to reconsider fucking with her. The vibe was way too good for her to fuck it up so soon.

"So what you're saying is if we decided to take things further, it wouldn't be an issue between me and brah?" Honcho was glad she confirmed that Mercedez was the one pregnant and not her because he never even bothered asking.

Taking a deep breath Alexus began. "Well, I'm not sure where T-Money's head is at because we haven't even had the chance to actually talk after I found out he had twins on the way. He kind of just dipped out and been avoiding me, so I haven't really got any closure."

Honcho replied, "Hmm, okay, I feel ya. Well, until you find out what's what on that end, we'll just stay low-key. A nigga fuckin wit'cha heavy though."

Alexus was loving everything he was saying. "Okay, daddy, we can do that. I'm fucking wit; you too." She smiled before leaning across the table to kiss him on his mouth.

From the outside looking in, you'd think Honcho and Alexus had been together for years.

Le'Monica Jackson

CHAPTER TWENTY-SEVEN

T-Money and Mercedez had been out shopping for the twins all day. Not wanting her twins to be like most babies, Mercedez tried to stay away from the blue and pink shit, which made shopping for them a lot more difficult. Although T-Money had other shit he needed to do besides shopping all day, he wasn't doing or saying anything to get back on Mercedez's bad side, especially while things were finally trying to get back to normal.

T-Money had already run the shit by Cedez about putting Rodger, a.k.a. Hot-Rod, on and he explained the fact that he was Snoop's brother. Mercedez was still working on falling back from the streets so she heard T-Money out, giving him her opinion and suggestions, but she chose not to get involved in no type of way. He peeped the changes in Mercedez and he kind of liked it because it was for the better. Although he was so used to her being his ride or die bitch, he was getting used to her just being a mother to his children. Normally T-Money would've had Mercedez taking the pack to the prison and meeting up with the officer that was going to be on payroll, but because he respected her mind and knew she wanted no dealings with it, he decide to put Quan and Quay to the test to see if he could trust them with a task like that.

Mercedez received a message from Janicka with the details about the baby shower, making a mental note to give Janicka a call once she and T-Money were done shopping. They'd already spent damn near $5,000 in one day on just clothes for the twins. The baby shower would be more for the celebration because they had just about everything they needed plus some.

Mercedez had finally agreed to let T-Money spend the night with her only because she was too lazy to do much on her own anymore. They stayed up all night setting up the room for the twins and putting their stuff away.

"I don't even know why you want all this stuff set up, Mercedez. I'm buying a house for my kids to live in, man," T-Money said as Mercedez lay stretched across the twins' bedroom floor watching T-Money organize everything while she gave him orders.

"Okay, Tevin, we are taking things slow and as of right now, they are living right here," she replied. She wasn't trying to hear all that.

T-Money just shook his head. He wasn't about to go back and forth with her. It took him another couple hours before he was done setting everything up. *Lazy ass just wanna lay there and give a nigga orders. I hope my baby's rip her all the way to her asshole.*

Mercedez had a hair appointment the next morning at 9:00 a.m. with Nay-Nay. She lay in her bed and fell straight to sleep as soon as her head hit T-Money's chest. He was so glad to finally be able to sleep next to her again. Even though he would've rather her come to his spot, it was all good as long as they were sleeping together. He stayed up flipping through the channels and holding Mercedez in his arms. She went to sleep totally forgetting to hit Janicka back up about the baby shower.

T-Money planted soft kisses on her forehead and whispered, "I love you," before he finally dozed off.

The alarm went off at 8:00 a.m. and T-Money felt like he'd just fallen asleep.

"Get up, baby," he said as he rubbed Mercedez's belly while she was spread across the bed, sleeping wild with her mouth wide open. She hadn't slept that well in a long time. "Baby, get up, you got a hair appointment." He attempted to wake her up again.

Mercedez sat up in bed, still halfway asleep, reaching for her phone on the nightstand. Nay-Nay had already texted her reminding her about the appointment. She had two missed calls from Janicka and a good morning text from Ms. Hogan. T-Money got up, brushed his teeth and rolled his first blunt of the day while Mercedez returned Janicka's call. She needed thirty more minutes before she actually got out of bed.

"Good mornin', sis. Well, me and Tonya decided we're going to do your baby shower in Atlanta so you don't have to keep jumping on the road. We already found a building that's a pretty good size. We figured we'd do it for the first Saturday of next month and the theme will be Kings and Queens. The colors will be silver and rose gold." Janicka was the perfect event planner.

"Oooh yes, that sounds nice! Shit, just send me the invitations through the mail and I'll start getting them out to people." Mercedez knew between her family and the people T-Money knew, her baby shower was going to be on swole.

After she and Janicka got off the phone, she began getting ready for her hair appointment while telling T-Money about the shower.

"Oh yeah, that sounds good, bae. King and Queen shit for my babies. Sis knows what time it is. Look who they pappy is," T-Money joked. All this shit was new to him but he was loving every second of it.

Mercedez didn't feel like driving so she had T-Money drop her off at Nay-Nay's salon.

"Wassup, Nay?" Mercedez said as she entered the salon. She was the first client to come in.

"Hey Cedez!" She paused, looking Cedez up and down. "Girl, look at you looking all good, pregnant and all. Girl, you look great," Nay-Nay complimented her, giving her a hug.

Mercedez sat down as Nay-Nay draped her with a hair cape and combed through her long pretty natural hair. Mercedez began telling Nay-Nay about the baby shower, making sure Nay-Nay would be free to attend.

"Oh, girl, you know I'm not missing that!" Nay-Nay said. She was a friend of T-Moneys and he'd always told her whenever he had kids, she would be the godmother. Nay-Nay didn't have kids of her own, so she was excited about her god babies. Nay-Nay didn't even have a boyfriend. The only nigga Mercedez ever really heard her talk about was a nigga that was up the road. She always heard Nay-Nay tell the nigga things like she couldn't wait for him to come home. Other than that, Nay-Nay lived for the hair salon. She was a little on the heavier side, but she had a pretty face and she definitely wasn't insecure about her size. When niggas did try to shoot their shot, she usually turned them down.

"Girl, I gotta make sure I get me a nice outfit for the baby shower. You know anything with T-Money face on it gon' have ballers pullin' up," Nay-Nay joked. She had been friends with T for a while so she already knew what time it was and what type of crowd he brought out.

Cedez laughed. "Girl! I'm so ready to have these babies." She rubbed her belly.

Nay-Nay changed the subject. "Girl, can you believe they still didn't find out who killed the girl Nicole who used to get her hair done here?" Nay-Nay usually had all the tea. Hell, most hair stylists did.

"Damn, that's crazy! She was pretty too. I saw on the news she had kids and all," Cedez responded, shaking her head. The first thing that came to mind was when she'd first seen Nicole at the salon and that was the only time she'd seen her alive.

They changed the subject as two other clients walked in.

"Hey Nay-Nay, how are you doing?" The two women walked in, heading straight to the back.

"I'm doing good. How y'all doin?" Nay smiled.

Mercedez saw new faces every time she went to her salon. Nay-Nay always got hella business.

Spinning Mercedez's chair around, Nay-Nay turned her to face the mirror. "You like?"

"Bitch, yes! You always do your thing, sis." Mercedez ran her fingers through her bone straight red frontal that hung all the way to the crack of her ass. Nay had her shit looking like it grew right out of her roots. Natural as hell. Mercedez pulled three blue faces out of her Chanel bag and gave them to Nay. She was always pleased with her services.

"Keep the change, girl. Thank you." She'd already sent T-Money a text letting him know she was ready so he was already outside waiting for her.

Normally he would've come in and chopped it up with Nay, but he had to make it to the lab in the next thirty minutes to holla at Quay and Quan about the prison run he was putting them onto.

"Damn, bae, I love seeing you," T-Money said as soon as Mercedez climbed in the passenger seat of his Range Rover.

"You do, bae," she said, letting down the sun visor, taking another look in the mirror at her new hairstyle.

"Hell ya, girl, you lookin' good as fuck." T-Money reached over and squeezed her thigh. "I gotta stop by the lab for a minute, baby."

Mercedez looked over at him and rolled her eyes. "Okay, Tevin, but I'm hungry and ready to go home."

"Alright, alright, I just gotta handle something real quick," he pleaded. He thought, *I can't stand ha ugly ahh.*

Mercedez sucked her teeth and folded her arms over her breasts. "Mm-hmm, and you better not take long," she demanded. She was so spoiled and bossy and her hormones were not making it any better. She always had to have her way.

Quan and Quay were already waiting outside of the lab smoking a blunt when T-Money pulled up. He hopped out of his truck, leaving it running for Mercedez.

"And if you take long, I'ma pull off!" she yelled out as he made his way up the driveway to the front door.

Quan and Quay laughed at Cedez as they dapped T-Money up. "Wassup, Boss?"

"Wassup, young bloods? I'ma give y'all the rundown. I gotta make this quick though. My crazy-ass baby mama——"

"Gon' leave yo' ass," Quan finished the sentence, clowning T-Money's ass.

They all laughed.

Quan and Quay followed T-Money in and joined him at the round table. He didn't waste any time, jumping straight to the point, letting them know what had to be done

"I'm gonna give y'all some shit wrapped up and ready to go, and I need y'all to take it to the prison. I'ma give y'all the address, but first I need you to fill out a visitation form to see Rodger Douglas. Y'all gon' be straight. I got an officer already up on game who y'all gon' be passing the pack off to at the visit. Y'all go together and take turns going or however you choose to do it, it don't matter to me. I just need da shit done and y'all already know I'm gon' throw y'all something extra for doing it."

"Okay, boss, bet! We gon' get on it ASAP," Quay assured him.

T-Money fucked with them. They were clearly down for whatever. Quan ain't say much. He just went with the flow.

Mercedez was in the driver seat laying on the horn.

"Okay, hit me up if anything changes. Lemme get up outta hear before my dumb ass be walkin'," T-Money joked.

T-Money, Quan, and Quay all got up and headed out the door. Quan and Quay hopped in their mobbed-out Ford Explorer rental car and sped off.

"Aye, chill out, man." T-Money laughed, hopping in the passenger seat since Mercedez had climbed her ass over to the driver seat, ready to pull off.

"No! Your ass was 'bout to get left. Quan and Quay ugly asses was gon' have to be givin' you a ride today," Mercedez said with attitude.

T-Money thought the shit was hilarious, and knowing she was dead-ass serious is what made the shit funny as hell.

CHAPTER TWENTY-EIGHT

T-Money already had shit in motion to get things done for Truck and Hot-Rod.

Meanwhile, Hot-Rod was still trying to find out who killed his brother. The officer he was fucking with had put a bird in his ear, showing him a picture of a bad-ass light-skinned chick, informing him that it was the girl his brother was supposed to swap out for him to give his time back and that she could possibly have something to do with his brother getting killed. Hot-Rod had been fucking with Officer Standley for the past five years and she always kept him in the loop about whatever the streets or the crackas were talking about. Hot-Rod stayed on beat with everything.

"Damn, shawty bad as fuck," he said to himself as he looked at the mugshot of Mercedez that Officer Standley had printed out for him to keep. He showed the picture to Truck.

"Aye brah, you know this chick?" Hot-Rod asked.

Truck grabbed the picture looking closely at it. "Naw, I don't know her, she badder den a bih doe, wassup wit' her?" Truck replied.

Hot-Rod shook his head and responded, "Shit, Officer Standley said she heard a bitch might have sumthin' to do with my brother getting killed."

There was an awkward silence as both men took a good look at the photo of Mercedez. She was even sexy in her mugshot. The picture was taken years ago when she had been arrested on drug charges that eventually were dropped.

Hot-Rod put the picture away under his mat, making a mental note to keep his ears open to see if he heard anything about a bitch having something to do with his brother's murder. Officer Standley didn't always have accurate info and before Hot-Rod put a word on the streets to have shawty killed, he wanted to be sure she was involved.

Hot-Rod had so much on his mind. He couldn't wait to be called out by Officer Standley to go and do his night time job, which was cleaning the officer stations, which also consisted of him and her ducking off in the cleaning closet so he could relieve some pressure. They were damn near in a full relationship. Officer Standley would work double shifts just to move shit for him or to give him some pussy. She had a whole man at home, but lately she seemed to be falling hard for Hot-Rod. He had her just where he wanted her: wrapped around his finger.

***

It had only been a few weeks since Alexus had been back in Hawaii and she was missing the hell out of Honcho. They were caked up on the phone Facetiming every chance they got.

Mercedez and T-Money's baby shower was two days away and as bad as Honcho wanted Alexus in his presence, he knew he would have to wait to link up with her until after the baby shower. It was mandatory that he attended his main man's first baby shower. The twins were definitely a big deal.

Alexus was feeling some type of way about Honcho going, but she had to put up a front as if she was unbothered. Alexus wished she was the one carrying T-Money's babies, but she would never admit that to Honcho though. He'd already put Alexus up on game, informing her that if he didn't answer his phone, it was because he would be at the celebration.

***

The big day was finally here. Mercedez and T-Money were being escorted in a limo to the building the baby shower was being held at.

"Oh my gosh!" Mercedez cupped her hands over her mouth as they arrived.

Tonya and Janicka had really done the damn thing. Mercedez and T-Money hadn't even made it inside yet, but the parking lot was full of foreign cars. Everyone was standing outside on both sides of the red carpet, waiting for T-Money and Mercedez to step out.

The first person Mercedez spotted was her mama, standing there with her big beautiful smile. Everyone was dressed in either silver or gold. Mercedez and T-Money wore gold Versace outfits. After getting out of the back of the limo, they walked hand in hand down the red carpet towards the glass double doors as all of their guests clapped and took pictures. Mercedez had tears in her eyes. She was impressed.

Upon entering the building, Mercedez halted at the threshold. She couldn't believe her eyes. The place was decorated to the gods. There were king and queen crowns everywhere and a table full of different kinds of foods, not to mention the gifts. Everyone had really done it big for the twins. Janicka and Tonya had even set up a whole picture booth.

Nay-Nay was the first person ready to flick it up. "Congrats, y'all! Lemme get a picture with the parents of my god babies!" She pulled Mercedez and T-Money in, standing on one side of Cedez, holding her belly, while T-Money stood on the other side with his arm around Mercedez. The photographer snapped the pictures. Printing them out, he gave Nay-Nay one and held on to the other two so he could build the baby shower album.

The baby shower was lit. The women played the games and shit while the men gathered around, posted up, drinking and talking.

Mercedez excused herself as she noticed a late guest walking in. "Oh my gosh!" Mercedez halted. "This woman came way down here, wow! I can't believe this! Hey, Ms. Hogan!"

Mercedez embraced her with a hug. She hadn't seen Ms. Hogan since the day they'd met on the airplane. Ms. Hogan had three gift bags in each hand.

"Congrats, baby!" she said as she handed Mercedez the gifts.

"Thank you. I'm so glad you could make it," said Mercedez. She'd never told T-Money about Ms. Hogan, so she decided she'd introduce them to each other since Ms. Hogan had already planned to be there for the delivery. She grabbed Ms. Hogan's hand and led her over to where T-Money was posted with his homies.

"Baby, I want you to meet——"

T-Money turned around to acknowledge her and instantly locked eyes with Ms. Hogan.

"My baby! Oh my goodness, I have been looking for you for years, Tevin!" Ms. Hogan cried as she hugged T and cried real tears.

Confused, Mercedez stood to the side. "So you know her already?" Mercedez asked.

"Bae, this the woman who raised me," T-Money responded.

Cedez couldn't believe what she was hearing. T-Money had never mentioned Ms. Hogan before. She was his very last foster mother when he was thirteen. She had him and Truck at the same time. Ms. Hogan was the only foster mother he ever had that actually gave a fuck about him. Even when he got in trouble, she never gave up on him, but the minute he turned sixteen, he hauled ass and never came back because he wasn't used to anybody who cared. At the time, he felt like she was too strict, but looking back, he realized she was just trying to save him from the streets. Patricia Hogan, a.k.a. Ms. Patty genuinely loved him and Truck. Crazy he'd just found Truck and now there he was standing in front of Ms. Patty at his baby shower event. It was a beautiful moment. They did minor catching up, but they definitely had to get together at a better time.

Ms. Hogan felt like her prayers were being answered. She'd been asking God to help her find Tevin for a long time. She already had plans on being a part of the twins' lives, but now it was on a whole 'nother level.

"Those babies are my grandbabies, Mercedez. Tevin is my son!" Ms. Hogan was beyond happy. She didn't even have any biological children. Tevin and Truck were the closest thing to her own children she ever had.

T-Money hadn't told her he'd been in contact with Truck, but he was going to be sure to let her know. Mercedez walked Ms. Hogan, around introducing her to the family. Ms. Karen held a conversation with Ms. Hogan as Mercedez got back to playing the games. The women measured Mercedez's belly while Ms. Karen and Ms. Hogan prepared the tables for everyone to eat. They seemed to really be clicking.

Mercedez was loving everything about the shower. Great things were definitely taking place. T-Money couldn't even keep his eyes off of the woman who he called "Mama". He couldn't believe she was really there. He still didn't know how Mercedez knew her, but that was a conversation that he would be sure to have later on.

Le'Monica Jackson

CHAPTER TWENTY-NINE

T-Money and Mercedez were pleased at how the celebration turned out. It was definitely something to remember, but they were glad it was finally over. Mercedez was ready to go ahead and have the babies and T-Money was ready for her to as well. He missed putting blunts in rotation with her and staying up late nights sipping her favorite drink with her…Hennessy, where Henny thing can happen! Most of all though, they were ready to meet their bundles of joy.

Everyone who attended the shower was killing the timeline on Facebook with pictures. Of course Alexus was salty as fuck when Honcho posted the pictures he'd taken with T-Money and Mercedez. She sent him a text. "I hope you enjoyed ya folks baby shower hit me up when you got time for me. Damn, I miss you."

He hadn't spoken to her all day, but he peeped that she was liking every post he made. He shot her a quick text back. "A'ight… I miss you too and stop 'cause I told you what I had to do today, tighten up."

Alexus read the message and rolled her eyes. *I'm not even gone respond to that,* she thought to herself.

Honcho hit her up as soon as he got from around T-Money. He was feeling flaw for knowing he even had to fuck with her low-key, but it was a little too late for all that.

Alexus was calling T-Money private, but of course he never answered. At this point, she wasn't even surprised. It was obvious he was willing to lose her for Mercedez. He never said anything about divorcing her. She had no idea what his intentions were, but it would only be a matter of time before she turned all the way up on his ass. She needed closure more than anything because now she was actually trying to move on with her life with Honcho. She knew T-Money feared if he divorced her, she would try to take everything he had, but she was past all that shit. She just wanted closure and a divorce. Alexus couldn't stand it any longer knowing that she was, in fact, number two the entire time they were married. It never really was genuine. He pretty much married her because he felt bad for her.

All Alexus saw down her timeline was everyone posting photos from the baby shower. That shit was going viral. "Well damn, they actin' like these mothafuckas celebrities or something," Alexus said to herself, sucking her teeth as she scrolled.

Nay-Nay had posted damn near fifty pictures and Alexus was following her. She read Nay-Nay's last post that was posted thirty minutes ago.

T-Money and Mercedez baby shower was nice asf, proud to say I'm the godmother. Free Bae can't wait til it's our turn.

"Phony-ass hoe don't even got a man," Alexus chuckled.

***

Nay-Nay was looking good as hell in all the pictures, so it was mandatory that she send some flicks to the prison. "Oooh, Hot-Rod gon' love this one, my stomach looking flat and my ass is pokin'."

Nay-Nay was picking out every picture she knew he would like. As soon as he called, that was the first thing she let him know. "Hey baby, I was just thinking of you. I went to a baby shower today, I'm going to send you some pictures from the celebration."

"Alright, baby," Hot-Rod replied. "I know you was lookin' good, but I called to let you know I'm gonna be able to start takin' care you from in here, bae. I got some shit in motion."

Hot-Rod had Nay-Nay's nose wide open for him and for that reason, she was willing to wait a lifetime for him to come home. "Okay baby, that's wassup. I know things gon' work in ya favor, bae. I'm still praying for you to come home sooner. I'm ready to have your baby, Rodger," she replied. Nay-Nay was the true definition of a rider. She and Hot-Rod weren't even together before he got fucked up. They actually started talking through Nicole before she got killed. She was at Nay-Nay's one day on a collect call with Rodger, who was her brother-in-law. He heard Nay-Nay in the background and asked to holla at her, and they'd been talking ever since then.

After the call ended, Hot-Rod lay on his bunk staring at the picture that Officer Standley gave him. "I don't know who dis bitch is, but a nigga 'bout to bust on her face." He laughed as he whipped his dick out. Grabbing lotion from his locker, he lathered up and jacked off to Mercedez's picture.

***

It had been three days since the baby shower. Blaze, Quan, Quay, and Honcho were all making shit shake in the streets and T-Money was pleased at how much Money they were bringing in. Honcho was good for upping the prices on mothafuckas and he was doing so well out there. He'd made enough money in one week to take a break without T-Money jumping down his throat. He'd booked his first flight to Hawaii and he was ready to see how Alexus was really living. She'd made him so many promises about when he finally came to Hawaii. Now he was ready to see what Hawaii was really all about. With all the bragging she did, it kind of had him ready to consider packing up and hauling ass to be with her. Every time he considered it though, he thought about his grandma.

Hawaii was exactly how he imagined it: palm trees and lots of water. Beautiful!

"Damn, I could get used to this," Honcho said as he sat on the balcony of Alexus' mini mansion.

She put her hand on her hip and responded in a soft voice, "And it could be all yours, baby. Whenever you're ready." She sat on his lap straddling him.

It all sounded so good. What Honcho didn't know was that it already partially belonged to T-Money.

He sparked up a joint, enjoying the cool fall weather. Honcho had never experienced such a peaceful atmosphere in his entire life. It even smelled fresh in Hawaii. No gunshots, no kids running around, no ratchet hoes screaming from one apartment to another. He was in paradise. Lost in his imagination, he was interrupted by the sound of his phone going off. Checking his caller ID, he saw that it was Ms. Gladys.

"Hey Ma," he answered.

"Jadarrius, I need a ride to the hospital," she whined.

Putting his joint out, tossing Alexus off of him, he began pacing back and forth. "What's wrong, Ma? You alright?"

Ms. Gladys responded, "Baby, I ain't been feeling well the past couple of days. You don't come home that often these days. I was gonna wait till you came home, but…"

Honcho was panicking. "Alright, Ma, alright, say no mo'. I'm out of town, but I'll be there ASAP." He hung the phone up and instantly began to gather his shit.

"Baby, I'm going with you," Alexus said as she snatched up her things and booked a same day flight for the two of them.

Honcho's trip came to an end sooner than he expected. Alexus hadn't even shown him half of the things she'd planned to show him. It would have to wait until another time because there was nothing more important in Honcho's life than his grandma, and he stressed that to her, off rip. Alexus had never met Ms. Gladys and here she was headed to Georgia with Honcho to see her.

CHAPTER THIRTY

Quan and Quay were approved for visitation and had two days before they had to transport the package. T-Money had already rented a 2019 Camaro for them to use to jump on the road with. They agreed that both of them would go on the first run to make sure everything played out right. Hot-Rod had already given Officer Standley the rundown so she was on point. Truck didn't have to get his hands dirty. Off the strength of him being T-Money's brother, he was getting bust down regardless.

"Mail call" an Officer called out.

The inmates scurried from their cells and huddled around the table, waiting for their name to be called.

"Rodger Douglas!"

He was always the first name to be called. Between his moms and Nay-Nay, he was guaranteed mail every day. Hot-Rod got his mail and went back to his cell. The mail was from Tenaya Rivers, which was Nay-Nay. He'd received pictures from the baby shower.

"Sexy ass," he said to himself as he skimmed through the pictures until he got to the last one. "Wait a minute!" He stared at a picture with Nay-Nay holding a pregnant woman's belly and a nigga on the other side. Reaching under his mat, he pulled out the picture he had just jacked off to yesterday. Looking from picture to picture he compared the pregnant woman to the woman's mugshot. "Mannn...this the same bitch!" Hot-Rod thought about calling Nay-Nay up and seeing what the fuck was up. He decided to just sit back and see for himself. He flipped the picture over. "Me and the parents of my godchildren, T-Money and Mercedez," he read out loud. "Man, this hoe trying to snake me or what?" he questioned in his mind.

"The same nigga that's putting me on baby momma name all tied up in my brother's murder." Hot-Rod sat up on his bunk, trying to put everything together. He jumped up, placing the pictures in the envelope and stuffing it under his pillow as Truck walked in the room.

"Yo nigga, ya pack touching down soon. Just talked to T-Money. We're gonna be supa stars, bro," Truck said.

"Yeah, I know, I got a visit with the niggas Quan and Quay." Hot-Rod was still trying to process what kind of creep-ass shit was going on. He trusted Nay-Nay for the most part, but he'd never fully trust nobody, so for now, everyone was suspect. He had to keep his mouth closed because he still needed T-Money to supply him.

As soon as Truck left his cell, he pulled out his cell phone and immediately called his mama. "Hey Ma, I got a word in here that a chick named Mercedez may have something to do with Robert and Nicole's murders." He gave his momma the whole rundown. "I got some pictures. I'ma send 'em to you. I'm doing a lil business with the girl baby daddy. They call him T-Money. So if anything happens to me in here, that nigga and his lady behind it." Hot-Rod really felt like Truck was low-key setting him up. Meanwhile, Truck hadn't even talked to his brother in years. Shit was just coincidental.

Hot-Rod snapped a picture of the photo and sent it to his mom's phone.

Nurse Douglas was speechless when she realized that the woman was a patient of hers. "Oh my Lord! This is just so, so, so disturbing. Hot-Rod, who told you this girl was involved?" she asked.

"Mama, that's irrelevant. Just listen to what I'm telling you, I'm gonna do my own investigation. You just be safe out there and don't mention anything to anybody!"

"Okay, baby, I love you," Nurse Douglas didn't bother telling Hot-Rod that Mercedez was the patient. She sat on the edge of her bed, stuck in a daze. Ms. Douglas thought back to the day when she did Mercedez's sonograms. "Wait, that girl's name was Chantel Jackson," she said to herself Ms. Douglas became distraught. Mercedez had an upcoming appointment and Nurse Douglas was going to make sure she was on the schedule to work that day.

***

"Ma, open the door!" Honcho was beating on the front door of his grandma's apartment. After knocking for about thirty seconds, he reached in his pocket and pulled out a ring of keys. He tried each one until he found the right one that fit. "Ma!" he yelled as he walked through the apartment with Alexus right on his heels.

Nothing was in a disarray, everything was where it should have been, but his grandma was nowhere. She usually sat in her recliner right by the front window, but on this day her chair was empty. Her coffee mug was empty and the window shade was closed when it usually would have been open so she could be nosy. All of his senses came alive. He knew something wasn't right, so he rushed to his grandma's bedroom, busting in her room. He went crazy, seeing his grandma laying on the bedroom floor.

"I'll call the ambulance!" shouted Alexus, pulling out her phone from her back pocket.

Honcho was down on one knee, cradling Ms. Gladys' head in his lap, checking her pulse. She was still breathing, but they were very shallow breaths and she wasn't even responding. "Fuck! Fuck! I should've never left."

Alexus instantly felt guilty for convincing him to come to Hawaii.

"Yes, yes, she is breathing, but she won't wake up," Alexus said to the 911 operator.

"Man, tell 'em to get they ass here right fuckin' now!" Honcho roared, tripping out. He looked out the front window.

Alexus yelled, "Calm the fuck down, the paramedics are here!" She opened the front door and the paramedics rushed inside with a stretcher.

They asked Honcho a bunch of questions about Ms. Gladys' health as they lifted her onto the stretcher. They wheeled her out the door and Honcho piled inside the ambulance with them all. There was no way he was leaving his grandma's side.

Alexus was doing the dash in Honcho's 2016 Maxima, being sure to stay right behind the ambulance. Honcho needed her support and she was gonna be right there.

***

Arriving at the doctor's appointment, T was right by Mercedez's side. This would be the first appointment they attended together. Cedez had been having back pains, so she was glad she would be seeing her doctor today. Holding her hand, T-Money helped her up each step. They made their way to the hospital's elevator to get to the doctor's office. She signed in and waited to be seen. She was used to the whole routine now.

T sat next to her, reading an email from Quan. "Everything 100!" T-Money answered "100" and stuffed his phone back in his pocket.

"Chantal Jackson," Nurse Douglas called her name.

They made their way to the back. Nurse Douglas checked her vitals before the doctor came in.

"You need to stay off your feet and stay hydrated. And this must be dad?" The doctor shook T's hand.

"Yes sir." T-Money laughed.

The appointments were pretty much all the same. Cedez was ready to start dilating already. She was 7 ½ months along, looking like she would bust any minute now.

Nurse Douglas had got a real good look at both Mercedez and T-Money before she left the room. She pulled out her phone that she kept in her pocket that day, praying her boss didn't catch her. She was trying to see if they resembled the picture. They were most definitely the same people, but the girl in the room was certainly Chantal Jackson. Nurse Douglas was totally confused and lost. She was going to get down to the bottom of it somehow.

Mercedez and T-Money met her back at the front desk to get their next appointment time and date. When she saw them coming, she quickly exited out of the gallery. "Okay, Ms. Jackson and Dad, I'll see you guys in two weeks," said Nurse Douglas. She handed her an appointment card and she walked them to the door. She wanted them out of her sight as soon as possible.

She seems a little on the edge today, Cedez thought to herself.

Getting off of the elevator, she had to stop at the vending machine. Mercedez grabbed herself two packs of M&M's and a Pepsi. She held the packs up in T's face. "Two packs, nigga, 'cause I'm having 2 kids at one time while you calling me fat in your head." Cedez held up head and stuck her tongue out.

"Aww man, she knows me too well," T mumbled to himself.

"Excuse me!" Paramedics were rushing in someone on a stretcher, bumping into T-Money. He turned around and realized it was Honcho's grandma and Honcho was running behind them.

"Brah, brah, she good?" asked T-Money.

Honcho kept running. He had tunnel vision. The only thing he was worried about was Ms. Gladys.

Mercedez popped the top on her Pepsi, turning and locking eyes with Alexus. She thought her eyes were playing a trick on her until she heard the tramp's voice.

"Baby, hold up, I'm right behind you." Alexus brushed past T-Money and all of them disappeared around the corner

Mercedez and T stood there to process the scene of Alexus and Honcho together.

T didn't know if he should stay to make sure Ms. Gladys was good or not. Then again, he didn't need Cedez thinking he was trying to get up with Alexus.

It was silent for a moment until Cedez spoke up. "Um, if I heard and saw correctly, your wife was just running behind your right hand man talking 'bout 'hold on, baby'?" Mercedez mimicked, chuckling. "That's what happens when you try to put a ring on a slut."

T remained silent because that shit threw him for a loop. He was hardly ever thrown off balance. He was always in control and had the ups in any and every situation.

Cedez stared at T with an amused looked on her face. The only thing that could be heard was the beeping from the elevator. "Or am I tripping?"

"Shit, I'm just as lost as you. I'm taking my Queen to check on my shorties, while you trying to rank on a nigga. I'on' even give a fuck. You my only concern." T-money mushed Mercedez in the back of her head.

"Yeah, uh huh, nigga, lemme find out!" she said, rolling her eyes and neck.

"Damn, you trippin', girl, ain't shit to find out!"

"Oh well! Oh well!" Mercedez tried talking over him.

He shrugged his shoulders as they made their way to the car. He knew Honcho would hit them up later and give him the whole run down. That shit kinda fucked him up, running into Alexus, and her not saying two words to him. Was she really with Honcho? *Hell, I hope Ms. Gladys okay.*

Cedez sat in the passenger seat with her feet kicked up on the dash, popping M&M's in her mouth. She clearly didn't have a care in the world.

"Aye gurl, get them paws off my damn dash," T said.

"Boy, my feet cute. You wasn't saying that shit last night when you was licking the lint from my socks from between my toes."

"Whatever!" T responded.

"Besides, the doc said I need to prop them up."

Even though he was clowning, she could tell he was a bit worried. She knew him all too well. Frankly, she didn't give a damn. Her only concern was her babies. Actually, she found it funny that the bitch he put a ring was on T-Money's right hand man's dick. That was a downgrade. *Bitch s'posed to be in Hawaii but is in Georgia with Honcho's dick in her mouth, fucking the help*, Cedez thought to herself. "Fucking the help!" She laughed each word out.

T just shook his head because he knew Cedez was right. He also knew she was trying to be funny and petty.

Dropping Mercedez off at her spot, he went to meet up with Quan and Quay. He called up Quay's number.

"Hot-Rod received the pack and everything a go from here, boss man. He busted down the pack with Truck," Quay answered, informing him of the outcome without even a hello.

T loved the way Quay was all business, no play.

Quan and Quay made sure they gave Officer Standley her cut. She gave Quay her personal number, coming off a little flirtatious when she eyeballed how much money he'd pulled out. And he was with the shits all day, so he took it.

As soon as they left the prison, he shot her a text. "It's Q, lock me in." He knew better than to just give out his real name. At the end of the day, she was still a worker for the feds.

Thanks to Blaze, everybody was eating good off the prison hustle he'd put together.

Le'Monica Jackson

CHAPTER THIRTY-ONE

Mercedez was home preparing herself for company. Ms. Hogan had planned to come to town for three days for a women's seminar she would be speaking at. She wanted to spend a little time with Mercedez and possibly have a sit down with Tevin. Mercedez had already invited her to stay over instead of getting a room. She couldn't wait to have Tevin and his foster mom sit down and talk. They hadn't talked since the baby shower and according to their reaction, there was a lot that needed to be said. Cedez certainly could use Ms. Hogan's conversation and assistance for the next three days, since the doctor advised her to stay off of her feet.

"T will love the three day break," Cedez said to herself. She began thinking of how demanding and lazy she'd been the last few months.

***

Lying in the hospital bed, Ms. Gladys had finally woken up.

"And who is this heffa?" she said as soon as she opened her eyes.

Honcho gently rubbed her head. "Chill, Ma, you just woke up from a coma, man. Lemme get the doctor." He reached over and pressed the call button for the nurse.

"Well, what happened, Jadarrius, why was I in a coma?" Ms. Gladys said with a concerned look on her face. "And who the hell are you?" she asked Alexus directly.

"My name is Alexus. I'm Honcho's——"

"You're his nothing, and baby, his name is Jadarrius. I don't know no damn Honcho," Ms. Gladys interrupted, rolling her eyes.

All Honcho could do was drop his head. *She ain't got no damn filter, man, damn*, Honcho thought.

Alexus looked like she was slapped in the face. *I'm not about to go back and forth with an old-ass lady who I just went all out my way to make sure was good.* She was tight, so she just made light of the situation by remaining silent and smiling.

A nurse entered the room and started informing Ms. Gladys of her condition. "Ma'am, your sugar was low. Seems like you haven't been eating right or taking your insulin. Also, you had a mild heart attack"

Ms. Gladys wasn't taking her health seriously at all.

Honcho shook his head as tears welled up in his eyes. "Ma, I told you that you have to start taking care of yourself. Man, your health is important, Ma."

"Jadarrius I'm grown. I do whatever I wanna do!" yelled Ms. Gladys.

"Ma'am, he's right, you have to take care of yourself. It's no joke, your health is not to be taken lightly," said the doctor.

"Plus you're already at high risk, being a diabetic and all," the nurse said.

She had a 102 degree fever, so she wasn't leaving the hospital any time soon. The nurse put fluids into her IV and left Honcho, Alexus, and Ms. Gladys alone. She was very stubborn. There was no talking to her. After about thirty minutes, she'd finally calmed down and dozed off.

It had been on Honcho's mind all day about running into T-Money. He had to call him, but had no idea how he would explain being with Alexus.

Alexus spoke and said what was riding both of their minds. "So baby, are you gonna tell T-Money what it is between us?"

"Shit, he ain't blind, he already saw us." *He hasn't called me yet*, Honcho thought, pulling out his phone, only to see he had a text. "I hope your grandma straight, blood. HMU and lemme know when you get a chance."

Once Honcho read the message, he got up to leave. He needed to step out of the room to make this call just in case T questioned him. "Stay right here with her. I'll be right back. Matter of fact, what you want to eat?" he asked.

Alexus shrugged. "It don't matter, bae."

He grabbed his car keys and headed towards the elevators. He scrolled down to T-Money's name and dialed him up.

"Yooo," T picked up. "Whats good, brah? Everything good with your grandma?" T asked.

"Yeah for the most part. She had a heart attack and shit, man. A nigga found her passed out," Honcho replied.

"She gonna be a'ight though, right?'

"She should be. Hell, she woke up talking shit." Honcho laughed.

"Shid, that's Ms. Gladys all day every day. But shid, lemme ask you something. What was with you and Alexus today?"

The phone grew silent. Honcho felt fucked up about it but the little bit of real nigga in him wouldn't allow him to lie about tit. "Yeah, that was her."

"I ain't trippin' though, lil dawg. Just let shawty know she can get the divorce."

Honcho halted. "Divorce?"

"Yeah, divorce," T-Money stated.

Honcho was in disbelief. *Man, this bitch wild as fuck, man.* He couldn't even form his mouth to say what he really wanted to say. "Um, a'ight," he said before hanging up.

Honcho had lost his train of thought, forgetting he was even going to get food. He'd lost his appetite. He could choke Alexus's ass, but the timing was all fucked up. He decided he was gonna act like him and T-Money never had the conversation. But he most definitely was gonna put T up on game. Just the thought of knowing he'd back doored his homie with a shiesty bitch pissed him off.

After T hung up with Honcho, he got a phone call from a private number. "Yooo," he answered.

"So it's like that, T?" Alexus screamed into the phone. "You see me and don't even acknowledge me, Tevin!" She had been waiting all day to call him. She thought she was ready to let him go until she saw him with Mercedez, looking like a happy couple.

Tevin hung the phone up as soon as he heard Alexus's voice. He already knew the minute he gave her any conversation, she would continue to call. He couldn't risk Mercedez going ghost on him again, especially when he wasn't doing shit. He was sure Honcho would relay the message. T had nothing to say to her at all.

Honcho couldn't wait until everything was over with his grandma so he could handle the bullshit he put himself in fucking around with Alexus' lil creep ass. It was only a matter of time before he confronted Alexus about being married to T. The shit had him wondering what Alexus' real intentions were and why she wanted to fuck with him. Now knowing they were married made everything about her suspect. He didn't trust her and would be walking light around her from here on out.

"I knew I shouldn't have fallen for her bullshit, brah," he said out loud. At this point, he wanted her away from his grandma.

CHAPTER THIRTY-TWO

Weeks had passed, and Ms. Hogan was still at Mercedez's. She planned on staying until the babies were born. Cedez had been placed on bed rest and had already dilated 2 cm. The twins were expected to come a little early, which was normal when carrying two babies.

T-Money and Ms. Hogan were reunited and it was like they never missed a beat. Truck was even back around too. Life was really good for everyone.

T-Money's product was booming throughout the prison. Hot-Rod was still keeping quiet about his suspicion with his big brother's murder. He wanted to be 100% sure and he wanted to know Mercedez's involvement.

T-Money had finally linked up with Honcho and got the full rundown on how Alexus and him linked up. T instructed Honcho to go ahead with whatever Alexus was on. He wanted to see what her M.O. was. Although Honcho agreed, he had low-key fallen for Alexus.

He was stuck between love and loyalty. Alexus had shown him so much over the past few months, and yet he still hadn't asked her about being married to T-Money. Honcho was playing both sides.. He had T thinking he was keeping him in the loop when really he wasn't telling him half the shit he and Alexus really had going on. What he and Alexus had was far more than real. It was Treal Love.

Quay and Officer Standley had a thing going on, on the side. She was doing far more than just taking all the packs to the prison for him. She was throwing pussy at him every time he and Quan made a run.

Mercedez and Ms. Hogan were in Target shopping for the twins, although Cedez was supposed to be on bed rest. She couldn't just lay around all day. "Gurl, movin' 'round is what's gonna make them babies come. Doctors don't know nothing," Ms. Hogan said with Cedez waddling behind her, looking as if she would tip over at any minute.

Holding the small of her back, she stopped in the middle of the aisle. "Ma, I think I'm peeing on myself," she whispered.

Ms. Hogan turned around with amusement written all over her face. "Your water broke, Chantal." There were things Cedez still hadn't told her yet, like her real name.

Tears were streaming down Cedez's face. "Call Tevin!" she yelled.

Ms. Hogan dropped everything she'd picked up and called her son. "Oh, her water just broke and we're headed outta Target now, baby. Meet us at the hospital." She was thinking fast, trying to hurry and get Cedez out the door.

Mercedez sat in the passenger seat, calling everyone, letting them know the twins were on the way. Tonya and Janicka were already headed to the hospital while Ms. Karen jumped on the road. There was no way she was missing it.

T met them in the front by the E.R. T-Money ran with a wheelchair. Cedez could barely make it out of the door of the car. Her contractions were taking her breath away. T was panicking as he helped her out of the car.

"Aye, aye, my gurl in labor!" He waved his hands, getting the nurse's attention.

They dropped what they were doing and got Cedez to the labor and delivery floor quickly.

"Breathe, baby! Breathe!" T-Money instructed her as she squeezed her eyes shut.

Her screams were ear piercing, so everyone knew when a contraction hit and just how long it lasted. After transferring her from the wheelchair to the bed and getting her comfortable, the nurse checked to see how far she'd dilated.

"Okay, ma'am, you're more than halfway there. We have you at 6 cm, but doc's gonna want you at a 10, okay? But would you like the epidural? If so, we're gonna get you all set up." The nurse was so calm.

"Yes, please, that'll be great," T spoke up. *My Pooh takes that pain like a champ, but fuck all that.*

Janicka, Tonya, and Ms. Hogan were in the hard-ass ugly green guest seats, waiting for the babies to be born. T had pulled up a chair next to the bed, comforting his life line every time a contraction hit. He wasn't leaving her side until he saw his babies' little faces.

Hours passed, then Ms. Karen came running in just in time. "Is she okay?" she rushed out in one breath. Ms. Karen dropped her purse and ran over to Tevin as the doctors were setting everything up. They were suited up, getting ready for Cedez to push. "She's at 9 cm, it's time."

"My grandbabies weren't coming without me being here." She laughed as her eyes began to water.

With Janicka and Tonya surrounding her, the whole room was packed. Cedez felt so special. T-Money had one leg and Ms. Karen the other, both comforting her. The doctor was giving her instructions on how to push.

"On the count of three, let me get one really big push, okay? Remember, you're made to have babies. Your body is opened up 10 cm. Now 1, 2, 3, push, Mommy. I need you to take deep breaths."

Sweat rolled down Cedez's face into her eyes. Her ears, nose, and cheeks were red. Her knuckles were white. "Okay, okay." She breathed deep, shaky breaths. Cedez pushed as hard as she could. "Oh my God, I can't!" she screamed.

The scene in front of Tevin pulled on his heart strings. He would always have a certain extra respect for women from that day forward. His eyes began to burn with tears and his mouth became dry. He swallowed and his throat closed and knotted up with tears upon seeing his woman go through that kind of pain.

"Again, Mom, 1, 2, 3 push!"

Everyone one was yelling and encouraged her to push a little harder.

"That's my baby!" Janicka yelled out as T-Money cut the cord. T-Money turned to her with a shit-eating grin. "Boy, I wasn't talking to your ugly ass, nigga, mushy ass, I see them tears. Boy, please, you ain't do nothing." Everyone burst out laughing when T looked around to see if anybody heard her.

"Whatever, girl, shid, I thought you were talking to me for cutting the cord.

Everybody burst out laughing again. "Man!" they all said. The nurse took baby number one and cleaned him off as he screamed at the top of his lungs.

Mercedez was exhausted but she still had one more. Baby number two was only minutes away.

"Okay, on the count of three. We're not done. 1, 2, 3, push, push, push. Okay, babies all out," he tried to joke.

Nobody found it funny. Baby boy, young king, London Tevin Carter, and baby girl, young queen, Paris Taylor Carter, made their grand entrance into the world. Their birthday was February 1, 2021 at 6:15 p.m. London weighed in at 5 pounds, 3 ounces and Paris right at 5 pounds. They were seven minutes apart.

Honcho was on his way to the hospital to meet London and Paris when he got an unexpected call from his grandma's doctor. "Sir, you need to get back here ASAP."

He started doing the dash to get there. His heart was racing and he began to sweat. He turned his A/C up a little higher.

Making it to the third floor, Honcho ran into T-Money. Ms. Gladys had been there about a month now

"What's going on, man?"

Honcho was already spazzing. Seeing the look in T-Money's eyes, he knew it was bad news. T-Money had stopped on the third floor already and got the news.

The doctor met Honcho in the hallway. "Sir, we did everything we could."

Honcho broke down before the doctor could even finish speaking. "Nooo! Nooo!" He banged his head against the wall as T-Money stayed by his side, comforting him.

Damn, just gonna put a hole in the people's wall, the fuck? T-Money thought, looking around at who all noticed it. "Bruh, we gonna get through this, I promise you."

The best day of T-Money's life turned out to be the worst day of Honcho's life. Ms. Gladys had taken her last breath on February 1, 2021 at 7:03 p.m. *How ironic is that? That's weird as fuck,* T-

Money thought to himself. Life had a funny way to it that T-Money never understood. He really was not good in situations like this. He didn't know what to do or say. He was a little uncomfortable even witnessing his mans so weak like that.

Honcho's heart was broken. Ms. Gladys's death was very unexpected. He was thinking she would've been home in another week or so. She had improved a lot over the last week. Nobody held his heart. Ms. Gladys was the main reason he got up every day and went hard in them streets. She was his purpose in life. His whole world had crumbled within a matter of minutes. His cries came from somewhere deep within his soul.

T just remained quiet. You would've thought this would be a wakeup call for Honcho, losing the main person who lived for him.

Honcho took a few minutes to get it out of his system. He took deep breaths, trying to fill his lungs up with some air. He wasn't breathing; just crying. Shit was sad as fuck.

Le'Monica Jackson

CHAPTER THIRTY-THREE
JULY OF 2021
(5 MONTHS LATER)

It had been 5 months since Honcho laid Ms. Gladys to rest. On February 1, 2021, she took her last breath. Ms. Gladys was all Honcho had and since she'd been gone, he was wilding the fuck out.

With the help of his main man, T-Money, Ms. Gladys' home going celebration was beautiful. T-Money had been very supportive through the whole ordeal. Although T-Money was still skeptical about his wife Alexus and Honcho kickin' it, it didn't affect him having Honcho's back as he went through the most tragic situation of his life.

Watching Alexus sit front row at the funeral with Honcho was the most disturbing shit T-Money had ever encountered, but shit, what could he say when the bitch his heart belonged to, Mercedez, was glued to his hip, not to mention she'd just given birth to his baby boy and baby girl on the same day Honcho had lost Ms. Gladys.

Baby girl London and baby boy Paris were now five months old. T-Money and Mercedez were loving life as parents. The twins were moving so fast and were really giving Mercedez a run for her money.

With T-Money head first in the streets, his mom Ms. Hogan had really stepped up and was helping Mercedez out a lot with the twins as she focused on getting her shit in order. Mercedez threw her flag in and she gave the street life up for good.

"Heyyyy, Mama girl...Londonnn...I wuv you, ma-ma!" Mercedez held her right underneath her arms, standing her up as she bounced up and down, pushing up on her legs. London was such a happy baby while Paris spent a lot of time sleeping. Mercedez never got a break when it came to London, so Ms. Hogan's help was very much needed.

Carrying London on her chest, Mercedez went into the twins' bedroom to find Ms. Hogan in the rocking chair asleep with baby Paris fast asleep in her arms.

"That's beautiful," Mercedez whispered as she stood in the doorway, falling in love with the scene before her.

Ms. Hogan had temporarily moved into Mercedez's two bedroom loft with her while she was building relations with her long lost foster child T-Money. She was also bonding with her new grandchildren.

"Baby, put something on, I need you to ride somewhere with me." Mercedez opened her phone, reading a message from T-Money. Not wanting to interrupt Paris and his grandma from napping, Mercedez cleaned up and packed her diaper bag to take London along with them.

"Uhhh, he would want me to ride somewhere with him. While I'm all comfortable," Mercedez said to herself. She slipped on a pair of jeans and a comfortable Tommy Hilfiger shirt and shoes to match. Mercedez ripped a sheet of paper from her notebook and posted it on the fridge. It read: *Hey Ma, you and Paris were sleeping so well I didn't want to disturb you. If you guys wake up by the time we get back, just letting you know me and London stepped out with Tevin. We'll be back soon. Love you!* Mercedez and Ms. Hogan had a bond that every baby mama would love to have with their baby daddy's momma. But y'all know nowadays a bitch is about ready to fight their baby daddy momma.

Yeah, I know some of y'all reading this part like "Yessss, sis!" Okay, back to the story though…

"Outside." T-Money texted Mercedez grabbed London's car seat and diaper bag, locked the house up, and made her way to the parking garage where T-Money was parked in his Range Rover with it still running. He hopped out of the truck, opening the door to the back seat as he grabbed London's car seat to strap her in. London's face lit up as usual upon hearing her dad's voice.

T-Money got back in the driver's seat and started looking over at Mercedez. "Let me guess: Paris fat ass sleep, ain't he?"

Mercedez laughed "You know he is. Yo' mama was sleeping too, holdin' him in her arms."

T-Money shook his head. "You gon' let her spoil the hell outta him."

Mercedez replied, "You know Paris is her baby. Now where are we goin'?"

Tevin turned the music up, ignoring Mercedez's question. Mercedez knew that meant just ride and don't kill the vibe. Kevin Gates' "Fatal Attraction" was playing throughout the car. Normally T-Money would have it so loud the windows would be shaking, but for the sake of London, it was loud enough just to tune Mercedez out.

Mercedez rolled her eyes as she leaned against the passenger door, waiting to reach their destination. The ride seemed to last forever. London had fallen asleep and Mercedez was damn near dozing off herself. As soon as Mercedez had drifted off to sleep, she felt the truck turn off. She assumed T-Money was just handling something and wanted her to ride and now they were back home, but surprisingly, she opened her eyes to a big house with security gates around it.

"Turn the car back on, baby, me and London gon' sit out here and wait for you," Mercedez said, stretching as she made herself comfortable.

"No, you and London get out. I need my two girls with me for this one," he responded.

Mercedez sucked her teeth, getting out of the car and unbuckled London from her car seat. *What the hell could he possibly need me and a five-month-old baby for?* She went with the flow, carrying London in her arms as she followed T-Money. He punched in a code and the double doors opened. Pushing the doors all the way open, he grabbed Mercedez's free hand and led her in. "This is all yours, baby!" T-Money said.

"Ohhhh my gosh, Tevin!" Mercedez yelled, causing London to wake up, lifting her head up.

"You scared my baby," T-Money said as he reached for London so Mercedez could do what she really wanted to do. She jumped up and down in disbelief

"I love it, baby! I love it!" Mercedez repeated over and over. T-Money had previously told her way before the twins were even born that he was going to buy a house for her and the babies, but

Mercedez was expecting it to be a house he already owned that he would maybe just add hers and the twins' name onto it.

T-Money had really gone all out. The house had ten bedrooms and five full bathrooms. There were five floors in the house, spiral stairs and an exclusive playground in the backyard. Mercedez was in love. She was used to living lavishly, but her new mansion was beyond what she'd imagined

"We only have two kids. What's the ten bedrooms for?" Mercedez asked as she took a tour around the house.

Slapping Mercedez's ass, T-Money responded, "You never know. We might have more."

"Boy, please, Paris and London are already something else," Mercedez said.

She was impressed and ready to decorate the new home. She could already picture London and Paris running around the house. There was more than enough space for them.

"Ma can have one of the rooms," Mercedez said, insisting on Ms. Hogan moving to the mansion with them.

T-Money responded, "Naw I already paid the rent up at your loft for the rest of the year. We already talked, and she agreed on staying there."

Ms. Hogan had come to Georgia with no intentions on staying but for the sake of London and Paris she just couldn't leave. She got too attached and ended up staying.

Mercedez couldn't wait to get back to Ms. Hogan and Paris. She was missing her baby and she was also ready to tell Ms. Hogan about her new home. Mercedez had taken plenty of pictures to send to her sisters Tonya and Janicka and she couldn't wait to share them with her mama. She definitely was going to need all their help to decorate that big-ass house, and that was right up her mom's Ms. Karen alley.

T-Money handed Mercedez over a set of keys and a piece of paper with the twins' birthday month and the date 0201 written down on it, which was the code to the keypad.

Cedez checked her phone, noticing she had a text message from Ms. Hogan along with a photo attached. The message read "Hey sweetie me and Paris just woke up not too long ago I got the note you left on the fridge. We'll see you when you get here love you." She threw in a picture of Paris laying down with his mouth wide open trying to smile. The twins had deep-ass dimples and a smile to die for, just like their daddies. They had smooth tan skin just like Mercedez and heads full of jet black curls with slanted chinky eyes just like Mercedez too. You could hardly tell them apart. The only difference between the twins was that Paris had a birthmark on his left cheek and London didn't.

"My son is so handsome," Mercedez said as she looked at the picture.

Mercedez and T-Money made their way to the car. Cedez hopped in the passenger seat, admiring her new home as T-Money strapped London back in and pulled out of the long red brick driveway. T-Money was glad to finally be moving his baby mama out of the loft she'd moved in just months before. Everything was going great for them, however, T-Money still had some things he needed to put an end too as far as Alexus before Mercedez would fully allow him back into her life the way they used to be before she'd found out about him being married to Alexus.

Pulling back up to Mercedez's loft, she got out of the car, grabbing London's car seat and diaper bag. She couldn't move fast enough; she was so ready to see Paris.

"I'll be back a little later, baby. I got to hit the lab. Lemme get a kiss," T-Money said as he rolled his window down.

Mercedez stuck her head in the car and T-Money kissed her passionately.

"Daddy gon' see you later, ma-ma." He reached down in London's car seat, gently rubbing her chubby cheeks. He sat there until Mercedez and London disappeared before he pulled off.

Le'Monica Jackson

CHAPTER THIRTY-FOUR

It had been two weeks since the last time Honcho had been in T-Money's presence, but it was mandatory that he meet him at the lab. Honcho was getting low on product and he also had to give T-Money his cut from what he'd made off of the new shit T-Money was throwing on him. Even though T-Money handled the situation with Honcho fucking with Alexus like a G, Honcho still avoided going around T-Money as much as possible because the vibe just didn't feel right, but that was clearly his guilty conscience.

Pulling up to the lab, Honcho pulled up right behind T-Money.

"Perfect timing," T-Money said to himself, looking in his rearview mirror, seeing Honcho's Maxima parked behind him. T-Money tucked his 9mm in his designer jeans, making sure it was secured right beneath his Gucci belt before hopping out of his Range Rover. Meeting Honcho in the driveway of the lab, they dapped each other up before proceeding inside.

As soon as they made it inside, Honcho pulled a MCM bookbag off of his back, emptying it out on the center table. He counted out 40 thousand dollars for T-Money.

"Damn, dat's wassup lil homie. How you been holding up, man? You ain't been yaself since you lost Ms. Gladys," T-Money said as he sat directly across the table from Honcho, looking him straight in his eyes.

Honcho folded his hands together and dropped his head. "Man, that shit fucked a nigga head up," he said.

"I know, man. We gonna get through it together. I know Ms. Gladys was everything to you," T-Money said.

Honcho felt like shit knowing T-Money genuinely cared about him and here he was plotting to take his place in the streets as well. It's like at first he wasn't with the shit Alexus was trying to do, but ever since Ms. Gladys had passed away, Honcho didn't give a damn about anything. He just shook his head, fidgeting with his fingers. He didn't even know what to say. There was nothing no one could say to take away the pain he was feeling. There was an awkward silence in the room when T-Money got up and made his way to the kitchen. He had to cook up more dope. There was something about T-Money's wrist game that made his shit lock up like no one else could make it do.

Honcho was stuck for a second. Shaking out of his thoughts, he left his phone and book bag at the table and met T-Money in the kitchen. He learned something new every time he watched T-Money cook. T-Money dipped his fork in a little bit of dish detergent and beat the bowl, repeatedly until his shit locked up like he wanted it. Honcho sat back and just watched, making a mental note to dip his fork in dish detergent next time he cooked his own shit.

Taking the bowl off the stove, T-Money set it to the side. "I'll be right back, brah. Let me grab this other shit I want you to check out." He walked back to the room, where Honcho counted out the money.

Lifting up a piece of the tile floor where he stashed at, T-Money grabbed a small key from his pocket, unlocked his safe, and pulled out a big Ziploc bag of heroin that he'd been sitting on for a while. He was ready to throw it on Honcho before he put it on Blaze, Quan, and Quay. He had planned on waiting until his brother Truck was released to just front it to him, but he needed to see how it sold first and then he was just going to cop some more for Truck if Honcho moved it quickly.

Locking his safe back up and placing the piece of tile back in place, He realized the phone Honcho left on the table next to his MCM bookbag was lighting up. He reached for the phone to take it to Honcho when he looked down and noticed it was a text message from Alexus. As bad as he wanted to mind his business, he couldn't help but open the message.

"Baby call me when you leave from the lab, I have the code to his main safe out here in Hawaii all that shit gon' be yours when we get done with his ass. Be safe daddy, I love you."

T-Money couldn't believe what he'd just read. He never thought Alexus would cross him like that. Deleting the message, T-Money set the phone right back down. *Good thing I changed all my codes before I even left the dumb bitch in Hawaii*, T-Money thought to himself. "Okay, this nigga playing under me with the hoe," he said to himself.

He walked back into the kitchen and presented the heroin to Honcho as the bowl sat to the side cooling down. His mind told him to just go ahead and draw down on Honcho and light his ass up right there in the lab, but one thing T-Money didn't do was move sloppy. He played right along because in the end, he was going to have the last laugh.

"So this all yours, lil homie. Hit me up when you get off of it," T-Money said, placing the bag of heroin in Honcho's hands.

Honcho's face instantly lit up. "Damn, brah, this is love! I got'chu. You know I'm gonna flood the streets," he said. Looking around for his book bag, he realized he'd left it in the meeting room. He quickly grabbed his phone, stuffed it in his pocket, and put the bag of heroin in his book bag. Struggling to zip it up, all he could think about was how much money they would profit off of it. "Okay brah, I'll hit you up!" he said, throwing his book bag over his shoulders.

T-Money responded, "Say less, lil homie," and dapped him up before leaving the lab.

Lately Quan and Quay were getting closer to T-Money and with the creep shit Honcho was on, he wouldn't be around that long anyway. T-money was big on loyalty and Honcho was proving to be snake as fuck.

Quay had maneuvered his way in with Officer Standley at the prison, which was exactly what T-Money needed. Every trip Quay and Quan made to supply Truck and Hot-Rod at the prison, Officer Standley made sure she made time for Quay to dick her down as well. Their relationship was beyond business at this point. Although she was still giving Hot-Rod pussy on the clock, she and Quay were linking up on the outside, going on dates and really getting to know each other. Besides, Quay had way more to offer and Officer Standley was clearly money hungry. To Hot-Rod she would always be Officer Standley, but to Quay she was Aaliyah. Hot-Rod thought he had her exactly where he wanted her. Meanwhile, Quay was nutting in her and some days, she had Hot-Rod sucking Quay's cum right out of her. She got a thrill out of having shit her way.

Hot-Rod had grown to trust her so much he had her looking into the murder of his brother. He confided in her, telling her that Quay and Quan were workin for the nigga T-Money, who might have something to do with Snoop's murder. Aaliyah Standley was all for Quay and she was getting as much information out of Hot-Rod as she could.

Quay had just dropped a pack off at the prison when he received a phone call from Aaliyah. "Yo, wassup, shawty?" he answered. "Damn, you looked so good, daddy, meet me at the at the 7/11. I want some dick and I also got some info for you that you may want to hear. I'm going on my lunch break in 5 minutes meet me there or beat me there," she replied.

Quay busted a U-turn right in the middle of the street, heading in the direction of the 7/11 gas station.

"Okay baby you got it," he said before hanging up.

Backing into the parking lot in the truck that T-Money rented him, he watched for Aaliyah to pull up. His truck was mobbed up and had more than enough room for him to get her just how he wanted her: ass up/face down.

Aaliyah came pulling in, in her 2013 Honda Accord. Flashing his lights, Quay got Aaliyah's attention. He was in a different ride each time they met up, so she never knew what he was riding in. She backed in next to his Audi and jumped in his passenger seat. Quay was laid back in his seat, waiting for Aaliyah to unzip his pants and give him some sloppy head like she always did.

She looked him in his eyes before making a move and said, "Baby, before we get started, I want to tell you the tea I got first."

Quay was laid back in his seat and leaned on the arm rest. "Okay, wassup, ma? Talk to me."

Aaliyah reached in her purse and pulled out the picture of T-Money, Mercedez, and Nay-Nay at the baby shower. She had stolen Hot-Rod's picture, made a copy, and got it back to his cell before he even noticed it was gone. "Well, Hot-Rod says this nigga in this picture name is T-Money and the pregnant chick is his baby mama

Mercedez," Aaliyah said, pointing at T-Money and Mercedez in the picture.

"Yeah, uh huh, and...?" Quay responded, wishing that she'd hurry up and get the shit out. Aaliyah rolled her eyes and finished

"Well, apparently T-Money is who you're working for and Hot-Rod says T-Money and Mercedez have something to do with his brother Snoop getting killed."

Quay studied Aaliyah's face for a second and responded, "Naw, man, Snoop and T-Money were cool, brah trippin'!" Quay had no idea that T-Money had killed Snoop. The streets weren't saying shit about nobody being a suspect and especially not T-Money and Mercedez. "Let me see that picture," Quay said, grabbing the baby shower picture from Aaliyah. "And how did you get this shit anyways?" he asked suspiciously.

Aaliyah sucked her teeth. "Someone sent it to Hot-Rod. I'm not sure who though."

Quay had a serious look on his face. He wasn't even in the mood to fuck no more. "Aye, check this out, if I find out you got any creep shit going on dat's yo' ass," he said between clenched teeth, squeezing Aaliyah's jaw line

She shook her head, frightened at the terrifying look in his eyes.

Quay stuffed the picture in the sun visor above his windshield. "Let me handle this. I'll get up with you later," he said.

"So we not gon' have sex?" she questioned.

"I said I'll get with you later!"

Aaliyah knew he meant business. She quickly opened the passenger door, hopped out of his truck, jumping back in her car, she sped off.

Aaliyah was the one who initially brought it to Hot-Rod's attention about Mercedez being linked to his brother's murder, not knowing Mercedez was T-Money's people. *Damn, what I done got myself into?* she thought.

Quay shot T-Money a text. "Link up ASAP big homie I gotta holla at you."

T-Money was on the phone with his brother Truck when the message came through. "Yeah, brah, I ain't think I'd see the day coming so soon that I'll be out this bitch next week. Hot-Rod holding shit down though, so everything still gon' be a go," Truck said.

"Yeah, I'm glad it's over for you, brah. When you get out, you just got to move low-key. You know I'm gon' make sure you good when you come home," T-Money replied. "But shit I'ma chop it up wit' you later, brah. Quay just texted me." He dialed Quay's number, impatiently waiting for him to answer. He handed Paris to Mercedez. "Bae, get him real quick," he whispered, motioning for Mercedez to grab the baby.

Mercedez rolled her eyes, putting London in her basinet, and grabbed Paris.

T-Money stepped out on the balcony of Mercedez's loft to talk to Quay. "So what's up, Quay, everything good? The pack made it through?" The first thing T-Money suspected was the pack didn't make it to Hot-Rod and he had to take a loss.

"Yea everything 10-4 with dat homie, but shit, da bitch Aaliyah ran some shit by me about Hot-Rod, I don't want to talk on the phone though so when you free, hit me up so we can link up," Quay said.

"Hmmm, a'ight, I'll call ya in 'bout three hours. I'm handling something with my family right now." T-Money loved the fact he was able to finally claim a real family. He had a strong feeling whatever it was Quay had to tell him was something that was going to cause him to snap.

T-Money ended the call and stepped back inside. As bad as he wanted to just link up with Quay, he knew Mercedez was going to be jumping down his throat because she and Ms. Hogan were trying to pack up everything and watch the twins at the same time. "Aye Ma, you know Truck getting out next week," he said to Ms. Hogan as she sat on the floor in Mercedez's bedroom, packing all of her shoes and clothes to move to their new home,

"I know. He called me a couple days ago. I told him I want him to come stay here with me when he first gets out. It's such a blessing to be reunited with y'all, Tevin." Ms. Hogan smiled, thinking back to when they were young boys. She couldn't have children, so Tevin and Truck were all she knew. Blood couldn't have made her love them anymore than she already did.

Mercedez lay across the bed breastfeeding Paris, waiting to be alone with T-Money so she could ask what the phone call between him and Quay was about. T-Money avoided telling Mercedez anything that had to do with the fast life, trying to respect her change and the fact that she didn't want anything to do with it, but for some reason, she always made it her business to still stay up on what he had going on.

Ms. Hogan sealed a box full of Mercedez's high heels and pushed it out by the front door for the movers T-Money had hired to move everything. As soon as Ms. Hogan was out of sight, Mercedez began. She cleared her throat.

"Sooo, what Quay wanted?" she asked. "Ya vibe seemed a lil off when you stepped back in the house."

"Oh, nothing, he was just telling me about how fast he was moving the new shit I supplied him with," T-Money lied.

Cedez knew him so well she knew he was lying, but decided not to say anything "Mmm, okay," she replied, sucking her teeth.

T-Money knew the question would come up again later on, but at that moment, he remained quiet. The only thing on his mind was getting to Quay to find out what the fuck was going on.

T-Money left the room, leaving Cedez wondering. He spent time with London and Paris before meeting up with Quay. As bad as he wanted to put more time in with his kids, he still had to balance out being a father and tending to the business he had going on in the streets. After kissing London and Paris, T-Money grabbed his keys to head out.

Le'Monica Jackson

CHAPTER THIRTY-FIVE

The day had finally come. T-Money and Ms. Hogan were on the road, heading to pick up Truck. His prison sentence was finally over. Ms. Hogan's heart was beating out of her chest. She was nervous as hell. She had custody of Truck a little longer than she had Tevin. Truck was truly Ms. Hogan's weakness. She loved the ground that boy walked on.

Mercedez was at her new home, preparing a nice meal for when Truck arrived. T-Money had invited the whole team over to help welcome his little brother home: Quay, Quan, Honcho and Blaze were getting ready to head over to T-Money's and Mercedez's home. Of course Quay was bringing Aaliyah along. He'd already given T-Money the rundown about what Aaliyah told him, so T-Money informed Quay to keep Aaliyah around. She could be very useful. Truck had no idea that Officer Standley had any relation with Quay, but he damn sure was going to find out.

"Oh my gosh!" Ms. Hogan halted, cupping her hands over her mouth as tears ran down her cheeks.

Truck had really grown into a man over the years. He walked out of the prison gates with a nice fresh haircut. He was short and stocky. It was obvious he spent a lot of time working out in the pen. T-Money remained in the car, giving Ms. Hogan a moment with Truck. Standing in front of the Rover, Ms. Hogan stretched her arms out, embracing Truck for the first time in years.

"Mama! You lookin' good, girl," he said as he wrapped his arms around her. He released her by one hand, spinning her around as she did a little twirl. The last time he saw her, he wasn't even big enough to wrap his arms around her.

T-Money stepped out of the truck and stood to the side, admiring the view in front of him, rubbing his hands together. He was excited to see Truck. They embraced each other with a clap of the hand followed by a hug. T-Money stepped back with his chest out and he looked Truck directly in his eyes. All was silent for a few seconds.

Truck broke the silence. "Thanks, brah, a nigga happy to see y'all for real."

"Let's get up off this prison ground. Come on, y'all," Ms. Hogan interrupted as she hopped in the back seat, allowing Truck to ride shotgun.

Truck climbed in looking around as if he'd never seen nothing so flawless before. "Damn, bra, dis bih nice," he said, rubbing the tips of his fingers across the peanut butter seats.

Ms. Hogan slapped Truck across the back of his head. "Watch ya mouth, boy!" She laughed, but had a seriousness to her tone

"Oh, my bad, Ma." He threw his hands up in defense.

T-Money laughed. "Thanks, man, you'll be sliding in something nice real soon."

Truck had already stacked a couple thousand from moving drugs in prison, so he was ready to jump head first in the game with T-Money. He had to get his feet back wet ASAP.

T-Money couldn't wait to get Truck to his welcome home gathering. It was nice bringing Ms. Hogan along, but he was ready to fire up his first blunt of that zah in the free world. Truck let his window down, enjoying the fresh air, appreciating his freedom.

"Damn, bro, a nigga blessed to be back out here," he said under his breath.

"So you know not to take freedom for granted now baby," Ms. Hogan replied. She never led him wrong.

There was an awkward silence until T-Money turned the music on. Ms. Hogan was going to have to deal with it T-Money wasn't gonna let the ride home be boring because their mom was Christian. "Aye Ma, you might wanna plug ya ears," T-Money insisted as Kodak Black "Last Day In" began quaking thru the speakers.

Ms. Hogan sucked her teeth waving T-Money off "Y'all do y'all thang."

Truck bopped to the music, feeling every word. T-Money glanced in the rearview mirror, laughing to himself as Ms. Hogan sat in the back seat shaking her head. Truck's anxiety was through the roof. He never imagined coming home to the only people he'd ever claimed as family.

T-Money stopped at a gas station five minutes away from their home. Pulling in the parking lot he reached in his pocket and pulled out a knot of cash. "Aye, come on, brah, come grab what you want. You ain't been in a gas station in a few years. I know you ain't gon' stay in the car," T-Money said. He turned around to the back seat. "Ma, what you want outta here?" he asked Ms. Hogan before getting out.

"Bring me out some, uh…boiled peanuts and a Pepsi," she replied.

They hopped out the car and made their way inside the store. Looking around Truck appeared to be amused. Everything felt so weird to him. T-Money laughed. "Yo ass stuck."

"Hell yeah," Truck replied, pinching the bridge of his nose.

T-Money went straight to the counter, approaching the clerk. "Let me get five packs of them Backwoods, please," he said, pointing behind the counter on the back wall where the smoking section was. He called out to Truck, who stood in the middle of the store looking around. "Aye, snap out of it. You home now, man. Get me a large cup of peanuts and her Pepsi and you grab what you want," T-Money said.

The store clerk smiled, looking in Truck's direction. "You good, sir?" the girl asked Truck.

"Yeah, yeah, I'm good. I just came home from prison. Just trying to adapt to shit, man." He rubbed his hands across the waves in his hair and licked his bottom lip.

He made his way to the boiled peanuts and began making Ms. Hogan a cup while T-Money stood at the counter making small conversation with the store clerk, whose name tag read "Tammy". She was about 5 feet tall with long pretty hair and gold teeth on her fangs. She had smooth pretty chocolate skin and she was nicely groomed in her work uniform.

"Yeah, my brotha just got out. He gotta get used to being in the presence of a beautiful woman and shit again, feel me?" He reached down his pocket and pulled out a hundred dollar bill. "Here, for the Backwoods and whatever else he bring up here to the counter." T-Money set the bill down and made his way out the door. "Truck, I already paid for everything. Grab what you want. I'll be in the car waiting," he announced before exiting.

Truck grabbed a can of Sprite and Pepsi, a pack of Air Heads, and the boiled peanuts and made his way to the counter.

"Welcome home, handsome." Tammy batted her lashes as she rung up Truck's items. They locked eyes immediately.

"Thank you lil baby," he responded, licking his lips as he admired the beautiful black queen before him.

Their energy instantly clicked. Tammy wrote her number down on Truck's receipt and slid it across the counter to him as she bagged his items. "Call me sometime."

Truck glanced at the receipt and put it in his pocket. "Most definitely, baby girl," he responded and made his exit. Getting back in the car, he handed Ms. Hogan her boiled peanuts, popped his Sprite can open and turned the music on.

"Aye, you ever heard this before, T?" Truck went on YouTube on T-Money's phone and typed in an upcoming rapper out of Orlando, Florida by the name of "2Cap". T-money knew whatever song was about to play, Ms. Hogan was definitely about to trip. The song began playing as Ms. Hogan waved her hands in the air.

"Hey, hey, hey, that's enough. Come on, Truck, that's too much!" she shouted.

T-Money paused the song. "Yeah, brah, I heard of da nigga. He just had an interview on I.G. with the producer Zaytoven," T-Money responded.

The rest of the ride they decided to jam Yung Bleu's new album.

Pulling up at Mercedez's mini mansion, nothing but nice-ass foreign cars were parked in the front yard.

Truck sat up in his seat, amazed at how nice the home was. "Dang, bro, dis you?" he asked.

"This the house I just brought my baby mama. I got a couple other spots," T-Money responded, bragging without even trying.

Truck couldn't believe how good his brother was living, considering where they'd come from. T-Money was ready to put his brother on so he could live good as well. When they entered the house, everybody was posted in the back in the lounge with several blunts in rotation. The twins were in their second room downstairs sleeping while Mercedez was in the kitchen, fixing up the food and mixing different alcoholic beverages. Truck was definitely going to be fucked up for his first day out. He followed T-Money through the mini mansion, looking around like a kid in a candy store.

"Damnnn, brah," he said to himself, stopping in the kitchen

T-Money softly rubbed Mercedez's ass. She turned around to acknowledge him and Truck.

"Hey baby," she said, greeting her man and placing a kiss directly on his lips. She stepped back, extending her hand to Truck. "And you must be Truck? I've heard a lot about you, welcome home."

Truck pulled her in and gave her a hug. "Thank you, yeah, I'm Truck. I heard a lot 'bout you too. You sis now. Ain't no handshakes. We family. It's all love."

Mercedez handed T-Money and Truck plastic red cups with Remy Martin on the rocks. "No chaser! Y'all enjoy ya selves," she said.

They grabbed their cups and made their way to the twins' room, where Ms. Hogan was standing over them as they slept peacefully. T-Money motioned for Truck to come closer to the crib. He whispered, "Dis ya niece London and ya nephew Paris."

Truck's face lit up. "Wow, I'm an uncle too! They're so cute, brah. God been really blessing you." Truck reached in the crib and gently rubbed the twins' backs.

"Okay, y'all go enjoy yourselves. I'll be in here with my babies." Ms. Hogan took a seat in the rocking chair as she shooed them away.

"Alright, Ma, we out. Come on, Truck, lemme introduce you to the team," T-Money said.

The music was bumping as they made it closer to the lounge area. The first person Truck spotted was Blaze. "My nigga! What's good, brah?" They dapped each other up.

Blaze passed Truck a fat-ass Backwood. "Man, welcome home, my nigga, hit dat shit!"

Truck pulled long and hard on the blunt. He began coughing uncontrollably. Everyone laughed.

"Take ya time Das dat Zah. It's been a while since you had dat good shit in ya system," T-Money joked as he beat on Truck's back.

T-Money introduced Truck to everyone in the room. "And dis is Quay."

Truck's eyes shot straight to Officer Standley, who was sitting right next to Quay. "What you doin' here Ms. Standley?" Truck was confused as hell seeing her at his coming home gathering with a blunt and cup of liquor in her hand.

"It's Aaliyah when I'm not in working attire." She laughed.

"Good to finally meet you face to face, dawg. Welcome to the team. You gonna eat good, fam. Aaliyah here wit' me, no worries," Quay informed Truck. They dapped each other up.

"Okay, shit, dat's wassup. Good to finally meet all y'all too. Blaze told me everybody like family 'round here. I know we all gone rock out," Truck replied.

Everybody refilled their cups and toasted to a real nigga coming home and a new member joining their team.

Mercedez had finally finished in the kitchen and joined everyone else to celebrate. Truck was getting fucked up quickly. He was already stumbling and carrying on. He was definitely enjoying himself.

Cedez's drink was sneaking up on her as well. She was pushing up on T-Money, grinding on his dick to the music. Aaliyah was busting it open to the beat as Blac Youngsta ft. Money Bagg "You 1, 2, 3" blasted throughout the room, her ass was bouncing on beat. She certainly was not the Officer Standley Truck knew from the prison. She was dancing like that's what she did for a living. The only thing Truck could think about was being the lookout every time she and Hot-Rod fucked.

He pushed the thoughts in the back of his head and his mind drifted off to the store clerk Tammy. It had been a while and it was mandatory after the celebration he ended his night in some wet-ass pussy. Blaze had given Truck an iPhone 8 plus that he'd already activated for him. Truck pulled the phone out, trying to remember how to work it. He pulled the receipt out of his pocket, put Tammy's number in his contacts, and shot her a text.

"Wassup baby girl. This Truck. I met you at the gas station earlier." He put the phone down in his pocket and waited for her response. Being locked up for a few years, he'd forgotten a lot of shit, but he didn't forget how to get him some pussy, that was for sure.

Honcho was vibing out, checking his phone every thirty minutes, making sure Alexus hadn't hit him up.

T-Money was keeping Honcho close for a reason. He'd been a little standoffish the whole time and T-Money made sure to keep a close eye on him .

The celebration turned out really nice. Everyone ate well and really enjoyed themselves.

It was getting late and T-Money had gotten Truck a suite for the night. Tammy agreed on spending the night with Truck and he definitely didn't plan on taking her to the loft he was going to be living at with Ms. Hogan. T-Money threw Truck the keys to his 2016 Kia Optima.

"Call me if you need me, brah."

Truck departed and headed towards the gas station to pick Tammy up. He had sobered up a little bit and was ready to get his rocks off.

Le'Monica Jackson

CHAPTER THIRTY-SIX

Ms. Hogan was enjoying her new home. She was keeping London and Paris through the day while Mercedez spent a lot of time taking online classes to become a realtor and looking for a spot to open up a hair store. Cedez invested a lot of money on hair throughout her life and decided she wanted to join the hair business herself. She was finally finding a legit way out of the game. Between trying to find different hair vendors, staying up on her class assignments, and tending to her babies, she had no time for anything. Mercedez was kind of loving life as a normal woman. Leaving the streets alone, some days she didn't pick the twins up until the sun went down and most days, T-Money was bringing them home.

With everything T-Money had going on in the streets, he was managing to put as much time in with his kids as possible. He hadn't received any calls from Alexus in weeks, which was great because he and Mercedez were back to their normal routine, sleeping together every night at their new home, and the last thing he needed was Alexus trying to interfere with that.

It had been three days since T-Money had last seen Truck. They talked every day, but Truck was still at the hotel with Tammy, obviously enjoying himself. T-Money didn't bother interrupting him either. He had plenty of time to put him on some money. He decided he'd allow Truck to enjoy his first couple of days out.

On another note, T-Money had been spending a lot more time with Quay than usual. Quay had Aaliyah on point and she was willing to do whatever it was Quay instructed her to do as far as Hot-Rod. As badly as T-Money wanted to let Hot-Rod eat, he had no choice but to start putting a play into action to get rid of him. The nigga knew way too much and letting him live would be putting not only T-Money and Mercedez at risk, for Snoop's murder, but his whole team's freedom would be in jeopardy since Hot-Rod knew about their organization. The only problem was how would T-Money be able to touch Hot-Rod behind the prison walls. The last thing he wanted to do was put a hit out on him in the prison because it wasn't shit to make it happen. *Shit, it gotta be anotha way*, he thought.

T-Money called Quay. He had to have a sit-down with him. "Yo Quay, you free?"

"Wassup, man? Yeah, I'm free, what's good wit'cha, Blood?"

"Shit, I'm chillin right now. If you got a minute to meet me at the lab, I need to holla at'cha."

"Okay, say less."

A bright idea came to T-Money's mind and he had to run it by Quay just to be sure. When T-Money pulled up to the spot, he noticed Quay had Officer Standley in the passenger seat. "Da fuck jit got goin' now? He know I'on' even move like dis," T-Money said to himself. Normally he would've snapped because the only chick that ever been to the spot was Cedez, but in this case, Quay was right on point since T-Money's idea required the help of Officer Standley. Quay hopped out of the car, leaving it running.

"I'll be out in a few, baby," he told Aaliyah.

Following T-Money, inside Quay could tell he had something on his mind. T-Money pulled out a chair for Quay after flipping the light switch on. "Sit down, lemme run some shit by you," he instructed, jumping straight to the point. "So Q, how tight you and this chick is?"

"Shit, I'm fucking wit' her, boss, a lil more than I expected." He chuckled, but the serious look on T-Money's face told Quay he meant business. "Why, wassup, T-Money, everything good?"

Clearing his throat, T-Money went on. "Is she still fuckin' wit Hot-Rod? Do you know?"

"I make sure she keep da nigga close just to keep me in the loop about everything he saying as far as you and sis." He paced back and forth.

T-Money was taking in what Quay was telling him. "Aaliyah 'bout her money, right?" T-Money asked, already knowing the answer before even asked. Shit, she was taking drugs into the federal prison for a couple hundred.

"Yeah, yeah, of course, brah," Quay assured him.

"Okay, well you know I can't let da nigga live. He too dangerous to our team right now and with all dat time brah got, I don't too much trust him. For da time being, you and Quan are to continue making sure he's straight on product, but in the meantime, I got a proposition for Aaliyah."

Quay nodded in agreement. "Okay, she out in da car, you want her to step in?

"Yeah, go get her. By the way, never pull up to the spot with anyone outside of our team again. We don't move like dat. Ya heard me?"

"Alright, boss man, you right, I'm trippin'."

Quay got up and went to his car to get Aaliyah. He approached her on the passenger side, motioning for her to let the window down. "Come in, my nigga wanna holla at'cha."

"Okay bae." Aaliyah leaned to the driver side and pushed the push to start button to turn the car off and then followed Quay in. She couldn't imagine what on God's green earth T-Money needed to holla at her about. Stepping through the threshold of their spot, she could smell what seemed to be a mixture of cocaine, weed, and Creed cologne. She figured that was where they did their dirty work.

"Hey, how are you doing?" She smiled at T-Money as she took a seat next to Quay. "Wassup?"

"I'm straight, what about ya'self?"

Shit seems real awkward since Aaliyah had never really held a direct conversion with T-Money. "I'm fine." She kept it short, wishing he'd go on with what he needed to holla at her for.

T-Money leaped up on the counter and began, "So Aaliyah, clearly you fucking wit' my nigga Q heavy."

She blushed, glancing over at Quay and back at T-Money. "Yeah, I am."

"You wanna keep him out here in these streets? Or you wanna see him behind the gates like ya boy Hot-Rod?" T-Money knew exactly what he was doing.

"Of course not!" she replied, not exactly sure where T-Money was going with that.

"Okay, okay good. Well apparently you know dat he tryna give some time back and you also know he is willing to bring whoever down, right?" T-Money continued, "You wanna make an easy 50 G's?"

Aaliyah's eyes widened. *Shit, 50 thousand sound good,* she thought to herself. "Hell yeah, what you need me to do?"

"I need you to get rid of Hot-Rod."

The room grew silent for a second.

"Umm, what you mean by——"

T-Money interrupted, "I mean kill dat nigga."

Aaliyah lowered her head "Uh, oh, okay, I can do that," she answered without even thinking about how the hell she would make that happen. Whatever she had to do she was on it for those 50 bands.

T-Money chopped it up with Quay and Aaliyah for a while, informing them that whatever they discussed was not to go anywhere else. He didn't even plan on telling Truck about it. It was to stay between them.

CHAPTER THIRTY-SEVEN

It was early Monday morning, the start of a new work week for Officer Standley.

"Inspection, inspection, make sure you're wearing your face mask when I come around!" she shouted as she walked through Alpha dorm where Hot-Rod was housed at the Federal Prison. Covid-19 was serious and they'd already lost three inmates due to the virus, so wearing it was mandatory.

Walking past Hot-Rod's cell, Officer Standley discreetly winked at him as she always did. The only thing she could think about were those 50 bands T-Money promised her. She'd never killed anyone before and wasn't even sure how she was going to accomplish the task, but she definitely wasn't passing up the money.

Hot-Rod had no idea his days were numbered. All he knew was that Officer Standley was so caught up in her own life she ended up leaving her man at home in the midst of everything which was probably a great idea since she was sleeping with Quay unprotected and had previously fucked Hot-Rod unprotected as well. Hot-Rod wasn't worth leaving her man at home. However, Quay was worth it.

She finished her inspection right in time. Her supervisor was coming through with an important announcement for the inmates,

"Attention! Attention! Everyone step to the door of your cells," Sgt. Nixon demanded.

The inmates did as they were told, giving Sgt. Nixon their undivided attention as she stood there with a mean mug on her face.

"Okay gentlemen, we have lost loved ones and other inmates to Corona. Three inmates have passed away. Covid-19 is only getting worse. The compound will remain being run by controlled movement. However, there is a vaccination for the virus. Although it is not mandatory that you get it, I do highly recommend it. The shot is free, so each and every last one of you all need to consider getting it. I'll leave the forms with your dorm officer for you all to fill out. Once you turn them in by placing them in the sick call box, you'll be seen within five business days."

Inmates lined the officers' station to get their forms. Almost half the dorm wanted one. Surprisingly, Hot-Rod was not one of them. Officer Standley made a mental note to spend some time with him soon. Hopefully when everyone went out to rec, they could get some one on one time. She made sure she wasn't acting any way out of the normal.

As soon as rec was called, she gave Hot-Rod the signal as a code and he knew to fall back. The other inmates made their way outside as Hot-Rod got ready for a shower. He grabbed his shower bag and played it off. He didn't want to look suspicious.

The dorm was nice and quiet. Everyone went out of rec. He put his bag in the shower area, then headed into the day room. He made sure to sit at the table that was in a blind spot from the camera.

"Mr. Douglas, is everything a'ight?" Officer Standley tried to play it off in case anybody was around observing that she didn't know about.

"Yeah, I'm a'ight." Hot-Rod smirked.

She approached him walking sexy and climbing on the day room table. She crossed her legs at the ankles, looking down at Hot-Rod as he sat down at the table. She began making conversation with him. "So why didn't you come get a form to get vaccinated?"

"I don't know, I really wasn't planning on getting the shot honestly," he replied.

"But in a place like this, you should go get it just to be on the safe side." Not that she gave a fuck. She was just trying to show concern.

"You right though, ma. Fill the form out for me bae. I'ma go ahead and get it."

"Will do," she replied.

"But shid, I miss that pussy, girl. When you gon' let daddy get some?" Hot-Rod licked his lips and grabbed his dick, looking her up and down.

"I miss that dick too, daddy. As soon as my cycle go off, I got'chu," she lied. Her cycle wasn't on; she just honestly didn't wanna give him no pussy. Quay was dicking her down so good that she didn't have no pussy left over for nobody, let alone Hot-Rod.

"How 'bout you just gimme some head before they come back in from rec then?" he insisted.

She wanted to say no, but knew it would raise a red flag. "Okay, let's go." Knowing she wouldn't have to entertain him much longer, she hopped off of the table and made her way to the officers' bathroom with Hot-Rod right behind her.

They peeped the scene, then vanished inside the bathroom. Officer Standley put the seat down lightly and sat down on the toilet. Hot-Rod stood frozen in front of her with his dick out standing at attention. She had no time to waste so she began stroking his dick from the base to the head. She toyed with him for a few before she wrapped her lips around the head of his dick. She bobbed her head up and down around and around sucking hard with a lot of slob. She just wanted him to cum to get it over with. His body begin tensing up. He locked in one position and she felt his cum rising to the tip of his dick. She grabbed a napkin and caught his seed in her hands on top of the napkin.

"Ahhh damn!" he whispered.

Officer Standley held her index finger up to her lips to silence him. She flushed the napkin and waved him off to exit the bathroom before her. He made his way back in the dorm and jumped in the shower before everybody came back. She maneuvered her way back to the officers' station, sitting behind the computer as if nothing happened. She filled out the form for Hot-Rod to get vaccinated.

***

Truck had been home a week now and things were going good. Keeping in touch with Tammy and doing his lil 1-2 in streets, he was surely getting used to society. He was spending most of his time in the lab working with T-Money. His main focus was running his bag up. He didn't want Ms. Hogan paying one bill.

"Ma, what you cooking today?" Truck walked in the kitchen, where Ms. Hogan stood over the stove stirring a pot.

"Just some rice, lima beans, and neckbones," she replied, not taking her eyes off the pot.

Truck rubbed his hands together. "Yeah, it's smelling good too."

"I figured you would love to eat a home cooked meal. You've been ripping and running all week." Ms. Hogan made sure she kept a hot meal for Truck.

Someone was knocking at the front door.

"You expecting company?"

"No, baby, see who it is."

Clutching on his .45, Truck made his way to the front door. He peeked through the peephole. It was Blaze. He swung the door open and pulled his gun out, joking with Blaze. "Aye nigga, don't pop up on me unannounced!"

"Stop playing, man, I just hopped off the phone with you. Grow up, nigga," Blaze said, laughing.

Truck burst out laughing too. "I'on' want no smoke, don't shoot." He put his hands up in the air, acting like a little scared girl

"Nah, nigga, you need to grow up." Dapping each other up, they walked in the house "How you doing, Ms. Hogan?" Blaze greeted with a wave.

"I'm a'ight, Blaze and you?"

"I'm making it," he replied.

"You might as well stay and eat," she insisted

Blaze plopped down on the sofa and went to read a text from T-Money. "Truck, I came by cause T-Money wanted me to come get you. He wants to link with us around 8:00 p.m." He showed Truck the message.

"Okay, after Mama done cooking, we'll slide then," Truck had plans on meeting with Tammy at the same time, but he had to take a rain check. He was really feeling Tammy far more than he had planned on. Being gone for three years he definitely didn't have plans on coming home being under a bitch. Tammy kept Truck under her, but most of all, she understood business came first. That's what he liked most about her and was one reason why he kept her around.

"Here you go." Ms. Hogan passed the boys their food with steam floating from the top. The smell of her food always took her down memory lane where she had a house full of foster kids. She leaned back against the sink and watched her boy eat with a pleasant smile on her face.

"Thank you, ma'am." Blaze licked his lips, ready to devour it.

Truck held his head down and blessed his food. "Thank you, Ma!" he said after saying his grace.

"Yeah, no problem, y'all boys eat up," she said and walked into the bedroom.

The dining room was quiet while they bust down their food. The only thing you could hear was them sucking the meat and broth out of their neckbones.

Truck's phone was ringing non-stop so he licked the juice from his finger and wiped his hands on his Levis. He pulled his phone from his pocket. "Yo, wassup, T? We 'bout to be out in a minute."

"Okay, bet, I'm already here. Tell Ma send a nigga a plate and Cedez's need her own. I ain't sharing!" He laughed.

"Say less, I gotcha," Truck replied.

They both went and dumped the only thing left on their plates in the trash. "Ma, T wants a plate for him and Cedez."

"Okay, gimme about five minutes to make them." She fixed their plates, humming an old song that gave Truck a flashback of his childhood. She covered each plate with foil and put them in a plastic bag. She handed Truck the plates. "Okay, baby, be safe out there."

"I'll be back later, Ma!" he yelled, locking the door.

Between Honcho and Alexus and all the shiesty shit they had going on and the Hot-Rod situation, T-Money had a lot going on and his plate was full. He was never the type to keep a bunch of drama going on so he wasn't used to all the bullshit. It would only be a matter of time before he had everything nipped in the bud.

T was packing up his work and preparing Blaze's and Truck's cut as he waited for them to arrive. He had to find out Hot-Rod's drug of choice. He wanted to poison him, so drugs were his number one option. Even though he'd already put Aaliyah on it, he needed a backup plan. T-Money checked his cameras when Blaze and

Truck pulled into the driveway. He left out their piece of the pie and put the rest away.

"Wassup?" T dapped each one up and led them to his bar. T refused to do business at the home he just bought for Mercedez, so he invited them over to his own personal spot.

"Damn, bro, how many spots you got?" Truck asked as he looked around, admiring his place.

T-Money had a nice lil set up. Black, white,gold, and a little red. A real man cave. His spot looked just like the DMX spot on the movie *Belly*.

T-Money just laughed. "Shit I got a couple spots, not too many, brah." He pulled three shot glasses with Scarface pictures on them from the black granite cabinets. He pulled out a bottle of Patron and poured each of them a shot. "Okay, I got the packages already set up for y'all." Blaze and Truck nodded in agreement. T-Money went on, "So Truck, I'm really fuckin' wit ya boy Hot-Rod. I was thinking 'bout throwin some otha shit on him for personal"

Truck sat silent, taking in everything his brother was telling him. Blaze relaxed in his chair and considered the fact that T was speaking directly to Truck.

"So what's his drug of choice? I know a nigga be needing to escape reality up that road sometimes."

"Shit, Rod be fucking with them Percs but he straight on them now. He has his own plug on that," responded Truck.

The room grew silent. T-Money knew his first plan was a no go. He cleared his throat. "Okay, I just wanted to run that by you, but y'all come on follow me to the front lemme throw dat pack on y'all boys."

They followed him to his sitting room. Truck was hyped. He was getting his first major pack since being home. He was ready to jump in the game head first and show T he still had the dope game on lock. Now that Truck was out, T wasn't worried about a right-hand man or the next one up. He didn't need Honcho as part of his team. There was nothing better than putting his brother in position.

The boys talked business and discussed numbers before T wrapped the sit down up. He sent them on their ways with the best product in the south. He stood in the threshold with his hands in his pockets and watched Blaze and Truck leave.

"Damn, I hope Aaliyah follow through with this shit, or I'ma have to take a different approach to get at homie," T spoke out loud. He disappeared back inside when Blaze's car was no longer in sight.

Aaliyah had been playing her role perfect, keeping Hot-Rod right where she needed him. Hot-Rod was on the call out the next day to be vaccinated. Aaliyah had already put her plan into play. She'd ordered rat poison online after reading up on how fast it would kill a human. She'd been stationed in medical care the past few days. The only thing she had to figure out now was how the hell was she gonna mix it with his vaccine, being sure Hot-Rod got the specific dose to take him out and nobody else. God forbid an innocent inmate got it and died behind her. She sat behind her desk in deep thought. She had to get this shit into his system in less than 24 hours. She watched the clock tick by.

She had been paying attention as the nurses vaccinated the inmates. She noticed they already had the vaccine set up and ready for injection as soon as they stepped into the room. *Okay, that'll be my chance to step in when the nurse steps out to call in the next inmate*, she thought. She snapped out of it when she heard a door slam. She went on break and texted Quay. "Hope ur having a good day bae... Just letting you know IMU." Aaliyah had been feeling like she was stuck on a love boat fucking with Quay. She smiled to herself and blushed just thinking about him reading the text.

She began feeling really confident in her plan. She hadn't even run it by Quay or T-Money, yet she knew it would work. She only promised T she would get it done no later than the end of the week T-Money was definitely depending on her.

She smiled as she warmed up her food just thinking about how she was gonna spend the money. T-Money was paying her 50 bands for the job. "Easy work, no sweat, bet," she said to herself. Life would be so much easier for her. *I could pay off my car and college, and do a rent to own. I need this money*, she thought to herself.

Le'Monica Jackson

CHAPTER THIRTY-EIGHT

Honcho was heading to the airport to visit Alexus in Hawaii for the second time. Now that Ms. Gladys was gone, he had no worries at home. Alexus had fallen madly in love with him and was ready to cross the man she shared a last name with. Honcho was no longer second guessing or questioning Alexus' plan. He was ready to take T-Money's throne in the game and would stop at nothing to get T-Money's safe that was in Hawaii that Alexus had in her possession. It held over 3 million dollars in it. Honcho couldn't even dream of millions. The most he ever possessed was $300,000. That would be more than enough to put them exactly where they wanted to be.

T-Money made the mistake of allowing Honcho to meet the plug. He'd sent Honcho to meet with them a few times, trusting him not to ever cross him. But little did he know the plug was set up for life with money and product. They weren't hard up. Loyalty meant more to them and once they got word of Honcho's betrayal, he wouldn't have made it out of the meeting alive. The only way for their plan to prosper was to turn T-Money's lights out for good. It couldn't be an undercover low key thing where they just robbed him and disappeared and lived happily ever after. T-Money had to die.

***

Mercedez was almost done with her real estate class. She had just found a building she was interested in purchasing to open up whenever she wanted to. "Mercedez's World of Weaves," she said out loud. "Yeah, this would be the hottest hair store in the State of Georgia." She snapped her fingers, dancing in her seat. She had visualized it over and over again, now she was ready to bring it to life. The building she found wasn't far from Nay-Nay's salon. With that alone, she knew it would bring her plenty of business.

Ms. Hogan had found herself a new church home in Georgia. Mercedez attended service with her whenever she could. Dressing the twins for church was the most beautiful thing ever to her. Cedez was still fighting her demons, praying her past didn't catch up to her while she was in the process of cleaning up her life.

London and Paris had really changed her perspective on life. With Tevin still in the streets, she was definitely keeping their father and her man prayed up, although he was being a little distant and acting funny lately. She respected the fact that he respected her mind when she said she wanted no dealings. But a part of her didn't like feeling left out. It made her feel like he was being sneaky. T-Money took good care of the household and the twins financially. However, Cedez wished he would spend more personal and physical time as a family man. She was easy on him knowing first hands down the streets could be a full time job. T held a high position in the game and being the boss required his full attention at times. Cedez couldn't complain though. She had the help of Ms. Hogan. She couldn't have found someone more reliable.

Even though she had fallen back from the streets, she couldn't forget the charges that hung over her head or the fact that she killed Buddy Ro and Snoop and his wife. She kept her eyes and ears open to what the media was saying about it. Thank God no fingers were being pointed at her and Tevin. She kept her lawyer on top of it. He hadn't heard anything on his side of the fence either. Mercedez kept in mind Karma always comes back around. She never cared about Karma because it had always been just her. Now with the twins, she didn't want her shit falling on her babies. She prayed to God it never came knocking at her front door. Her faith was very strong. She knew her higher power had her.

***

Aaliyah peeped the scene. The nurse was already prepping her set for the next person.

"Good morning." Aaliyah peeked in the room greeting the nurse.

"Hello, good morning," the nurse replied while continuing to prepare her tray for the upcoming inmate.

She was trying to see when would be a perfect time to sneak in and steal a little glass bottle of vaccine. She needed to mix the poison and have it back in place before Hot-Rod went in. The nurse stepped out of her office, making her way to the storage closet.

"Really, how easy is this," Aaliyah said out loud with a little chuckle. The nurse gave her enough time to ease into the office. Looking over her shoulder, she quickly slipped into the office. Her hands were sweating and her whole body shook as she skimmed the desk of a bottle of medicine. Snatching up a bottle with a needle, she stuffed the items down her pants. "Got it, bitch," she said to herself. Peeking her head out, looking both ways making sure the coast was clear, she slid into the bathroom, pulling the tube out of her pants and the rat poison from her bra that she turned into liquid the night before. YouTube was a motherfucker. It's crazy what you could learn. She popped the cap off the needle and took a seat on the toilet. She made sure the door was locked. Her hands were trembling as she mixed the vaccine with poison. She shook the bottle up, making sure it didn't look funny. She didn't want them to suspect it had been tampered with and throw it out. Her plan was going great so far. Exiting the restroom, she was sure not to show any signs of nervousness. She placed the empty tube in the pocket of her jacket, making a mental note to be sure to throw it out. She put the poisoned vaccine in her shirt, hiding it right between her breasts. She returned back to her desk, surprised to see inmates already seated waiting to be seen.

Hot-Rod was the first person she spotted. "Morning, Officer Standley," the inmates said all at once. Hot-Rod winked at her and she winked back. He took it as a flirtatious wink but it was really a goodbye, you're dead wink on her end. She smiled and took a seat at her post, getting comfy at the desk.

"Martin." The nurse called the first person back to be seen. An older black man stood and went to the back to get his shot. "Douglas, you'll be next," she informed Hot-Rod.

Aaliyah was getting antsy in her seat, shifting from side to side. Her anxiety was through the roof. The inmate Martin came back to the waiting area within seconds. Aaliyah got up from her desk and made her way towards the nurse's station. She eased close to the door as the nurse walked out. "Mr. Douglas, your turn," Aaliyah heard the nurse say.

She quickly pulled the bottle from her bra and replaced it with the one on the metal silver tray. She was out of the nurse's office before they made it back; she moved swiftly to have been so on edge. She puckered up her lips to blow him a kiss, not caring that the nurse saw her as she passed them.

Hot-Rod licked his full lips as he admired her frame from head to toe. He was always ready to get in her pants. She wasn't nothing more than a quick fuck for him. He knew if she was fucking him she was fucking another inmate too. "We definitely don't do no kissing," he mumbled to himself.

The nurse still heard him. She'd peeped them flirting and found it so funny. Honestly, she didn't give two fucks about them and their lil fling.

It was something about her sex game Hot-Rod couldn't resist. Little did he know she'd be the last person he ever fucked. A piece of ass was his downfall.

Aaliyah felt relieved. She took a deep breath and day dreamed about her new life with the extra cash the remainder of the shift. Now all she was waiting on was seeing how long it took for the poison to take effect. She watched as Hot-Rod left medical rubbing his upper arm in a circular motion. That must be where he got the vaccination at. "Have a good day, Mr. Douglas." She waved him on, he looked back over his shoulder before closing the door.

"You too, Officer Standley, you too."

***

Ms. Douglas's phone ringing woke her up. She rolled over in bed, awakened in the middle of the night. She squinted her eyes looking at her alarm clock on the nightstand. 4:00 a.m. "What in the world?" she mumbled. Ms. Douglas reached over for the phone. She jumped up, resting her head on the headboard. Her heart dropped thinking the worst when she realized it was the federal facility that

Rodger was being held at. She cleared her throat. "Hel-hello?" she answered.

"Ms. Douglas, this is Sgt. Nixon here at——"

Ms. Douglas interrupted, "What's going on with my son?"

"Well, I hate to have to be the one to let you know the bad news…"

Ms. Douglas jumped out of her bed, heart racing. "Please, please!" she cried.

The phone grew silent. Sgt. Nixon exhaled and spilled it out in one breath. "Your son Rodger Douglas was found unresponsive during 3:30 count this morning. He was rushed down to medical, but unfortunately, he had no pulse."

"No Lord! Please no!" She dropped down to her knees as the phone fell to the floor. She couldn't stand to bear any more.

"Hello?" Sgt. Nixon realized Ms. Douglas was no longer on the line. Sgt. Nixon eventually hung up.

Officer Standley's plan worked out successfully. She heard the news the following day. She wouldn't be at ease until he was in the ground. She still couldn't believe she actually went through with it. She'd called out of work the next few days claiming symptoms of Covid. It was believable since she had been working the medical post. Inmates had tested positive and some even had lost their lives from the virus. In reality, she really just needed to clear her head.

She hit Quay up as soon as she got the news. "Quay baby, I need to see you and your mans ASAP." She wanted her bread. With the position T-Money held in the streets, everyone knew not to say his name over the phone. With all the murders he and Cedez had committed, she heard they were animals. So she refused to speak either of their names involving crime period. She loved and valued her life.

Quay already knew what it was about. He didn't even respond, he just hung up. He grabbed his keys and headed to the lab. He hit T's line instantly.

"Damn, ya bubble head ass can never sit still!" Cedez complained as Tevin jumped out of the bed, passing the baby girl to her.

"Cedez, chill, lil mama, I'ma be right back. This an emergency." He leaned over, trying to kiss her.

She turned her head, rejecting her man's kiss. "Yeah, uh-uh! Whatever, Tevin," she responded. She laid London across her lap and began playing with her as if he wasn't in the room and like she wasn't bothered. She didn't care what the emergency was. As far as she was concerned, as long as his family was good, it wasn't a damn emergency. She was getting fed up with how Tevin was moving when it came down to his home life. He wasn't spending time with the twins. She had no idea what was going on but she didn't give a damn. He was so busy with his own shit she didn't bother informing him on how far she'd come with the store. Her real estate classes were going well and she had already bought the building for the store. Mercedez's World of Weaves was filled with hair, the electricity was on, and the grand opening right around the corner. Tevin didn't know shit though.

CHAPTER THIRTY-NINE

"Baby, I've missed you." Alexus greeted Honcho with open arms as she stood in the doorway of her beautiful home.

Honcho embraced her, cuffing her soft round ass, snuggling his face in the arch of her neck. He placed soft kisses on her as she inhaled the smell of his expensive cologne. A man wearing Creed was an easy way to get a woman's attention without even saying a word.

"I missed you too, girl. Damn, what you got on under here?" Honcho responded, realizing Alexus didn't have any panties on under her cotton dress.

"Whatever you want me to have on," she responded flirtatiously as she lead him inside, closing the door behind him.

Honcho felt good to be out in Hawaii with Alexus, leaving all of his problems in Georgia. He was still working for T-Money, but they hadn't chilled much in the past few months. Honcho was moving differently since Ms. Gladys had passed, which was partly the reason he hadn't been coming around, but the main reason was he was too far into what he and Alexus had going. She was the only person who seemed to keep his mind in a clear space. Honcho had never had a bitch on Alexus' level that submitted to him the way she did. Sure he was used to bitches submitting, but they were always basic bitches who were looking for a come up, meanwhile Alexus didn't need him for a gotdamn thang.

Honcho took off his shoes, kicked his feet up and got comfortable on the red leather sectional Alexus had in her sitting room. She rolled him a nice fat blunt as she went on   and on about how much she missed him. She really had the nigga feeling like he was T-Money's equal when in reality, he wasn't even close. Honcho caressed Alexus' thighs, licking his bottom lip. He gave her a lustful look as he sparked up the blunt. He couldn't wait for everything they'd talked about to finally be in his possession. T-Money had no idea Honcho was way out in Hawaii and that's just what Honcho wanted, for T-Money to be in the blind. Honcho blew the marijuana smoke in the air before putting the unfinished blunt out.

"Damn Lex, you claim you missed a nigga, when you gon' show me how much you actually missed me?" he questioned. Before Alexus could give an answer, he was easing his hand under her dress.

She spread her legs, giving him easy access to her love button. Honcho slid closer to her on the sofa and began rubbing her clit. She was already wet just as he expected. Parting her pussy lips, Honcho gently eased his two fingers inside. "Ahhh," she gasped softly as she reached for his manhood,

Honcho knew exactly what she wanted. He quickly pulled his dick out, allowing it to stand straight up out of his pants Alexus definitely was what you called "the throat goat". That bitch head game was out of the world. She licked her lips, seductively gazing into Honcho's eyes before going down on him, taking the whole thing into her mouth. Honcho raised his hips up off of the couch, making sure she had the whole entire dick in her mouth. Honcho thrust in her mouth for a good three minutes, enjoying every second of her performance, not wanting to cum so fast he forced her to stop and decided he'd give her some head in return.

Alexus laid back on the couch, throwing her legs over Honcho's shoulder as he gently wrapped his lips around her pulsing clitoris. He was surprised by how sweet her pussy juices tasted. "Mmm," he moaned with passion as if he had just bit into one of Ms. Gladys' famous pies or something.

"Daddy...daddy," Alexus cooed as she moved her hips in a circular motion, making love to Honcho's face. She ran her fingernails through his neatly groomed dreadlocks. Everything about him was a turn on.

Honcho knew she was genuinely enjoying it, realizing that she had a nice size puddle of cum on the couch and it definitely wasn't coming from his mouth because he was trying his best to slurp up every bit of her juices. *Damn, this pussy good*, he thought to himself, backing away from Alexus' pussy. He just looked at it, admiring how pretty it was as she begged him to continue. Honcho loved how she seemed to be feening for him.

"Why'd you stop?" Alexus whined.

Honcho responded in a demanding manner. "Come ride dis dick."

Alexus quickly hopped up, pulling her dress off over her head, straddling Honcho. She slowly slid down on his pole while he palmed her ass cheeks, spreading them apart, making sure every inch of his dick was deep inside of her.

"Ahh fuck!" he moaned and threw his head back against the headrest of the couch.

Alexus looked down at him and smiled, feeling confident in herself. *I'ma have dis nigga head gone*, she thought to herself as she bounced up and down on him, causing her ass to sound off every time she came down on it.

Honcho was pumping inside of her, matching her rhythm. The pussy was so good he didn't even bother pulling out as he reached his climax. His body jerked and his toes curled as he exploded inside of her. Alexus' smile told it all. She knew for a fact he was definitely falling for her. Alexus had never told Honcho that she couldn't have children so him nutting in her proved that he didn't give a damn about losing T-Money as a friend when it came to her.

With the wealth and money that Alexus had promised Honcho, it was enough to make him switch up on his day one nigga. She hadn't checked the safes since T-Money had left her to be with Mercedez and it was only a matter of time before she emptied his shit and gave Honcho everything she'd promised him.

Le'Monica Jackson

CHAPTER FORTY

Ms. Douglas was in a daze as she headed to the police station to confirm the death of her firstborn son. Tears slowly ran down her cheeks. She hadn't even had enough time to grieve over the loss of Robert and here it was she had to bury Rodger in less than a week.

"Lord, you said you wouldn't put no more on me than I can handle. I need you, Father. I can't handle it!" She was waiting on the autopsy to find out exactly what happened to Hot-Rod. She refused to believe that the same girl who was at her doctor's office had something to do with the death of her son. According to what Hot-Rod had told her though, Mercedez was definitely a suspect.

Ms. Douglas arrived at the police station, bracing herself before going in to see Hot-Rod's body lying lifeless on the cold steel slab. "My son!" she cried, standing at the glass window staring at Hot-Rod. He seemed to be at peace. He looked as if he was just in a deep sleep. Ms. Douglas stood there for at least 13 minutes, trying to come to her senses and accept the fact that Hot-Rod was really dead.

"Take as much time as you need, ma'am." An officer walked up to console her, giving her Kleenex to wipe away her tears.

Ms. Douglas was not mentally ready to prepare another home going celebration. A mother should never have to bury her child, but things ain't how it used to be back in the days. The cemeteries housed more young folks than old folks these days.

Nay-Nay was the second person to get the call about Hot-Rod's death. She waited in the parking lot of the police station hoping to see Ms. Douglas for the first time. This definitely was not how she'd picture meeting Hot-Rod's mom. "Damn, who do I introduce myself as?" Nay-Nay said to herself as she stepped out of her black BMW truck, walking in the direction of the lady who she assumed was Ms. Douglas walking to her vehicle with her face washed in tears. "I'm so sorry for your loss. I'm Nay-Nay. Rodger's, uh close friend. Ms. Douglas, I've heard a lot about you." "I heard a lot about you as well," Ms. Douglas responded.

The two ladies stood in the parking lot crying, discussing Hot-Rod. Ms. Douglas reached in her purse and pulled out her phone.

She went to her photo gallery, pulling up a picture of a mugshot. "Do you know her?"

Nay-Nay's heart dropped when she saw Mercedez's mugshot "Uh…no I don't," Nay-Nay replied.

"Well, Hot-Rod told me if something happens to him, this girl may have something to do with it."

Nay-nay was just as confused as Ms. Douglas. *How the hell would Cedez have something to do with Hot-Rod's death?* Nay-Nay thought to herself. She couldn't wait to get back in her car and hit T-Money up. The ladies exchanged numbers "Call me if you need anything, Ms. Douglas," Nay-Nay said as they separated.

Nay-Nay planned to help Ms. Douglas with Hot-Rod's funeral. Nay-Nay was worried about the baby shower picture she'd sent Hot-Rod because the last thing she needed was his personal belongings being released to Ms. Douglas and her finding out that Nay-Nay really did know who Mercedez was. That would instantly raise a red flag and make Nay-Nay look suspect when in reality she was in the blind about the whole situation. She was just as anxious about the autopsy as Ms. Douglas.

Nay-Nay's head was all over the place. *Oh my gosh, did his mama show me the mugshot because she's already seen the baby shower picture? She said she's heard so much about me. Did Hot-Rod tell her bad things about me? Oh my Lord, what if he kept me around thinking maybe I was trying to get him knocked off?*

Nay-Nay didn't know what to think at that point. All she knew was that she loved Hot-Rod and planned to have a future with him when he came home. She wanted so badly to talk to T-Money, but she needed some time to sit back and think everything over. Although she loved T-Money like a brother, with a situation as serious as this, she had to be sure she approached him in the right manner, being sure not to make him feel like she would ever fold on him or Mercedez. When it all boiled down to whether T-Money and Mercedez had something to do with it or not, it would break Nay-Nay's heart, but her loyalty would always lie with Tevin Carter.

CHAPTER FORTY-ONE

"He was poisoned? I-I-I'm confused. I just don't understand," Ms. Douglas cried as she held the phone to her ear.

The autopsy showed that Rodger had rat poison in his system. The whole federal facility was under investigation and Officer Standley had yet to return to work. Ms. Douglas was completely blown away. Any and everyone was suspect at that point. She didn't know who was responsible for Hot-Rod's death. She knew for a fact he didn't do it to himself.

"We were working on getting him home. He would've never taken his own life," Ms. Douglas said to herself.

Something in her spirit just wasn't sitting right. She knew her child, and knew for a fact someone had poisoned her son. She just couldn't imagine who would do something like that

Officer Standley grew terrified. The last thing she needed was her name coming up in anything that had to do with Rodger Douglas. Truck was the only one who had any idea about the affair between the two - well, at least to her knowledge.

***

Time was ticking and Honcho was desperate to begin living the life Alexus had promised him. He was getting attached to her and loving the new environment. It's like none of his problems existed when he was in Hawaii. Lying back in the bed that T-Money once shared with Alexus, Honcho crossed his legs at the ankles, feeling very relaxed as he flipped through channels on the 75 inch plasma that was mounted on the wall. Alexus genuinely enjoyed his company. "So baby, what happened, when we going to put our plan into action?" he questioned Alexus, hoping it would be sooner than later.

"Good thing you brought that up because I was thinking this weekend. We could go ahead and at least clean the safes out. Some kind of way I gotta get him down here so we can get rid of him. The only problem is he won't answer for me, so I don't know how I would be able to make that happen."

Honcho thought hard about everything she was saying. He knew he had to outsmart T-Money, and he needed a plan. "A'ight, check it, he's not picking up for you, but I know he's gonna read your texts," Honcho said.

"No, he's not, I think he has me on the block list!" cried out Alexus.

"Ummm, okay, go to the next door neighbor's house and use their phone and call him. Tell him somebody has robbed the house," instructed Honcho.

Nodding her head, she agreed with a sneaky smile on her face while she rubbed her hands together.

***

"Aye T, wassup? I need you to pull up on me, it's a 911." Nay-Nay called up T and requested his attention as soon as possible.

"Bet," replied T.

They met up at a low-key sports bar. "Wassup, baby girl, you good?" he questioned.

"Yeah, I'm Gucci, but check it. I was holding down this nigga in the pen and he just recently died," Nay stated.

T-Money lowered the hood off his eyes and leaned back in his seat. He knew off the rip that she was talking about the nigga Hot-Rod. "Keep talking," he demanded once she paused for a little too long.

From reading his body language and the change in his demeanor, she already knew it was true. "Well, I went to meet his moms and she pulled up a picture of Cedez saying that he had sent her the picture and said if anything happened to him, Cedez was responsible," Nay-Nay revealed. T-Money sat silently, which made Nay-Nay's mind run wild. "Look, T, I'm just putting you up on game is all. I'on' wanna see ya family fucked up. I know y'all are so happy and in a good place in life right now."

T-Money raised his hand, silencing her mid-sentence. "Good looking out, baby girl. I'ma drop some bands on you for this information," said T.

"Man, don't try it. It's called being a friend. You don't owe me anything. I'm good. You've done enough for me over the years," Nay-Nay responded.

"A'ight, I'm 'bout to get outta here and handle this, Nay," he said, lifting out of his seat and kissing her on the forehead. He dropped a blue face on the table and exited the bar.

Walking out of the bar, T-Money's cell rang and he didn't recognize the number. But he knew only people he knew had the number, so he answered.

"Hello, Tony Turner's Funeral Home, how may I help you?" T answered in a professional tone.

"T!" cried Alexus.

Yeah," he answered in an unhappy dry tone, not fazed at all by the tears in her voice.

"We've been robbed! Somebody broke in our home. I know you don't want the police involved. What should I do? You need to get over here," a frantic Alexus said.

"Damn, the fuck? A'ight, bet, I'm on my way. Don't touch shit. I'ma kill me a ma'fucka today!" T screamed He knew it was all bullshit, but didn't want to let her know that he was hip to the creep shit she and Honcho were up to. With that being the case, he called up Honcho. "Aye bruh, a ma'fucka had the balls to break in my crib in Hawaii. I'm 'bout to head over there. I need you to ride shotgun wit' me." said T.

"Bro, I'm not even in the state right now. I'm down in MIA with my lil bitch," Honcho lied.

"I can't wait for you, man. Just get back here and hold shit down. You the only person I can trust right now," T stated

"Say no mo', I'm on my way," said Honcho.

T ended the call and shook his head. *Fuck nigga in Hawaii!* T thought to himself.

"Hey baby, where are you going?" asked Cedez. She walked in on T packing a very small luggage.

"Um, to handle something down in Florida. But I'm only gonna be gone two days tops, no need to worry."

"Shid, I wanna slide. Wassup? You been acting real funny lately," questioned Cedez.

T-Money got up and walked towards the room door and closed it. He sat down on the mini couch in their room and patted the seat for Cedez to join him, and she obeyed. "So Nay-Nay came to me with some information that could end up ruining us. Apparently, she was dating Hot-Rod when he died. His moms had a picture of you that he sent, saying if anything was to happen to him it was because of you," T informed her.

"Fuck, man, how? What are we gonna do now? I'm trying to be done with the street life and just be a mom," Mercedez groaned.

"I'ma handle it, trust. I got you. Just sit pretty and take care of my shorties."

"Okay, but if you need me, you know I'on' mind doing whatever to protect what's mines, and my family is #1 for me," she reminded him.

"Girl, I know," T said, laughing at his gangsta baby momma with milk leaking from her titties. He hit her with a pillow and got up.

"So just fuck the fact you acting funny? Don't think I ain't pick up on you changing the subject, my nigga!" Cedez said with her eyebrows up to her hairline and lips poked out.

"Just chill, lil momma. I just want you to stay a housewife, so I leave the street shit where it's at, ya feel me?" he asked.

"I guess you have a point, T," she said, walking to the door. She twirled around suddenly, remembering. "So what about my grand opening?" she asked.

"I'ma be there, sweet baby."

"You better, T, or I'ma knock ya ass out, on God, don't test me," Cedez threatened.

"Man, burn up. You know I'm not gonna miss that shit, girl." T-Money laughed, taking her threat lightly.

She walked out to make the twins bottles before they woke up from their nap. Cedez walked back into their bedroom to take a

248

quick shower. She noticed T-Money's phone charging on the nightstand. *This nigga think he three quarters slick*, she thought, grabbing his phone to snoop because she had every right. "Ain't no secrets in my house," she said aloud, unlocking his phone.

I wonder where this nigga at anyway, she mumbled under her breath, searching through everything. She found nothing. Checking his email, she found a flight confirmation number to Hawaii. "Bingo." She made a mental note. She heard the shower turn off and jumped out of her skin. She closed out all his apps and placed his phone back down. Mercedez reached in her titties and pulled out her rose gold iPhone and connected her Pandora to her speaker as she prepared for her shower.

T-Money threw his bag in the passenger seat of his car and headed towards the airport. He picked up his phone and called up Quay to put him up on game.

"Aye bro, I got a plan," Quay said.

"Okay, lay it on me, bro."

"So you know medical in prison is laced with cameras, right?"

"Right," said T.

"So I'ma have the cameras pulled and let the bitch go down."

"Umm, good play," agreed T. "Handle that ASAP." T. ended the call and laid back and enjoyed the ride.

***

Ms. Douglas got a call informing her that someone was arrested and charged with the murder of her son. She was satisfied that it was all over with and the person responsible was caught. The fact that they were caught red-handed on camera meant the picture she had of Chantal was irrelevant now. "Well Lawd, I thank you for that closure," Ms. Douglas said out loud with her hand raised. She grabbed her phone and deleted Cedez's picture. She called the prison to request her son's things.

"Well ma'am, you had 3 to 5 business days to make a claim to Mr. Douglas's property and you are a day late. Everything has been discarded. I'm sorry."

***

"Ma, you ready to put the finishing touches on the grand opening?" Cedez asked Ms. Hogan.

"Yes I am, and I'm ready to see those babies too." She laughed.

"Okay, I'm on my way."

Everything was coming together.

"Hey, I need to do some personal shopping and pampering myself. Do you mind the twins staying overnight?"

"Gal, don't ask me that, of course I don't mind! I would love their company."

She said, "Thanks! Really do appreciate it."

"Anytime, Frankenstein."

They laughed together. She kissed her bundles of joy and left the loft.

***

Alexus and Honcho prepared for T's arrival. They trashed the house and broke some lights. They were hyped, thinking they had one up on T.

"Okay bae, go clean out the safe," instructed Honcho.

Alexus put in the code so many times it locked up for one min. "What the fuck? Did he change the code?" she screamed.

Honcho rushed into the room. "What?" He kissed her neck to calm her down. "We just got to make that nigga give us the code. No worries," Honcho said, comforting her.

CHAPTER FORTY-TWO

Mercedez's phone rang. It was her mom's friend, the detective down in Orlando. She exhaled a sigh of relief. "Damn, I been waiting on this call," she said out loud.

The lady next to her looked over and smiled. Cedez was in the biggest hair store in the city and she loved going there.

"Hey, young lady, how are you?"

"I'm good, and you? Are you still fighting the crime?" Cedez asked, chuckling.

"Well, you know, it pays the bills."

"Tell me something good."

"Well, I thought your case was over when I was told your eyewitness died. But apparently he left a recorded statement with the lead detective saying he had hard evidence that he left with someone, which is unknown to me. And he said if anything happened to him, you and Tevin Carter are the ones to blame. Now I'm still looking into this person, and their ID is top notch, but don't worry, I will get their name."

***

T-Money walked through the airport with his head held high without a care in the world, He was ready to get all the bullshit behind him and get all of the snakes out of his way. He caught a glimpse of a dude walking in front of him. Something about the guy's walk was very familiar. T-Money couldn't seem to put his finger on it though. He made sure to go to the luggage check right next to the guy to get a better look at his face. The guy had dreads and wore dark sunglasses.

Damn, I wish I could see this nigga face, T thought to himself.

"Um, excuse me, sir, that bag is technically a carry-on," the lady behind the desk said.

"Um, okay, yeah, right," responded T without even looking at her.

Something wasn't sitting right in his spirit about this dude. T-Money stood back, and when the guy turned around, he realized the guy was a stranger he'd never seen before. He just resembled Cedez's brother Kobe "Damn, I'm trippin'," T said aloud and continued on his way.

When he made it to Hawaii, he stopped at his stash spot, grabbing his guns, bulletproof vest, and ammo. Turning on the cameras Alexus had no idea who had been in the home. He began to watch his prey for about two hours. He couldn't wait to catch them by surprise.

T-Money sat there getting lost in his own thoughts. *Funny how you can be a motherfucka's bread, butter, and water and it still isn't enough. They want ya spot! Nobody is grateful anymore. People just believe they can do people wrong and get away with it. Karma scares nobody nowadays. Greed overrules.*

He shook his head. "They gon' learn today," he clowned out loud in his Kevin Hart voice as he exited his vehicle.

He crept through the back sliding glass door, never letting them know that he was there. He heard their voices upstairs in the master bedroom. He laughed, listening to the plans they made to make him open the safe and kill him. "Such amateurs," he whispered. He stood in the doorway, leaning against the frame with one foot crossed in front of the other. He didn't even have his gun out. He seriously took them for a joke. He sucked his teeth purposely, startling them both.

Honcho jumped and grabbed his gun. "Damn, bro, that's how we doin' it, homie?" T asked Honcho, not even addressing Alexus. She was such a non-factor at this point. His world revolved around Cedez and his kids. That really made her feel low, unwanted, and unloved.

"Brah, just open the safe!" Honcho yelled.

T-Money just stared at Honcho. Unbeknownst to all of them, someone else was in the house.

Pow! Pow!

Both Alexus's and Honcho's bodies dropped in slow motion. T-Money turned around to face the gunman, knowing he hadn't fired any shots. There the unknown person stood with a smoking gun. At loss for words, T-Money stood there wondering why someone he didn't know would have his back, low-key feeling some type of way that he even allowed a nigga to track him the way this dude did.

"Aye, wait a minute, ain't you the nigga from the airport?" T-Money walked up to the dude. The guy removed his sunglasses and pulled off the wig of dreads. "Mercedez! What the fuck? You followed me?"

"Hmph, well good thing I did 'cause yo' ass was about to be a goner," Cedez sassed rolling her neck. "Shid, T. I thought you were cheating. I just knew this was a replay of the shit that went down in Cali, and on God, you was gon' have to shoot me one, straight up." The room grew silent and then she continued. "Whew, and this bitch you married is sooo flaw."

"Was so flaw…was!" T corrected her. They smiled. "Girl, I told you I'on' want nobody but you. Trust me, baby."

"Well, I'm sorry for doubting you, T," Cedez apologized.

"Now what are we gonna do about these bodies?" T questioned.

"I mean, shid, we are in Hawaii with all this beautiful water surrounding us," replied Cedez.

That was all that needed to be said. They wrapped the bodies up, put them in the trunk, and drove to the darkest parts of the water. They rented a boat with Alexus I.D., loaded the bodies onto it, placed anchors at the bottom of their feet, and dropped the bodies together all at once.

"I hope ya bitch ass can swim," T said, mimicking the Lil Boosie video that went viral.

The two sparked a blunt, putting it in rotation as they watched the fish attack Honcho's and Alexus's bodies. They headed back to clean up the blood and soon after, Tevin put the house up for sale before leaving.

"Hawaii dead to me," he told Mercedez without looking back.

They made it back to Georgia in time for Cedez to cut her red ribbon, giving a birthday to her new hair store. The grand opening turned out great. Mercedez posed for a picture with her family followed by a group picture with her mother, siblings, nieces, and nephew.

"Congratulations, Mercedez!" they all said at once.

ONE WEEK LATER

Cedez's phone rang. T-Money and Mercedez were on cloud nine as they layed in bed butt naked, locked in each other's arms after a very hardcore sex session. Their bodies glistened with sweat.

"Hello," Cedez answered.

"Ms. Smith?"

"Yes, wassup?"

"Well, I found out who the mystery man was with the information that your eyewitness left behind."

T and Cedez locked eyes. Both of their hearts hit the bottom of their ass.

"Okay."

"Yeah, well, Mr. Rodgers Douglas, who is now also deceased, was the mystery guy," the detective stated.

A huge weight lifted off both their shoulders. The lines of worry disappeared from their foreheads as they interlocked fingers.

"So basically you're a free woman, Ms. Smith. Keep it that way!"

"Thanks," she replied, planting a soft kiss on T-Money's lips.

To Be Continued…
Treal Love 2
Coming Soon

Lock Down Publications and Ca$h Presents assisted
publishing packages.

BASIC PACKAGE $499
Editing
Cover Design
Formatting

UPGRADED PACKAGE $800
Typing
Editing
Cover Design
Formatting

ADVANCE PACKAGE $1,200
Typing
Editing
Cover Design
Formatting
Copyright registration
Proofreading
Upload book to Amazon

LDP SUPREME PACKAGE $1,500
Typing
Editing
Cover Design
Formatting
Copyright registration
Proofreading
Set up Amazon account
Upload book to Amazon
Advertise on LDP Amazon and Facebook page

Le'Monica Jackson

***Other services available upon request. Additional charges
may apply
Lock Down Publications
P.O. Box 944
Stockbridge, GA 30281-9998
Phone # 470 303-9761

Submission Guideline

Submit the first three chapters of your completed manuscript to ldpsubmissions@gmail.com, subject line: Your book's title. The manuscript must be in a .doc file and sent as an attachment. Document should be in Times New Roman, double spaced and in size 12 font. Also, provide your synopsis and full contact information. If sending multiple submissions, they must each be in a separate email.

Have a story but no way to send it electronically? You can still submit to LDP/Ca$h Presents. Send in the first three chapters, written or typed, of your completed manuscript to:

LDP: Submissions Dept
Po Box 944
Stockbridge, Ga 30281

DO NOT send original manuscript. Must be a duplicate.

Provide your synopsis and a cover letter containing your full contact information.

Thanks for considering LDP and Ca$h Presents.

NEW RELEASES

VICIOIUS LOYALTY 2 by KINGPEN
THE STREETS WILL NEVER CLOSE 3 by K'AJJI
THE MURDER QUEENS by MICHAEL GALLON
THE BIRTH OF A GANGSTER by DELMONT PLAYER
MOB TIES 6 by SAYNOMORE
A GANGSTA'S PAIN 2 by J-BLUNT
TREAL LOVE by LE'MONICA JACKSON

Coming Soon from Lock Down Publications/Ca$h Presents
BLOOD OF A BOSS **VI**

SHADOWS OF THE GAME II

TRAP BASTARD II

By **Askari**

LOYAL TO THE GAME **IV**

By **T.J. & Jelissa**

IF TRUE SAVAGE **VIII**

MIDNIGHT CARTEL IV

DOPE BOY MAGIC IV

CITY OF KINGZ III

NIGHTMARE ON SILENT AVE II

THE PLUG OF LIL MEXICO II

By **Chris Green**

BLAST FOR ME **III**

A SAVAGE DOPEBOY III

CUTTHROAT MAFIA III

DUFFLE BAG CARTEL VII

HEARTLESS GOON VI

By **Ghost**

A HUSTLER'S DECEIT III

KILL ZONE II

BAE BELONGS TO ME III

By **Aryanna**

KING OF THE TRAP III

By **T.J. Edwards**

GORILLAZ IN THE BAY V

3X KRAZY III

STRAIGHT BEAST MODE II

De'Kari

KINGPIN KILLAZ IV

STREET KINGS III

PAID IN BLOOD III

CARTEL KILLAZ IV

DOPE GODS III

Hood Rich

SINS OF A HUSTLA II

ASAD

RICH $AVAGE II

By Martell Troublesome Bolden

YAYO V

Bred In The Game 2

S. Allen

CREAM III

THE STREETS WILL TALK II

By Yolanda Moore

SON OF A DOPE FIEND III

HEAVEN GOT A GHETTO II

By Renta

LOYALTY AIN'T PROMISED III

By Keith Williams

I'M NOTHING WITHOUT HIS LOVE II

SINS OF A THUG II

TO THE THUG I LOVED BEFORE II

IN A HUSTLER I TRUST II

By Monet Dragun

QUIET MONEY IV

EXTENDED CLIP III

THUG LIFE IV

By **Trai'Quan**

THE STREETS MADE ME IV

By **Larry D. Wright**

IF YOU CROSS ME ONCE II

By **Anthony Fields**

THE STREETS WILL NEVER CLOSE IV

By **K'ajji**

HARD AND RUTHLESS III

KILLA KOUNTY III

By **Khufu**

MONEY GAME III

By **Smoove Dolla**

JACK BOYS VS DOPE BOYS II

A GANGSTA'S QUR'AN V

COKE GIRLZ II

By **Romell Tukes**

MURDA WAS THE CASE II

Elijah R. Freeman

THE STREETS NEVER LET GO II

By **Robert Baptiste**

AN UNFORESEEN LOVE III

By **Meesha**

KING OF THE TRENCHES III

by **GHOST & TRANAY ADAMS**

MONEY MAFIA II

LOYAL TO THE SOIL III

By **Jibril Williams**

QUEEN OF THE ZOO II

By **Black Migo**

THE BRICK MAN IV

By **King Rio**

VICIOUS LOYALTY III
By Kingpen
A GANGSTA'S PAIN III
By J-Blunt
CONFESSIONS OF A JACKBOY III
By Nicholas Lock
GRIMEY WAYS II
By Ray Vinci
KING KILLA II
By Vincent "Vitto" Holloway
BETRAYAL OF A THUG II
By Fre$h
THE MURDER QUEENS II
By Michael Gallon
THE BIRTH OF A GANGSTER II
By Delmont Player
TREAL LOVE II
By Le'Monica Jackson
<u>Available Now</u>

RESTRAINING ORDER **I & II**
By **CA$H & Coffee**
LOVE KNOWS NO BOUNDARIES **I II & III**
By **Coffee**
RAISED AS A GOON I, II, III & IV
BRED BY THE SLUMS I, II, III
BLAST FOR ME I & II
ROTTEN TO THE CORE I II III
A BRONX TALE I, II, III
DUFFLE BAG CARTEL I II III IV V VI

Treal Love

HEARTLESS GOON I II III IV V

A SAVAGE DOPEBOY I II

DRUG LORDS I II III

CUTTHROAT MAFIA I II

KING OF THE TRENCHES

By **Ghost**

LAY IT DOWN **I & II**

LAST OF A DYING BREED I II

BLOOD STAINS OF A SHOTTA I & II III

By **Jamaica**

LOYAL TO THE GAME I II III

LIFE OF SIN I, II III

By **TJ & Jelissa**

BLOODY COMMAS I & II

SKI MASK CARTEL I II & III

KING OF NEW YORK I II,III IV V

RISE TO POWER I II III

COKE KINGS I II III IV V

BORN HEARTLESS I II III IV

KING OF THE TRAP I II

By **T.J. Edwards**

IF LOVING HIM IS WRONG…I & II

LOVE ME EVEN WHEN IT HURTS I II III

By **Jelissa**

WHEN THE STREETS CLAP BACK I & II III

THE HEART OF A SAVAGE I II III

MONEY MAFIA

LOYAL TO THE SOIL I II

By **Jibril Williams**

A DISTINGUISHED THUG STOLE MY HEART I II & III

LOVE SHOULDN'T HURT I II III IV

RENEGADE BOYS I II III IV

PAID IN KARMA I II III

SAVAGE STORMS I II III

AN UNFORESEEN LOVE I II

By **Meesha**

A GANGSTER'S CODE I &, II III

A GANGSTER'S SYN I II III

THE SAVAGE LIFE I II III

CHAINED TO THE STREETS I II III

BLOOD ON THE MONEY I II III

A GANGSTA'S PAIN I II

By J-Blunt

PUSH IT TO THE LIMIT

By **Bre' Hayes**

BLOOD OF A BOSS **I, II, III, IV, V**

SHADOWS OF THE GAME

TRAP BASTARD

By **Askari**

THE STREETS BLEED MURDER **I, II & III**

THE HEART OF A GANGSTA I II& III

By **Jerry Jackson**

CUM FOR ME I II III IV V VI VII VIII

An **LDP Erotica Collaboration**

BRIDE OF A HUSTLA **I II & II**

THE FETTI GIRLS **I, II& III**

CORRUPTED BY A GANGSTA I, II III, IV

BLINDED BY HIS LOVE

THE PRICE YOU PAY FOR LOVE I, II ,III

DOPE GIRL MAGIC I II III

Treal Love

By **Destiny Skai**
WHEN A GOOD GIRL GOES BAD
By **Adrienne**
THE COST OF LOYALTY I II III
By Kweli
A GANGSTER'S REVENGE **I II III & IV**
THE BOSS MAN'S DAUGHTERS I II III IV V
A SAVAGE LOVE **I & II**
BAE BELONGS TO ME I II
A HUSTLER'S DECEIT I, II, III
WHAT BAD BITCHES DO I, II, III
SOUL OF A MONSTER I II III
KILL ZONE
A DOPE BOY'S QUEEN I II III
By **Aryanna**
A KINGPIN'S AMBITON
A KINGPIN'S AMBITION **II**
I MURDER FOR THE DOUGH
By **Ambitious**
TRUE SAVAGE I II III IV V VI VII
DOPE BOY MAGIC I, II, III
MIDNIGHT CARTEL I II III
CITY OF KINGZ I II
NIGHTMARE ON SILENT AVE
THE PLUG OF LIL MEXICO II

By **Chris Green**
A DOPEBOY'S PRAYER
By **Eddie "Wolf" Lee**
THE KING CARTEL **I, II & III**

265

By **Frank Gresham**

THESE NIGGAS AIN'T LOYAL **I, II & III**

By **Nikki Tee**

GANGSTA SHYT **I II &III**

By **CATO**

THE ULTIMATE BETRAYAL

By **Phoenix**

BOSS'N UP **I , II & III**

By **Royal Nicole**

I LOVE YOU TO DEATH

By **Destiny J**

I RIDE FOR MY HITTA

I STILL RIDE FOR MY HITTA

By **Misty Holt**

LOVE & CHASIN' PAPER

By **Qay Crockett**

TO DIE IN VAIN

SINS OF A HUSTLA

By **ASAD**

BROOKLYN HUSTLAZ

By **Boogsy Morina**

BROOKLYN ON LOCK I & II

By **Sonovia**

GANGSTA CITY

By **Teddy Duke**

A DRUG KING AND HIS DIAMOND I & II III

A DOPEMAN'S RICHES

HER MAN, MINE'S TOO I, II

CASH MONEY HO'S

THE WIFEY I USED TO BE I II

Treal Love

THESE STREETS DON'T LOVE NOBODY I, II

BURY ME A G I, II, III, IV, V

A GANGSTA'S EMPIRE I, II, III, IV

THE DOPEMAN'S BODYGAURD I II

THE REALEST KILLAZ I II III

THE LAST OF THE OGS I II III

Tranay Adams

THE STREETS ARE CALLING

Duquie Wilson

MARRIED TO A BOSS I II III

By Destiny Skai & Chris Green

KINGZ OF THE GAME I II III IV V VI

Playa Ray

SLAUGHTER GANG I II III

RUTHLESS HEART I II III

By Willie Slaughter

FUK SHYT

By Blakk Diamond

DON'T F#CK WITH MY HEART I II

By Linnea

ADDICTED TO THE DRAMA I II III

IN THE ARM OF HIS BOSS II

By Jamila

YAYO I II III IV

A SHOOTER'S AMBITION I II

BRED IN THE GAME

By S. Allen

TRAP GOD I II III

RICH $AVAGE

MONEY IN THE GRAVE I II III

Treal Love

By Martell Troublesome Bolden
FOREVER GANGSTA
GLOCKS ON SATIN SHEETS I II

By Adrian Dulan
TOE TAGZ I II III IV
LEVELS TO THIS SHYT I II

By Ah'Million
KINGPIN DREAMS I II III

By Paper Boi Rari
CONFESSIONS OF A GANGSTA I II III IV
CONFESSIONS OF A JACKBOY I II

By Nicholas Lock
I'M NOTHING WITHOUT HIS LOVE
SINS OF A THUG
TO THE THUG I LOVED BEFORE
A GANGSTA SAVED XMAS
IN A HUSTLER I TRUST

By Monet Dragun
CAUGHT UP IN THE LIFE I II III
THE STREETS NEVER LET GO

By Robert Baptiste
NEW TO THE GAME I II III
MONEY, MURDER & MEMORIES I II III

By **Malik D. Rice**
LIFE OF A SAVAGE I II III
A GANGSTA'S QUR'AN I II III IV
MURDA SEASON I II III
GANGLAND CARTEL I II III
CHI'RAQ GANGSTAS I II III
KILLERS ON ELM STREET I II III

JACK BOYZ N DA BRONX I II III

A DOPEBOY'S DREAM I II III

JACK BOYS VS DOPE BOYS

COKE GIRLZ

By Romell Tukes

LOYALTY AIN'T PROMISED I II

By Keith Williams

QUIET MONEY I II III

THUG LIFE I II III

EXTENDED CLIP I II

By **Trai'Quan**

THE STREETS MADE ME I II III

By **Larry D. Wright**

THE ULTIMATE SACRIFICE I, II, III, IV, V, VI

KHADIFI

IF YOU CROSS ME ONCE

ANGEL I II

IN THE BLINK OF AN EYE

By **Anthony Fields**

THE LIFE OF A HOOD STAR

By Ca$h & Rashia Wilson

THE STREETS WILL NEVER CLOSE I II III

By K'ajji

CREAM I II

THE STREETS WILL TALK

By Yolanda Moore

NIGHTMARES OF A HUSTLA I II III

By King Dream

CONCRETE KILLA I II

VICIOUS LOYALTY I II

Treal Love

By Kingpen

HARD AND RUTHLESS I II

MOB TOWN 251

THE BILLIONAIRE BENTLEYS I II III

By Von Diesel

GHOST MOB

Stilloan Robinson

MOB TIES I II III IV V VI

By SayNoMore

BODYMORE MURDERLAND I II III

THE BIRTH OF A GANGSTER

By Delmont Player

FOR THE LOVE OF A BOSS

By C. D. Blue

MOBBED UP I II III IV

THE BRICK MAN I II III

THE COCAINE PRINCESS I II III IV V

By King Rio

KILLA KOUNTY I II III

By Khufu

MONEY GAME I II

By Smoove Dolla

A GANGSTA'S KARMA I II

By FLAME

KING OF THE TRENCHES I II

by **GHOST & TRANAY ADAMS**

QUEEN OF THE ZOO

By **Black Migo**

GRIMEY WAYS

By Ray Vinci

Le'Monica Jackson

XMAS WITH AN ATL SHOOTER
By Ca$h & Destiny Skai
KING KILLA
By Vincent "Vitto" Holloway
BETRAYAL OF A THUG
By Fre$h
THE MURDER QUEENS
By Michael Gallon
TREAL LOVE
By Le'Monica Jackson

BOOKS BY LDP'S CEO, CA$H

TRUST IN NO MAN

TRUST IN NO MAN 2

TRUST IN NO MAN 3

BONDED BY BLOOD

SHORTY GOT A THUG

THUGS CRY

THUGS CRY 2

THUGS CRY 3

TRUST NO BITCH

TRUST NO BITCH 2

TRUST NO BITCH 3

TIL MY CASKET DROPS

RESTRAINING ORDER

RESTRAINING ORDER 2

IN LOVE WITH A CONVICT

LIFE OF A HOOD STAR

XMAS WITH AN ATL SHOOTER

Le'Monica Jackson

CPSIA information can be obtained
at www.ICGtesting.com
Printed in the USA
BVHW011533200522
637642BV00018B/53